GOLDEN WEB

Also by Simon Gandolfi

ALISTAIR MACLEAN'S GOLDEN GIRL

GOLDEN
WEB

Second in the Alistair MacLean
Golden Girl Series

SIMON GANDOLFI

CHAPMANS

Chapmans Publishers
A division of the Orion Publishing Group Ltd
Orion House
5 Upper St Martin's Lane
London WC2H 9EA

A CIP catalogue record for this book is available from
the British Library

ISBN 1 85592 110 3

First published by Chapmans 1993

Typeset by Cambridge Composing (UK) Ltd, Cambridge
Printed and bound by Clays Ltd, St Ives plc

ACKNOWLEDGMENTS

My gratitude to Captain Tracy Bowden, discoverer of the galleons *Guadalupe* and *Tolosa* (*National Geographic vol. 156, no 6*) for his assistance in plotting the underwater sequences and to Paul Wood of Coral Marine in Maidenhead, England, for his expert technical editing of the dive times. I thank the staff of American Airlines and American Eagle for their kindness and patience in shepherding me through the airports of the Caribbean. I must also thank the Saturday group at the Museum of Modern Art, Santo Domingo, for their companionship and support during the writing of this work, in particular Barbara Bosch and Idaljisa Polanco, and, in Havana, Luis Suardiaz, editor of Granma, and Gustavo Eguren, President of the Union de Escritores y Artistas. Lastly I thank Alesandro Morales and Eduardo Aliverti for a friendship unharmed by that horrific product of political incompetence, the Falklands/Malvinas war.

1

The seventy-three-foot motor sailing yacht *Beau Belle* had been designed by Charles Nicholson and constructed in 1931 of teak on grown oak frames at McGruer's yard on the Clyde. Long of counter and clipper-bowed, the *Beau Belle* had been commissioned by a successful Glasgow manufacturer of heavy machinery at a time when crew were plentiful and so poorly paid as to permit elegance to precede any thought for the cost of maintenance.

To excuse the prohibitive cost of her upkeep, the *Beau Belle* had been described by the selling agents, when she had last been on the market in 1982, as a classic 'gentleman's' yacht. Her purchaser and present owner was at that time a Lloyd's underwriter who might have been judged a gentleman prior to his recent and very necessary change of domicile from London to the Bahamas, whence Bahamian law made successful application for his extradition too costly and lengthy a process to be considered practical by the City of London's under-funded and short-staffed Serious Fraud Squad. Nor was there anything gentlemanly about the *Beau Belle*'s present role as she edged up the deep Old Bahama Channel that divides the vast coral shallows of the Great Bahama Bank from the north coast of Cuba.

Though she was ketch-rigged, the *Beau Belle*'s main power came from a massive Gardner diesel that stood dead centre in an engine room large for the size of the yacht and, in its meticulous attention to detail, provided evidence that her first owner, despite his demand for outward beauty, had possessed a typically Scottish respect and understanding for the needs of marine machinery.

Of the same vintage as the *Beau Belle*, the hand-built Gardner made little noise and was so perfectly balanced and free of vibration that an old-fashioned octagonal threepenny piece would have stood on edge on the top of her engine covers while she turned at her cruising revolutions of 850 per minute. These revolutions, in calm conditions, gave the *Beau Belle* a speed through the water of 8.2 knots.

Bill Hewett, skipper of the *Beau Belle*, had already placed two charges of gelignite armed with fulminate of mercury detonators six feet apart and a foot below the waterline against the hull in the engine room. All that remained was the wiring of the charges to the storage batteries boxed alongside the auxiliary generator. When the skipper had worked first with explosives during his National Service in the Royal Navy his youth had made for steady nerves and a belief that he was invulnerable. Now he was fifty-eight years old and unable to hide from himself the slight tremor in his fingers as he knelt to tape the naked ends of the wires to the battery terminals.

The big brass-framed thermometer on the bulkhead by the companionway registered in the low hundreds. Sweating profusely, he first wiped his face and hands on a handful of cotton waste, then meticulously cleaned the lenses of his reading spectacles on his vest before taping in place the second pair of wires. These wires were wrapped around the brass handhold on the companionway, leading up to the wheelhouse and ended in a solid brass bell push that he had found amongst the engine room spares.

His task completed, Hewett folded his spectacles into a metal case and again wiped his face and hands. He had earned his living as a yacht skipper for over thirty years and, in normal circumstances, would have cleaned the slight film of oil from the sole of his deck shoes before returning to the wheel-house. But now the soiling of carpets or deck was immaterial. In less than two hours the *Beau Belle* would be at the bottom and he would never again have to seek employment.

He turned off the engine room lights before opening the companionway door. The port-side windows were down and the rain-cooled breeze of the yacht's passage welcomed him into the darkened wheel-house. Automatically he checked their heading. From far away on the starboard bow came the sweep of Lobos Cay Light marking the edge of the Great Bahama Bank while the light on Punta Maternillos flicked at their stern. Two further beacons should have marked the Cuban coast but were either lost in the rain or broken.

'Hey, how did it go, Bill?' the young man at the wheel asked cheerfully. Well over six foot tall and supply muscled, he stood with his feet apart, balancing himself with practised ease against the yacht's motion. He wore his fair hair longer than shoulder length and his features were disguised by a full beard, but he was young, certainly a great deal younger than the skipper and, by his accent, North American. The smile he gave Hewett was relaxed and carefree. He was an inveterate slapper of backs, a good-time kid, a warm hug his standard greeting for both men and women; he was leader of festivities, boss of the beach party barbecue. But he was intelligent, very intelligent.

'OK,' the skipper began and, finding his mouth dry, left it at that. Taking his binoculars from their hook, he stepped out onto the side deck and checked the set of the sails: cruising jib, main, and mizzen. Close into the Cuban reef they were clear of the shipping lanes, so that, as he swept the horizon with his binoculars, the few navigation lights were dim and distant.

He had planned the voyage to bring them up-channel on a moon-free night but the thick cloud cover and rain were an added bonus, as was the comparative smoothness of the sea. Once her sails were stowed and with her lights off, the *Beau Belle* would be barely visible.

Hewett wore a pocket GPS on a cord round his neck together with a waterproof pouch containing the key to the safe in the owner's stateroom, nearly 6,000 American dollars

9

in travellers' cheques, and an Australian passport. The passport was in the name of William Green.

The position given by the GPS, tuned to seven satellites, was accurate within fifty feet. Hewett had no need to check the chart. He had planned and rehearsed every detail of the night a hundred times. Making his way forward, he knocked on the forecastle hatch: 'Wakey wakey. Deck time, boys. Let's get the sails in.'

Two young New Zealanders struggled sleepily up through the hatch into the rain. Pleasant, uncomplicated, and uncomplaining young men, world travellers, Hewett had found them on the beach in West Africa and signed them on for the voyage. 'Sorry,' he said. 'Better now when it's easy, the weather report's threatening squalls.'

Taking the wheel himself, Hewett slowed the engine and headed the *Beau Belle* up into the wind to take the pressure off the canvas. The New Zealanders had come off watch at midnight. Due back on watch at six in the morning, they made for their bunks in the forecastle immediately the sails were stowed while the young American returned to the wheelhouse.

Switching off the navigation lights, Hewett brought the Gardner back up to 850 revolutions and edged the *Beau Belle* closer to the Cuban coast. The compass glowed softly in the darkness. There were no other lights, and the only sounds were those of the sea bursting away as the *Beau Belle* dipped her prow, the soft creak of the yacht's timbers, and the purr of the twin spinning glass discs that threw the rain clear of the forward windows. With the young American standing close behind him, Hewett sought for saliva and moistened his lips: 'Not long now. You'd better get the Zodiac and the tender ready.'

'Hey, come on, Billy Boy, relax a little,' the American advised, clapping an arm round Hewett's shoulders, squeezing, and his soft chuckle grated across Hewett's stretched nerves. Barefoot, the American moved silently so that Hewett heard only the closing of the brass door catch as the young man slipped out into the darkness.

Hewett felt the slight change in the sea as they nosed in towards the edge of the reef and, peering forward, saw the dark tall shape of the American bent over the fourteen-foot sailing tender lashed in its teak cradle on the deck forward of the wheel-house. Having rolled back the sailing dinghy's canvas cover, the American made his way to the bows and crouched briefly over the forecastle hatch.

'Sleeping innocent as a couple of nuns,' he told Hewett as he returned to the wheel-house. 'This rain's great but I need a towel.' He dropped down the forward companionway that led to the *Beau Belle*'s two guest cabins and the crew's quarters.

Hewett checked their position on the GPS and brought the *Beau Belle* onto a heading straight for the Cuban coast. Her bows rose to the chop on the reef edge, then they were through into smooth water and Hewett swung the yacht back on a course parallel to the shore. An hour to go and, though only an occasional smoker, he fumbled on the shelf by the chart table for the tin that held his matches and cigarettes.

He struck a match and saw the American standing at the foot of the stairs with a towel draped over his head. The American's T-shirt rode up over his muscled belly as he grasped the horizontal brass bar above the companionway and in the moment before the match went out, Hewett saw the dull shine of an automatic stuck in his waistband. With a quick bunching of his muscles, the American swung himself effortlessly up to stand beside Hewett, tall and friendly, the towel draped like a cowl to hide his face in even deeper shadow.

Fear held Hewett and he shivered as he cursed himself now, too late, and for the first time since the American had first disclosed his plan. Cursed himself for having fallen so easily for the American's glib guarantees that they were friends and partners, the rewards to be split two ways, evidence of their coup buried beneath Cuban waters where no one would ever search for the truth while Castro's Communists shouldered the blame.

'Imagine the headlines,' the American had prompted: "British Yacht Sunk by Cuban Gunfire". Trust the boy genius, Billy Boy. You're going to be rich. No problems.'

'Jesus, you're uptight,' the American chided now as he kneaded Hewett's shoulders. 'Retirement time, Billy Boy. Nice house on the lake in Guatemala, couple of neat little teenage chicks to keep you warm nights.'

Above all else the American mustn't know, Hewett thought, mustn't know that he had seen the gun. There was a sick emptiness in his belly and the back of his thigh muscles trembled as he fought to keep his voice calm: 'My key to the safe is in the engine room. Take the wheel a minute.'

Hewett stepped back, leaving the American no time to argue. With one hand already on the engine room door, Hewett hesitated, fearful that the American would sense his panic. He must act rationally, he needed time to think and plan but if he stayed below for more than a couple of minutes the American would shut the engine down and come after him. As if guided by an afterthought, Hewett released the door latch and checked their position on the GPS.

'There's a current holding us back, may be a hour and a half more,' he observed, voice calm despite the dryness of his mouth. He looked up to see the American turned half round from the wheel, watching him, his face a black oval. And with that sixth sense developed over years at sea, Hewett glanced over the American's shoulder and saw the tall black bows of a fishing trawler burst out of the darkness, twin curls of spray spuming away from her prow, no lights. Hewett shouted a warning and the American cursed as he spun the wheel. The *Beau Belle* heeled to starboard while the bows of the trawler carved down her flank. The bow wave flung the *Beau Belle* far over, her side deck underwater, and the sailing tender crashed through the varnished side rail.

Hewett grabbed at the door frame. For a moment his grip held. Then his feet shot from under him and he pitched through the open doorway. Arms up to protect his head, he cannoned off the starboard bulkhead. His right knee struck the top step. His shoulder smashed into the bell taped to the handrail.

Less than a second separated the two explosions. The blasts slammed up the engine room companionway, hurling Hewett back, and he screamed as the pain lanced into his shattered eardrums.

The *Beau Belle* heeled further under the sudden weight of the sea pouring into the engine room, every window in the wheel-house shattered. With the deck almost vertical, the American plunged free, swimming hard for the sailing tender already dipping its bows as the sinking yacht dragged on its painter. One slash of his deck knife cut the painter. As he hauled himself over the gunwale, he could hear the despairing shouts of the New Zealanders, the thud of their shoulders beating on the underside of the forecastle hatch.

2

Lieutenant Rodrigo de Sanchez of Cuba's Naval Intelligence Service hummed happily to himself as he coasted his duck-egg-blue 1950s MG down the mountain road towards the sea that stretched like a plane of light away to the horizon. He drove with the hood down and wore sunglasses against the mid-morning sun. He was lean of face and figure, his eyes were deep brown, and his dark wavy hair broke over the collar of his sports shirt.

Soviet collapse allied to a strengthened US trade embargo had bankrupted Cuba. The stores were empty. Roddy de Sanchez had bought the blood-red Lacoste shirt, his designer jeans, and his trainers in Venezuela. His wardrobe and the fact that he drove his own car marked him as a member of the Revolution's second-generation élite. He owed his position to his easy charm, good looks, carefully directioned sexual prowess, sound rather than brilliant mind, and to his father, Admiral Antonio Maria de Sanchez, Commandant of Cuba's North Sector. Coasting down the mountain saved sufficient gas for two trips to the tennis club.

Roddy restarted the MG and drove along the coast road. A sentry saluted with more politeness than enthusiasm as the Lieutenant turned in through the gates to the small naval station. Roddy parked the MG in the shade of a palm tree and took a Samsonite briefcase from behind the driver's seat. With the tide out, a thick stench rose from the baked mud-flats and Roddy gagged and slapped at a mosquito as he crossed the parking lot.

The cloistered barracks had been whitewashed twice a year since their completion in the eighteenth century, but now even whitewash was in short supply and the walls were stained, their lower parts spattered with mud. An arch led through the barracks to a clay parade ground cooled by the trade winds. Football posts stood at one end and a half-dozen sailors practised shots at goal watched with little interest by a second group who lolled in the shade of the wind-bent palm trees that separated the parade ground from the mud-flats and a long wooden jetty. A pair of sixty-foot fast patrol boats lay in the shallows at the far end of the jetty. A sailor fished from the bows of one of the boats while frigate birds hovered overhead. Thanks to the shortage of gas and fuel oil, there were no combustion engines to disturb the peace and Roddy could hear the wing beat of a hummingbird as it dipped its beak into a red hibiscus that grew beside the door into the Adjutant's office.

Roddy drank black coffee with the Adjutant before following a marine to the cells at the far end of the barracks. The marine slid back a small panel in a cell door so that Roddy could inspect the Gringo prisoner. The prisoner lay on the narrow bed. He was dressed in Navy-issue shorts and a T-shirt stretched tight across the chest. He lay on his back with his head pillowed on his arms. In his early thirties, he was tall and well-muscled, his hair long and blond, and he wore a full beard.

Roddy thought of the man as the Gringo because that was what the arresting sergeant had called him when he'd called in his report, and thinking of the prisoner as the Gringo was safer than thinking of him by his name, which Roddy knew to be Marco Rocco. Roddy and the prisoner had never met but were in an alliance that could very easily put Roddy in front of a firing squad. A trained intelligence officer, Roddy was a great deal more experienced in espionage than Marco Rocco. Suspecting that the cell would be bugged, he took a tape recorder from his briefcase and switched it on before nodding to the marine to open the cell door.

Marco opened his eyes, blue and innocent, and grinned at Roddy as if grinning was what he did much of the time, and said, 'Hi, you another clerk? Or are you the man that says when I get to go home?'

'I'm the man,' Roddy said. He held up the tape recorder to make sure Marco had seen it and recited his rank, the name of the naval base, and the date and time of the interview: 'Formalities. I understand that you were on a yacht.'

'You people sank it,' Marco said without sounding angry. 'Buuff, buuff, two shells through the engine room.'

'We'll come to that,' Roddy said. 'For now, I'd like your name, nationality, and date and place of birth.'

'The same as they were when I got picked up on the beach and the same as they were each of the hundred or so times I've given them since getting picked up on the beach,' Marco said. Other than opening his eyes, he hadn't moved since Roddy had entered the cell. He looked relaxed and contented with himself, long tanned athlete's legs, narrow hips, wide shoulders, and that lazy lover's grin.

Insolent, Roddy thought, and for a moment pictured his sister with Marco and felt the bile rise in his throat. But he was expert in dissimulation and smiled easily: 'Yeah, it's a drag, all this repetition, but it's the way bureaucracy works. Most countries it's worse. Cuba, we don't even torture people except in *The Miami Herald*.'

He laid the tape recorder on the wooden table at the foot of the bed and sat down while still speaking, his North American English fluent and moderately colloquial: 'We get your story on tape so that a secretary can type it up and stick it in a file. There's a file, we can get the Admiral's signature and have it passed to the Immigration Department, where the Assistant Minister signs it and has someone take it over to whoever has the key to the cupboard with the rubber stamps. Once we have a couple of stamps on the file, I or someone like me, a Lieutenant, drives you out to the airport where we shake hands and you get put on a flight to Cancún in Mexico or a charter to Vancouver depending on available seats. Back in the United States, you can sell your story to the newspapers: "How Castro sank me. Imprisoned by Castro. Castro's victim." They'll print anything you can invent or invent it themselves.'

A lift of his shoulders dismissed anything the Yankies wrote. 'We're used to it,' he said. He took a legal pad and pencil from his briefcase and arranged them on the tabletop beside the tape recorder. Then he looked over at Marco on the bed and said: 'Come on, do yourself a favour.'

Marco swung his feet to the tiled floor and yawned as he stretched his arms back. 'McKinley Wilson,' he said. He slipped his feet into flipflops and stood up, six foot something of him, relaxed and friendly. Crossing to the table, he sat down opposite Roddy and flashed his grin. 'So what do they call you? Roddy?' His grin broadened, teasing: 'Yeah, you look like a Roddy.'

'Good guess,' Roddy said. He knew that a fellow intelligence officer, ordered to check the tape, might wonder whether it was a guess. He wanted to hit Marco for taking such a fool risk. He wanted to be out of the man's cell, away from him, away from his dangerous jokes and his arrogant over-confidence.

He took up his pencil and wrote Marco's name on the legal pad – or the name that Marco had given him: McKinley Wilson. Instrumental in getting Marco his false passport, Roddy underlined the name twice before taking him carefully through the details of the alias: born Chicago, thirty-three years old, single, employed as deckhand on the British regis-tered yacht *Beau Belle*. Last port of call, Angola. Intended destination, Newport Beach.

'How did the yacht sink?' Roddy asked, and warned Marco: 'Keep it short and simple. The secretary that types English translations has a new lover so she won't work overtime.'

Marco described the *Beau Belle* pushing up the Old Bahama Channel in the rain with the wind strengthening so that the skipper had ordered the sails stowed. He described the unlit

17

trawler charging out of the night and the two explosions that came seconds later low on the waterline, explosions that had blown Marco out of the wheelhouse. The yacht had sunk in seconds but he'd found the sailing dinghy and managed to clamber on board. He had lain on the floorboards, a roaring in his ears, half-stunned by the twin blasts. He thought that he had heard an outboard start but he wasn't sure. 'That would have been the skipper,' he said, and Roddy nodded.

'Name?'

'William Hewett, British.'

Roddy wrote it down, neat handwriting, capital letters. 'Other crew?'

'Two kids from New Zealand who needed a favour,' Marco said, shoulders slumped, the worry suddenly thickening his words: 'Nice kids. Backpackers. They'd ridden into Angola on the back of a truck, no visas, so the skipper picked them off the beach the day we sailed.'

Two extra witnesses! The operation had allowed for Hewett, enmeshing him so that he could never speak, but not these extra two innocents, who would gossip inevitably of their great adventure and might be able to describe where the *Beau Belle* had sunk. That was the one fact that mattered, the position of the *Beau Belle*, but Roddy held off, knowing that the transcript of the tape would be studied and that he mustn't sound too interested. So he kept to the backpackers: 'Let's hope that you did hear an outboard and that they got away with the skipper. Their names please, Mr Wilson.'

Marco told him and Roddy added the names to his report before looking up: 'Now describe the explosions.'

According to Marco he had been stunned by the blasts which had left his memory for detail empty but, however much Roddy reasoned with him, Marco stuck stubbornly to his belief that shell fire had sunk the *Beau Belle*. 'So you won't admit it, but what else?' he insisted angrily. 'If those kids didn't get off the *Beau Belle*, you murdered them.'

'Why would we do that?'

'How should I know?' Marco kicked his chair back and stood glowering up at the barred window high in the wall.

'Maybe you were shooting at the fishing boat. Probably a bunch of kids trying to escape your Commie dictatorship.'

'In international waters? Don't be a fool,' Roddy told him. 'We leave gunboat diplomacy to the United States.'

'Because the goddamned Russians can't protect you any more, Roddy Boy, and that's the truth.'

Marco was good for an amateur, Roddy thought. He said: 'We're getting away from the subject, Mr Wilson. You seem very certain of this gunfire. Is that guilty conscience? Were you in Cuban waters?'

Marco rounded on him: 'Christ, now what are you trying to pull? The skipper navigated. All I did was stand at the wheel.'

'And all I'm trying to do is establish the truth,' Roddy said. 'Three men may be missing. The British will want answers on their own behalf and on behalf of the New Zealand government. So will the yacht's owner and the insurance company.' Taking a chart from his briefcase, he unfolded it on the table: 'What course were you on?'

Marco told him.

'And which side of the channel?'

Marco hesitated, then admitted sulkily that they had been close in to the reef. He pretended to think back: 'Visibility was bad so the skipper kept us clear of the shipping lanes. He said something about a couple of shore beacons being out . . .' Marco shrugged irritably and looked at Roddy, his eyes deliberately unguarded so that Roddy could read his anxiety and know that it was real. 'I'm telling you the truth, for Christ's sake. I didn't even look at the goddamned chart. No point. The skipper had one of those new GPS's accurate to fifty feet. He wore it on a string round his neck, taking readings every few minutes. You want to know where the *Beau Belle* is, he's the man you ask. Closest I could guess is ten miles.'

Despite a fondness for bean soups and roast suckling pig, Admiral Antonio Maria de Sanchez, Commandant of Cuba's North Sector, retained a trim figure. An attentive barber kept the grey from his hair and moustache, his nails were manicured, shoes highy polished, uniform well-cut and fiercely starched. A patrician nose, dark eyes, and a sensual mouth completed the picture of a man who would have seemed less remarkable at a conference of senior NATO Commanders or members of a military junta than amongst Cuba's Revolutionary élite.

Deep in thought, he examined a china figurine on the drawing-room mantelpiece of the de Sanchez villa in Vedado, traditionally the most snobbish of Havana's suburbs. A family conference had taken place in this same room shortly after Castro's landing – the Admiral had been a Navy cadet at the time. The family had decided at that meeting that he should supply Castro with information while his brother continued to support Batista's dictatorship. Meanwhile his sister and brother-in-law would emigrate to Florida with the family's tuna boats, their father transfer the family's freight shipping to the Dominican Republic. Such understanding of power in preference to ideological commitment had enabled the de Sanchez family to profit through three hundred years of Cuba's turbulent history, and the Admiral had prospered under the revolution, rising to his present rank through a keen mind and diligent application to administration, a quality rare in revolutionaries.

A grey dust line marked the inside of the china figurine's arm and the Admiral wiped it carefully with the tip of his handkerchief before turning to face his son, Roddy, who sat on the couch. 'It would be helpful if we knew whether the skipper escaped.'

Roddy shrugged. 'I've told you what the American said. He thinks he heard an outboard.'

'And the skipper would have had sufficient fuel to cross the channel?'

'Ten gallons according to Rocco.' Nervous, Roddy got up and crossed to the double windows which opened to the swimming pool. His sister, Maria, lay face down on a sunbed at the far side of the pool. She had removed the top half of her bikini and Roddy tasted the hate sour in his throat as he thought of her with the American. His father was to blame,

Roddy thought, though there was no expression in his eyes as he looked back over his shoulder at the Admiral, nor any expression in his voice as he said: 'If Hewett got away, he will have made for South Andros.'

The Admiral nodded his agreement. The most southerly of the Bahamian Family Islands, South Andros lay forty-five miles north of the Cuban coast. The seas had been calm and Hewett carried a GPS, so there could be little doubt that he would have come safely to shore and he must know to within a hundred feet where the *Beau Belle* lay. As most probably did the American Intelligence Services.

'We need someone with access to the Americans' satellite surveillance,' the Admiral decided. 'Check the files, Roddy, and get word to Rocco that he'd better search Andros for Hewett.'

Estoban Tur rode a black upright bicycle that had been made in China. The bicycle weighed five times as much as those multi-gear fantasies favoured by young Americans and Estoban sweated heavily as he pedalled uphill past the empty shop windows of central Havana. At least the air was clean now that the fuel shortage had forced the ancient gas-guzzling Buicks and Chevies back to their garages.

Turning in through the gates to Cuba's Naval Intelligence Headquarters, Estoban propped his bicycle against an acacia tree by the steps. He wore the better of his two brown polyester double-breasted suits, a white nylon shirt yellowed at the edges, and a frayed red tie: one of his nylon socks was a deeper grey than the other and his scuffed brown shoes had been made in Bulgaria. In his late thirties and ten kilos overweight, he looked like an out-of-work clerk. In fact he was in his fifth year as Director of Bureau Three in the DGI, Cuba's Intelligence Service, and party to every left-wing guerrilla movement in Latin America.

A marine guard sneered disdainfully as Estoban unchained a battered plastic attaché case from his bicycle. Gripping the case between his knees, Estoban threaded the chain through the rear wheel and padlocked it round the tree-trunk. The padlock was Russian and Estoban gave the chain a couple of hefty jerks before climbing the steps.

The marine was about to tell him to shift his bicycle. Estoban's identity card brought him stamping to attention.

Estoban gave him a tired smile: 'Yeah, life's a real pig, comrade.'

He mopped the sweat from his face and looked across the car park, searching for Lieutenant Rodrigo de Sanchez's MG. The soft-top sports car nestled in the shade between a pair of Zim limos.

'Don't bother logging me in,' Estoban told a decorative receptionist with flag officer legs and dollar-shop make-up. Crossing the lobby, he found a small printed notice hung on the elevator doors:

To save electricity this elevator
is restricted to senior ranks.

Estoban climbed the stairs to Roddy de Sanchez's office on the fifth floor. It was an airy room; a couple of modern oil paintings on the walls, brightly coloured rug from Guatemala, bowl of roses on the desk. The desk faced a picture window with views over tiled roofs to the sea. An empty bulk carrier lay at anchor outside the harbour and a small trawler butted its way round the point. With no sign of Roddy, Estoban watched the trawler while he got his breath, then went back down the stairs to Records, buried in a bunker two levels below ground.

A marine checked his pass at the steel doors and Estoban stood back under the TV camera while a second marine inside the bunker cross-checked his identity. The two marines used their keys simultaneously.

Filing cabinets divided the bunker into narrow alleys, each alley leading to a small study area furnished with a bare steel table and two upright metal chairs. The elderly duty officer inspected the contents of Estoban's attaché case before directing him to Alley E, where the soles of Roddy's American

22

trainers greeted him from the tabletop between two piles of buff files.

Estoban said: 'Hola, Roddy. How's life treating the privileged classes?'

Roddy smiled with easy warmth as he laid a file aside and pushed a dark curl back from his forehead. 'Overworked and underpaid, but that's not a complaint,' he said.

'The work I heard about . . .' Estoban hooked a chair back from the desk with his foot, slumped down like a half-filled sack, and mopped his face on his sleeve.

'You walked instead of using the elevator,' Rodrigo, cool in an imported sports shirt, guessed.

'Principle,' Estoban told him, and nodded at the files. 'Something I'd be interested in?'

'Mostly reports from fishermen.' Roddy passed him a file from the top of a stack. 'I've been told to come up with a few names for the United Nations narcotics people.'

'Mending capitalist fences?'

Roddy shrugged: 'The Central Committee wants foreign investment.'

'Next they'll be inviting those fornicating millionaires in Miami back – your family excepted, of course,' Estoban said with a quick smile as he studied Roddy. Estoban's father and grandfather had worked in the cane fields, slaves in all but name. Despite this disparity in background, Estoban found Roddy easy to like. He took a file from his attaché case. 'Roddy, I want you to do me a favour. Here's a real pig I want set up – better still, lure him into Cuban waters.' Estoban almost spat the man's name as he dropped the file on Roddy's table: 'Trent.'

Estoban watched as Roddy studied a photograph on the inside cover which showed a heavily bearded man seated in the cockpit of a big catamaran. Roddy began to read and Estoban waited patiently. Halfway down the second page, Roddy whistled softly and Estoban nodded. 'A professional killer,' he said. He spoke quietly, seriously, and looked straight into Roddy's eyes as he pressed the younger man to break free of his dilletante's role and commit himself. 'He's killed a dozen of our people, Roddy. True revolutionaries. Get him for me. Do that and I am very seriously in your debt. He's short of funds so there's a chance we can tempt him into making a mistake.'

Roddy preferred working late to wasting petrol in the evening traffic and it was eight o'clock before he left his office. He had read the Trent file cover to cover a dozen times. The file reported sightings of the Englishman under many aliases and in countries as disparate as Syria and the Argentine. And it listed assassinations attributed to him, Irish, Germans, Arabs, Latin Americans, attributed because there was seldom any proof. Added to which the few witnesses gave descriptions at variance with other reports, so Trent was either a master of disguise or the file assigned more than one man's work to the Trent heading. Shave the beard and even the photograph would be of little help, but at least the catamaran *Golden Girl* was easily traced, and the set-up was perfect. Roddy sketched out the details of the approach before leaving the office.

The petrol shortage had taught him a new style of driving and he drifted with the traffic in the slow lane along the Malecon, foot equally gentle on the brake as on the accelerator. The cool sea breeze had brought the young of Havana out onto the esplanade and driving slowly, Roddy had time to admire the dark chain of entwined couples outlined against the paler grey of the sea wall. Politically he was uncommitted. If asked, without fear of being overheard, he would have admitted his fortune in being born into the élite and that the élite enjoyed their privileges more under capitalism than they could in Cuba. But whatever his family background, he was a child of the Revolution and had learnt to find joy in simpler pleasures than those open to his cousins in Miami and the Dominican Republic. In this he knew himself different from his father and sister, and it was a difference that disturbed him as he turned in through the gates and garaged the MG beside his father's official Volga. Cuba suited Roddy very well.

He entered his father's study from the garden and found the Admiral in his shirtsleeves and with his feet up on the leather sofa, cigar in mouth, engrossed in the previous day's *Miami Herald*.

Admiral de Sanchez smiled at his son and pointed with his cigar at the social page: 'Tony Ramón's daughter has married one of the Garcia boys.'

Roddy didn't know who Tony Ramón was and didn't give a damn for his daughter. For a moment he thought of walking straight on through and up the stairs to his own room. He could leave the Trent papers in his wardrobe and return them to his office in the morning. But despite a growing aversion to his father's scheme habit was too strong and he bent to kiss his father on the cheek.

The Admiral spotted the file. 'What's that you've got?'

'The man we're looking for,' Roddy said: 'Trent. He's an Englishman.'

3

The flight from Havana to Cancún in Mexico landed at 11.15 am. Roddy de Sanchez hired a Ford at the Budget desk and waited till 1.30 to leave the airport area. He drove out of Cancún and down the South Highway towards Chetumal and the frontier with Belize. Thick bush and low trees crowded both sides of the macadam which the heat bent into layered waves of shimmering black and silver. It was lunch hour and there were few cars and trucks on the road so Roddy was able to maintain a steady eighty kilometres an hour while keeping an eye on the rear mirror.

At the thirty kilometres stone he pulled into the shade of an acacia tree. Captain Pedro Gomez y Roig of Mexican Intelligence had set up the meet for Roddy and had instructed him to stay in the car. With no breeze, the Ford soon became an oven and the sweat poured out of him. His eyes stung and dark patches spread across his shirt and cotton drill slacks. Charm, good looks, and an excellent tennis game made Roddy a useful gatherer of intelligence on the Embassy and country club circuit. Stuck beside the road, he felt out of his depth and vulnerable. Finally he got out of the car and squatted amongst the bushes. Almost immediately a cream VW Beetle raced by, the driver beating two shorts and a long on his klaxon.

Roddy got back into the Ford, did a U-turn, and floored the accelerator. Five kilometres towards Cancún, he stopped at a thatched shack that served beer out of an icebox that had run out of ice. He parked the Ford behind the shack, went in, and ordered a club soda from a middle-aged bartender with a boxer's shoulders who looked too prosperous for his role.

Refusing payment for the soda, the bartender pointed Roddy to a table in the corner then stood waiting in the doorway so that his body blocked out most of the sunlight. After a couple of minutes a car drew up outside. The bartender stood sideways to allow the new arrival passage, then he went out and closed the door.

'Smith,' the new arrival said. His features were blurred by the deep gloom of the shack and he wore a straw sunhat and glasses. He stood facing Roddy rather than show a profile that the young Cuban might recognise, around five foot eight in height but chunky, dressed in a suit, and carrying a satchel. 'This had better be good,' he warned Roddy in an accent that retained nasal traces of down-market Boston: 'We get caught talking to each other, we'll be in deep dudu.'

'I've got names,' Roddy said.

'That's what the big Mex told me.'

'A couple of them are major players running coke into Florida from the Bahamas. The others smaller, but not fleas,' Roddy said. 'I've got account numbers at banks in the Cayman Islands and Dutch Antilles and I've got tracks back to Peru and Colombia – mostly civilian, but there's a general and two colonels. One of the colonels has lines open to your people.'

'My people?'

'CIA,' Roddy said, hoping to spread a little spice over his wares.

'Wrong initials. There's more agencies in Washington than Cuba has people,' Smith said. If he was relieved or interested it didn't show in his voice, but he hooked a chair back with his foot and sat facing Roddy across the table.

Roddy guessed that he was in late middle age. The big Mexican who had set up the meet had guaranteed that the American was sufficiently senior to make decisions.

Leaning back a little in his chair, the American said: 'It would be nice if it was Christmas and you were one of the three kings . . .' He paused while a truck with a faulty muffler roared down the highway, then continued: '. . . but this is for real so you've got a shopping list.'

'One man,' Roddy said.

Smith waited, silent, perhaps a little contemptuous, Roddy thought. It was always there in the Anglos. Roddy said: 'The man worked freelance for the CIA for a time but he's out now and he's not an American national.'

'So you want to give him a pension.'

'He killed a friend of ours in Latin America,' Roddy said.

'For the CIA?'

'They picked up the bill.'

'We're talking personal here?'

Roddy didn't answer and the American chuckled softly. 'How do you want him? Wrapped? In a body bag? For a couple of names? Grow up, for Christ's sake.' He took a handkerchief from his pocket and blew his nose. Roddy thought that it might be a signal to the bartender that the meeting was over, but Smith folded the handkerchief carefully and slipped it back into his pocket, then settled himself into his chair, waiting.

Bargaining time, Roddy thought. He said, 'Ten names and no body bags.' He felt no qualms at giving the drug smugglers to the American DEA agent, nor did he give a damn for the English murderer Estoban Tur wanted trapped. It was the why that disturbed Roddy, but he had never yet disobeyed his father and he wasn't about to start. 'The man we want lives on a boat,' he said: 'We've got something that we can use as bait to draw him into Cuban waters but he needs pointing in the right direction. He's an Englishman, Trent. Right now he's in the Dominican Republic.'

The Dominican Republic occupies the eastern two-thirds of Hispaniola, the largest, after Cuba, of the Caribbean islands. Haiti occupies the west of the island. The Dominican Republic is a country of rich farmland, pine-clad mountains, rivers, and palm-fringed beaches. The genes of the population are drawn mainly from the native Amerindians, from Africa, and from

Iberia. Eighty per cent of the population are under the age of thirty. Their language is Spanish. They drink rum and dance to the rhythm of the *merengue*, the Latino Caribbean equivalent of the samba. Their government is democratically elected within strictures enforced by the military supported by the hierarchy of the Roman Catholic Church. The military are armed and trained by the USA as the bulwark that defends the sweet flower of individual liberty against infection by Cuban communism. Corruption is endemic. There are no medicines in the public hospitals where the poor die in unlit corridors. The Haitian refugees employed on the sugar estates are slaves in all but name.

The Santo Domingo Club Nautico marks the western end of Boca Chica beach resort, twenty-five kilometres east of the Dominican Republic's capital, and is protected from the open sea by the reef and the small islands of La Matica and Pinos.

Six foot six and 250 pounds of solid muscle, Captain Pedro Gomez y Roig of the Mexican Police strolled down the beach to the right of the club. Broad cheekbones and a mop of black hair marked his Maya ancestry. He wore a pair of black stretch shorts that threatened to split with every step and a red T-shirt with the arms cut away to let his biceps through and the slogan 'A Many Splendoured Thing' printed in white across its front. Back in Cancún, where he was an expert on the foreign community, he was known to all and sundry by the diminutive Pepito. Two young German women stretched out on the sand looked at him with longing but Pepito had other interests.

The fifty-foot ocean racing catamaran *Golden Girl* stirred gently at her anchor fifty yards out from the beach. Catamarans depend for their safety on instant acceleration and *Golden Girl*, even at rest, projected an image of barely leashed power.

Sloop-rigged, she had been built in England of cold moulded marine ply and drew a mere two feet of water with her dagger boards up. What on a monohull would have been a cockpit was more of a patio on the big cat, fifteen foot square, with deep settees on three sides, white cushions, and a table that sat twelve for dinner. Raised high, the aluminium boom supported a white cotton awning that shaded the cockpit and the saloon cabin top from the sun.

The owner of the *Golden Girl* stood in the water, one hand on the rail, softly sanding with fine emery paper a minute scar on the hull. Watching him, Pepito thought of a lover caressing his love.

The catamaran's owner had lived under many names but had been born Patrick Mahoney. Now he travelled under the name of Trent. His age was difficult to judge because of his beard and the cut of his shoulder-length hair, which was thick and almost black as his eyes; a loose-cut light cotton smock and baggy calf-length pants disguised his figure. In fact he was thirty-eight years old and five foot eleven, no fat, and Pepito knew that he could hold his own in a fight. He also knew that the red coral beads Trent wore round his neck held a matt black throwing knife in a small leather sheath against the nape of his neck. Trent could hit a playing card dead centre with the knife at fifteen yards.

He was fluent in Spanish, French, and Russian. He spoke a German that was dialect from the Bavarian Alps, and could pass as an intellectual or peasant from most Arab countries including Libya and Iraq. He was capable of conversing in Italian and Portuguese and he was reasonably proud of his Gaelic. Trent's command of languages was a natural talent fostered by a childhood spent in the stables of jockey and polo clubs from Spain to the Persian Gulf, and honed to perfection by tutors in the employ of a department of the British government. He had served the Department for eighteen years. His prime expertise was in combating terrorism through infiltration. But he had also been lent by his Control to the Americans to undertake those jobs prohibited by Congress. Wet work, the Americans called them. Wet for blood.

The man who had brought him into the Department and who had been his Control had betrayed him and Trent had resigned. But he wasn't out. He would never be out. Too many people had died through his expertise. He was marked by their organisations 'Seek and destroy'. And he no longer had his Department to watch his back. To stay alive, he would have to be careful, very careful indeed.

Pepito watched him brush a finger across the hull. Apparently satisfied, Trent tucked the emery paper into his breast pocket and waded ashore, pants and smock tail drenched. A half-dozen bullet and knife scars lay hidden beneath the baggy clothes but Pepito's concern was for the invisible damage. A field agent's relationship to his Control was almost symbiotic in its dependency. Worse, Trent's Control had been the guardian in whose house the Anglo-Irishman had spent the greater part of his childhood.

Pepito and Trent had spent two weeks together immediately after Trent's resignation and Trent hadn't smiled much; nor did he smile now, six months later, as he sat down on the sand – no greeting of any sort, not even a nod.

'She looks good,' Pepito said of the *Golden Girl*, his voice a deep rumble.

'Thanks,' Trent said.

Pepito lay back and closed his eyes against the sun. He had shared moments of joy and splendour with many lovers but the secrecy and watchfulness essential to his job made friendship a rare commodity, apart from within his family. Trent was one of the few men he completely trusted. After a while he said, 'Trent, you speak Spanish but you remain a lousy Gringo. I have flown from Mexico to see you. In doing so, I have abandoned a beautiful Norwegian lady who is only in Cancún for ten days, so that is in itself a great sacrifice for which you should be grateful. I have flown here without the permission of my superiors, which is a potential sacrifice of my career for which also you should be grateful. I am here for one hour precisely. Now I refuse absolutely to tell you why I have come until you ask me why.'

'Why?' Trent said.

'Because I am stupid enough to wish you to continue living,' Pepito told him. 'I also wish you to have sufficient money to invite a poor Mexican to a good restaurant when he visits you.'

Eyes closed, Pepito catalogued a speedboat racing towards

the reef, the background chatter from the hotel beach bar to his left and, from the Club Nautico, the slap of halyards against aluminium masts as the yachts rocked in the almost imperceptible swell. One of the German sunbathers giggled.

'A job?' Trent finally asked.

'That possibility exists.' Pepito prayed that he was right in attempting to return the Englishman to his profession: 'There is an American I wish you to meet,' he said carefully, deliberately spreading his words in short sentences to give them the weight of his own belief. 'Drug Enforcement Agency. We have worked together. He is a man of trust.' Reaching out, he gripped Trent's elbow in a massive hand thick and tough as a butcher's block. 'Many people wish to kill you, Trent. Alone, you have no hope. Work with this man.'

The seconds ticked by; a full minute. Then Trent said, 'With rather than for?'

'Independent consultant. Active,' Pepito added, because truth was essential to their relationship. He thought that he heard a slight sigh and Trent said quietly: 'I won't kill.'

Pepito opened his eyes. With the sun high, he was unable to see Trent's expression. 'The Cold War is finished,' he said.

'Terrorism is on the increase.'

'We are discussing drugs, my friend. The American is in need of a man with a yacht. I make no promises,' Pepito warned. 'The meeting must be arranged through Washington. You should call one of your old contacts. Both the Americans and your old department believe that you are a man difficult to control, so he must be a man of some courage. Say that you seek work as an independent. Choose the right man and the probability exists that he will point you to my associate.'

'This associate, he asked for me by name?'

'No.'

'He knows of our friendship?'

Already it was back, the continual wariness that kept a field agent alive. Pepito said carefully: 'Not to my knowledge, but I am less expert in these matters than you, my friend. The American consulted me over a different case which we settled to our mutual satisfaction. Then the conversation became general and he told me of his need. I said nothing but naturally I thought of you. It fitted – perhaps too well?'

'Perhaps.'

Pepito checked his watch, rose smoothly to his feet and lifted Trent by the hand so that they stood facing each other. Had Trent been a Mexican, Pepito would have embraced him, but the British were shy of physical contact and Pepito was at a loss as to how to show his affection. 'I must get back to the airport. If the job is offered to you, take it. And if you require help, call me.'

Trent had little faith in coincidence and even less faith in a DEA agent accidentally mentioning to Pepito his need for a man with a yacht. Pepito's American had a reason for not making a direct approach – probably covering himself, Trent thought – 'Hey, it's not my fault. You guys in Washington sent him to me.'

He wondered who had given his name to the DEA agent. A member of his old department? Or one of the American agencies for whom he'd worked? Either way, he didn't feel safe with his name being bandied around and Pepito was right, he needed to cover his back and to do so, he required access to information. Information was an organisational prerogative so he was going to have to make a trade and all he had to trade was his expertise. For the past six months he had been avoiding the decision.

Having paid a beach guard ten dollars to stay out on the *Golden Girl* till he returned, Trent packed a light bag and rode his BMW motorcycle through the capital and parked outside the vast modern Embajador Hotel on the west side of town. Package holiday companies favoured the Embajador and most flight crew stayed there so there was a great deal of movement and little chance of long-distance telephone calls arousing interest.

Booking into a room on the fifth floor, he dialled for an outside line and called a number in Washington DC.

A man answered, mid-west American, and well-educated.

Trent said, 'Hello there. This is Nick Noel. We used to meet in Guatemala City. I worked with the telephone company.'

The American was immediately enthusiastic: 'Nick! Hey, great to hear from you. I heard you retired.'

'Not exactly,' Trent said: 'I'm setting up as a consultant covering the Caribbean.'

'Is that right?'

'There was a man we used to meet for lunch on Thursdays who had a house out on one of the islands,' Trent continued – Thursday was the day he wanted a meeting, it was up to the American to tell him where. He could almost hear the American's brain whirring as he considered whether to help.

'Older than us? Grey hair, five ten or thereabouts?'

'That's the man,' Trent said.

'Had a house on Montserrat. Damned if I can remember his name. I can't even remember the name of the bar we used to meet at – Desert something or other. The man's girlfriend flew for American Airlines out of Miami.'

'It's not that important,' Trent said: 'Next time I'm in Washington I'll look you up.'

'Do that, and listen, take *good* care of yourself.'

4

Trent's contact in Washington had mentioned the Desert Inn as their imagined luncheon meeting place in Guatemala City with the man who had a house on Montserrat and a girlfriend who flew with American Airways out of Miami. Trent flew American to Miami and found an Oasis Restaurant on Montserrat listed in the Caribbean Handbook he bought at the airport. He caught American Eagle connections onto Antigua via San Juan from where a nine seater Islander brought him to Montserrat at eight o'clock Wednesday evening. Four flights with reservations made at the last moment gave the Americans ample chance to check if he was being tailed. He booked into a guest house on the slopes of the Soufriere Hills, slept well with a chair jammed under the door latch, spent the morning on the beach, and walked into the Oasis at a quarter to one.

An elderly English foursome discussed a hand of bridge at one table and a man in his early fifties sat by himself with his back to the wall at the table farthest from the bar. He gave a slight nod and Trent crossed to his table: 'I think we met a couple of times in Guatemala.'

'Desert Inn,' the man said, and Trent sat down facing him. The American was short and thickset with a lot of muscle. His face had spent too much time outdoors waiting for something to happen to be surprised by anything new. He wore a seersucker suit and cotton shirt that had been over-laundered and sun-bleached; his shoes were well polished leather, heavy, with metal moons on the heels; a worn satchel briefcase lay by his feet. A salesman on the Caribbean circuit in something serious like heavy machinery or industrial chemicals would have been a reasonable guess.

'O'Brien,' he said in the almost regionless accent of the expatriate who has spent years fitting in. His smile was lazy and friendly except that it took a long detour round his eyes, which were very pale grey and very careful. 'A man up in Washington said we should meet.' He gave a slight shrug: 'I ran you through the computer, Mr Trent. Seems we could play around a little and come up with a few names in common, friends and enemies. The man in Washington said I should be a little cautious but that's what they know in Washington.' O'Brien wasn't bitter or critical, merely stating the facts.

A bartender, tall and stringy enough to have played pro basketball, came over from the bar. O'Brien ordered cold lagers, his tone of voice quiet and courteous. He waited for the beer, sipped, and wiped his lips on a clean white handkerchief that had been through the wash for years. 'Never could get used to tissues,' he said: 'Know what I mean? Disposable. As kids we looked after things or we got a slap over the ear.' He returned the handkerchief to his pocket and looked back at Trent: 'The file says you retired. Now you want in again but on your own terms, which I can understand.' A slight stress on the I. 'Long term, the man in Washington said, which is how I like it. Do I have things right?'

'Right,' Trent said.

'Well, that's nice. With men from Washington, most times you get information back to front.' O'Brien's eyes flicked round the terrace, checking from long habit that there was no one listening.

'Agency instructions for working with outsiders say I make certain you give me something good and I give you the minimum in return which is no way to run a relationship. My way I check you out like I'm consulting a matrimonial agency. Looks like we share a few interests so let's act like we're on the same side. We screw up, I lose a few years additional to the pension I've already earned but with thirty years in already I don't give too much of a damn.'

He'd had his say. He took a second sip at his beer and leaned back a little, waiting.

Trent said: 'A Mexican told me an American associate of his was looking for a man with a yacht.'

'This Mexican has a name?'

'Pedro Gomez y Roig.'

'Nice man. And you have a yacht . . .'

This last could have been a statement or a question. Either was fine by Trent. 'In the Dominican Republic – fifty foot catamaran,' he said.

The DEA agent nodded to himself and raised a finger at the bartender: 'You like clam chowder, Mr Trent?'

Trent said he did and O'Brien seemed pleased: 'So that's something else we have in common.' He placed their order, then played with his beer glass, moving it a half inch left and right, studying the patterns his finger tips made in the condensation.

The chowder came in deep bowls and O'Brien ate in silence and with the same concentration that Trent suspected he gave to everything he did. With the empty bowls cleared and coffee served, the DEA agent said: 'Files say you're good at action, Mr Trent. Some reports say a little too good.' He gave Trent a slight smile: 'We're not talking morality here so much as career structures. Time was we could act pretty much the way we liked just so we said we were fighting communists and kept the Agency off the front page. Nowadays we have to be a little more careful. I ask you to do me a favour and we end up with a shortage of body bags, we'll have questions asked in Congress. But that's something you know about.'

Trent knew only too well. His Control had plotted to have him killed rather than risk his giving evidence before a House Committee on the wet work he'd done for the CIA. That was the way of it – tools of the Cold War transformed by political fashion into pariahs of the new order and a good many Senators and Congressmen busy washing their hands of

37

activities they'd screamed for only a few years back. He felt no need to excuse his actions. He'd done what he'd been trained by his Control to do and he hadn't thought much about it until he'd been posted to infiltrate an IRA cell in Northern Ireland. Knowledge of Irish history was essential to his cover, added to which his father was Irish and he had been brought up a Catholic. And so he had come late to judging social conditions and prejudice equally as evil as the terrorism they bred. He said, 'Combating terrorism, you kill people. It's part of the job. I resigned because I wasn't prepared to do it any more.'

O'Brien thought a while before nodding to himself: 'You called the right man in Washington, Mr Trent. With your reputation for mayhem, most people would have dropped the phone. Fact is he worked for me way back. A little more ambitious than I am. Likes the big desk, air conditioning that works. Right now I have a situation developing that's not strictly within my terms of reference. It would certainly help to have you up at South Andros, that's the Bahamian Family Islands. What I'd like is for some of the people I'm interested in to charter your boat. That happens, you and I are in business, Mr Trent. Payment we calculate when it happens. For now you have me and my boys looking out for any of your old enemies that might come sniffing along your trail. How does that suit?'

Trent knew that it would have to suit if he wanted to work with the American. Secrecy and information on a need-to-know basis were part of the profession. His thoughts went back to his previous Control, cold, solitary, devious, expert in power games and emotional blackmail. In his early years with the Department Trent had allowed himself to be goaded to a point where loathing had fuelled his determination to excel, thus enabling his Control to manipulate him far beyond the official bounds of the Department's commission. Then he had learnt to play his Control at his own game while cutting himself free of supervision, a modus operandi that the Department hadn't liked. Nor had the Americans, and he'd made enemies in Washington, but he'd got the job done – whatever it was. Because of the enemies, he said: 'I work with you rather than with your Agency and you keep my name out of your reports.'

By way of agreement O'Brien dipped his head a half-inch.

'Then we need ground rules,' Trent told him: 'You supply information and special equipment, that's all. I run the operation. I don't like what's happening, I pull out. Something goes wrong, you cut yourself loose.'

Again O'Brien answered with the briefest of nods: 'That's how I like to play.' He slid his coffee cup to the side of the table as if clearing the decks. Then he looked Trent straight in the eyes, his smile fractionally broader: 'The way they think up in Washington nowadays, you and I are a little out of date, Mr Trent. We'll make a good team. Know what they say about the Dominican Republic? God created the world in six days. The seventh day he rested. The eighth day he tried to get the power working in Santo Domingo and he's still trying.'

He drew a line in the condensation on the table and an arrow back from the line: 'Let's make it the eighth day back from whenever you ask for a meet is when we meet, and eight hours prior to the time we arrange. If you have to fly, travel American any time you can. That may complicate your routing a little but they fly on time and are very tough on security, which gives me a reason to have one of my people check their reservations computer when I want.'

He nodded to the bartender to bring the check. Having paid, he took a ballpoint from his inside pocket and noted a telephone number on the back of the check: 'Call me from South Andros.'

5

The two islands of South and North Andros mark the eastern edge of that vast expanse of coral shallows known as the Great Bahama Bank. Only a few hundred yards east of South Andros lies the Tongue of the Ocean, a sheer-sided gash that plunges six thousand feet. Trent thought that diving the wall was the closest terrestrial experience to a space walk. Lungs filled, he piked and slid down the cliff face.

Forty feet below the surface and to his left lay a small cave. Trent swam beneath the cave, then drifted up with his spear gun ready. The mottled flank of a ten-pound grouper quivered in the shadows. Trent's spear pierced the fish through the gills. Feet against the cliff, he pushed hard and yanked the fish out. Surfacing, he cleared his snorkel and swam to the *Golden Girl*'s fifteen-foot inflatable Zodiac tender rocking at anchor in the coral shallows.

He dropped his weight belt and gun into the boat, heaved himself up, and rolled over the hot fabric side tube onto the floorboards. Cleaning the fish, he zipped it into his icebag and started the fifty-horsepower Mercury. With the throttle open, the lightweight tender lifted onto the plane, skittering across the surface like a flat stone.

The passage from the Dominican Republic had taken Trent four days. With a northerner forecast he had sailed west up the southern coast of Hispaniola from Santo Domingo, and crossed the south end of the Windward Passage before lancing back north north-east into the lee of Great Inagua. From the west tip of Great Inagua, he had sailed for Columbus Bank and South Andros in one long reach, wind blowing Force Three in the early morning and strengthening to Force Five by mid-afternoon.

For Trent there was a unique thrill and freedom in sailing the big cat. A monohull would have fought the sea and winds but the *Golden Girl* had no lead keel to drag her down and the flow of air under her bridge deck added lift so that she seemed almost to fly over the water, making twice the speed of a conventional yacht of the same length; nor did she need to circumnavigate the shallows so that her course was shorter by a hundred miles.

Cleared through customs and immigration, Trent had found a safe anchorge off the beach at Kemp's Bay, where the small settlement offered a shop and service station at which he could leave the BMW motorcycle he carried on davits, a few holiday cottages, and a small hotel. A week had passed since he had notified O'Brien of his arrival.

Boarding the *Golden Girl*, he cleaned and sliced the grouper and wrapped the steaks in clingfilm before putting them in the solar-powered icebox. The prevailing wind held the catamaran steady and kept the cockpit cool under its cotton awning. Trent streched out on the cushions with a book and notepad. An hour later, he laid his book aside and watched a swimmer head out from the beach. The white back strap of her swimming costume betrayed her sex and the sun flashed off the glass in her face mask, fins beating a foam trail across the silvery grey-green surface of the sand-bottomed shallows.

Despite the distance, a good many holidaymakers swam out to the *Golden Girl*, hoping to be asked on board. Most of them had rehearsed their opening remarks as Trent had rehearsed replies that, though polite, left them with no alternative but to swim back to the beach.

The swimmer circled the *Golden Girl* before finally treading water. She pushed her mask up to display dark humorous eyes and a smile that struck Trent as direct and open by nature rather than intent. She said, 'Hi, you've got a great boat, like a cheetah, you know? Really moving. All four legs off the ground.'

Her remark was new and accurate and Trent responded, pointing her to the stainless steel rungs that mounted the cat's transoms.

She held out a wet hand as she ducked in under the awning: 'Auria Rocco.' Her grasp was firm with a slight hint of tennis player's callous on thumb and forefinger. American, and in her mid-twenties, she was stockily built, her dark eyes warm as they met Trent's, laughter lines already engraved at their corners and etched into the bridge of a short, slightly snub nose; a wide mouth, generous lips, neat ears left unprotected by her cropped haircut. Nothing about her was classically beautiful yet Trent perceived in her a joyous enthusiasm and sense of fun that was deeply attractive.

'Trent,' he said and found her a towel before fetching coffee from the galley.

The bridge of her nose wrinkled as she scented the steam spouting from the Italian coffee pot and her smile broadened: 'I don't believe it. A great boat *and* real coffee. That's quite a package, Mr Trent. And you read Spanish.' She hadn't disturbed his book or notes, merely read the author's name and title: *La Española, 1493–1520,* by Frank Moya Pons. 'Professional interest?'

'Strictly amateur, and it's Trent, no Mr.' He poured the coffee, the local beans freshly roasted that morning in the galley oven.

Auria sipped appreciatively and, with American directness, asked: 'So what do you do? You don't look like the kind of man who made a killing on the stock-market and you're a little young to be retired.'

Trent said that he had been a civil servant: 'I've taken a sabbatical.'

'Till your money runs out?'

'That's about it,' Trent admitted.

'And then? Shave the beard, get yourself a straight haircut, and back behind a desk some place like London?' She dismissed the possibility with a smile and a quick movement of her hand that encompassed the yacht, the sun and sea, the presumed freedom of Trent's present life. 'You'd go crazy,' she said. 'Mind if I look around?'

The companionway leading into the saloon that bridged the twin hulls opened off the forward port-side of the cockpit. The chart table lay to port of the companionway with new Brooks and Gatehouse electronic equipment above it connected to repeaters on the cockpit bulkhead: speed through the water, wind speed, depth indicator, barometer, satellite navigation. The Sailor radio was to port of the navigation equipment.

At the forward end of the saloon the mast foot supported a table cupped by a horseshoe settee spread with handwoven Guatemalan covers. A vase of white hibiscus decorated the table. A second vase stood on the hip-high cupboards lining the after bulkhead along with a pair of wide-based ship's decanters for white rum and dark, and a row of cut-glass tumblers held in place by a fiddle rail. Two inflatable armchairs were drawn up to the table. Afghan rugs lay on the blue carpeting. There were bookshelves, a pair of nineteenth century oil paintings of shipping on the Thames. Big windows opened forward onto the bridge deck with domed hatches port and starboard in the cabin roof.

The long galley bench lay amidships in the port hull with double-bunked cabins fore and aft. The cabins had their own handbasins and a head. The lone cabin in the starboard hull lay aft and was longer than those to port and separated from the sail locker that opened to the foredeck by a head and shower. Mexican bedspreads covered the bunks, and there were matching curtains and bright rugs on the white carpeting.

Returning to the cockpit, Auria said: 'She's beautiful, a real home.' She leant forward a little, forearms on the cockpit table, keen like a gundog: 'Do you ever charter?'

So she was probably part of O'Brien's target. But Trent had lived in subterfuge for the past eighteen years and found her lack of pretence attractive. 'Where do you want to go?'

'We're trying to check on a yacht that may have sunk and find out what happened to the skipper. There's Marco, that's my brother, and the skipper's son, Rik. Rik's a Brit,' she said, not to persuade Trent, but because the information was of interest to her: 'The situation's kind of complicated. Why don't you come ashore and meet the others?'

Trent refilled her cup with coffee, leaving Auria to add her own milk: 'You didn't answer my question.'

'What question was that?'

'Where?'

She looked uncomfortable for the first time but she faced him, meeting his eyes. She gave a slight shrug, as if easing herself of a problem that wasn't truly a problem, or didn't need to be a problem: 'Cuba.'

O'Brien had made no mention of Cuba – Castro's Cuba, haven for every terrorist group that kept Trent at the head of its kill list. And this was hardly the routine loss of a yacht on a coral reef. 'You have permission to enter Cuban waters?'

Again she gave that small shrug as she shook her head: 'There's a report the Cubans sank the *Beau Belle*, that's the yacht we're looking for. There's no way they'd want us searching for proof and the State Department doesn't allow Americans to visit Cuba.'

'The skipper's missing, possibly dead. Any other crew?' Trent asked.

'Two New Zealanders, backpackers, and an American.' She looked away to the beach, and uncertainty deepened the lines across the bridge of her nose that had been born of laughter: 'Like I said, it's complicated. You need to speak with Rik and Marco.' She looked back at Trent, hands open on the table: 'Talking won't hurt.'

Without answering, Trent put their cups on the tray and carried the tray down to the galley. She said, 'Please . . .' and he looked up from the sink to see her seated on the step leading into the saloon. Her swimsuit divided her into white and suntanned pieces like a small child's jigsaw puzzle. He sensed the anxiety in her, fear almost, and he didn't like it. Fear was his province, his and O'Brien's. In Auria it was out of character. And he was certain now that she was involved in whatever interested O'Brien. But which side was she on?

Angels or sinners. He would have preferred to have seen her expression but the sunlight on the white awning above her was too bright.

'Why come to me?' he asked quietly.

'We were asking around. You know how it is. Your name came up.'

'Up as what?'

'Sort of adventurous – I think a man said he thought you needed the cash.'

One of O'Brien's operatives, Trent presumed.

Auria searched her memory: 'He said you anchored out so you didn't have to pay marina fees and that you didn't mix. Marco said a big cat would be perfect. He sails a lot, ocean racing. That's what he does, sort of for a living.'

'Where was this?'

'North Andros – the marina at Fresh Creek. Does it matter?'

Trent smiled: 'That someone told you I'd be happy to break the law if the price was right?'

'It didn't happen like that,' she said: 'Anyway we wouldn't be breaking the law, not really. It's Cuba.'

'Cuba's laws count in Cuba. And perhaps I like sailing more than I like crowds,' he said lightly.

Auria laughed, grateful that the inquisition had ended: 'Marco likes both. If we go ashore, he'll be with a bunch of people.'

'And the skipper's son?'

'Rik? He's kind of shy.'

6

Trent ran Auria ashore at the small beachfront hotel where she had left her companions. As she had expected, her brother was at the bar beside the pool, centre of a small crowd of jovial tourists. He waved at Auria, calling that he'd join them in a minute. The skipper's son sat alone at a table in the shade of a palm tree. He was unmistakably English, skinny, close to six foot, beaky-nosed, blue-eyed, nervous, and with the sort of pale skin that would burn in ten minutes of midday sun. A Panama hat shaded his face. He wore a white city shirt with the cuffs rolled up; his grey flannel trousers were ridiculously thick for the climate, and his heavy leather shoes would have been more at home hiking across the Yorkshire Dales.

As the Englishman rose to his feet, Trent read in his eyes his love for Auria and his fear of annoying and of disappointing her. A difficult partnership.

Auria introduced them: 'Richard Hewett, Mr Trent.'

'Trent will do. May I get you a beer?'

The Englishman was reluctant to meet Trent's eyes and a slight blush coloured his cheekbones as he checked his watch, as if the hour controlled his drinking. But Trent was already ordering cold Kalik lagers. 'Auria tells me you're searching for your father.'

It was up to Richard to carry the ball forward. He was hesitant. The beers came to save him. Insisting that he pay, he half rose to get at the wallet in his back pocket but Auria intervened, telling the waiter she'd pay by credit card when they left. Trent was sure that she was accustomed to money. She had the smell of it; perhaps not a great deal, but sufficient to have given her the early social security that he thought must have been absent in Richard's childhood as it had been in his own. And Richard's clothes were unsuitable for the Caribbean. Because he didn't intend the length of his stay to warrant a tropic wardrobe? Or because he was naturally careful? Or both?

'You need a boat. Tell me about it and perhaps I can help,' Trent said.

The story came slowly and with Auria prodding gently, protective of her companion's shyness. Richard's parents were separated though not divorced. His father was a professional yacht skipper specialising in delivery work. He had been employed by an English insurance broker at Lloyd's to deliver the broker's yacht, *Beau Belle*, from Angola to Newport on the Connecticut coast. Originally the owner had intended wintering in Cape Town, but the *Beau Belle* had put into Angola for major engine repairs. Some of the spares were unavailable and had to be made before being sent from England, so the owner had paid off the first delivery crew, flying out Richard's father once the work was complete, by which time the winter season had passed.

Here Auria's father entered the story. Owner of restaurants in New Jersey and Newport, where he had met the *Beau Belle*'s owner, he chartered the yacht for six months. 'The *Beau Belle*'s kind of old-fashioned,' Auria explained: 'Beautiful, a real classic. Dad had this idea of running super expensive day charters linked to the restaurant. Or maybe it was the owner's idea. If it worked out the first year, Dad had an option to buy. I guess he wanted to get Marco involved.'

Hewett senior had sent Richard a card from Angola. Next they received a report that the *Beau Belle* might have been sunk by gunfire off the north coast of Cuba.

'How did you hear?' Trent asked.

Richard took a letter from his pocket:

47

'Dear Mrs Hewett,

Your estranged husband, William Hewett, was employed as skipper of the motor yacht, *Beau Belle*. He was to have delivered the *Beau Belle* from West Africa to Newport Beach. I regret to inform you that the *Beau Belle* is now eight weeks overdue and that we must face the possibility that your husband has lost his life at sea.

At your husband's request his life was insured for $200,000 with yourself and your son, Richard, as co-beneficiaries. The owners of the *Beau Belle* carried employee insurance that should grant you a widow's pension of $250 per week. At this time the underwriters at Lloyd's are attempting to ascertain to their satisfaction the fate of both your husband and the *Beau Belle*. You may have seen a report in the *Daily Telegraph* suggesting that a yacht was sunk off the Cuban coast. Should this be true, it seems to me most unlikely that the yacht was the *Beau Belle*; however I understand that the underwriters have written to the Cuban authorities. I hope to be able to inform you of the results of their investigations in the near future.

At the time that she went missing, the *Beau Belle* was under charter. Under the charter agreement, the charterer is responsible for any losses to or claims against the owners of the *Beau Belle* not covered by the insurers. Should the insurers refuse payment for whatever reason, both you and the owners of the *Beau Belle* will be entitled to institute claims against the charterer in the American courts.

In expressing my deep regrets, I remain,

Yours sincerely,
David Rogerton-Smithe'

Two clippings were pinned to the letter, from the *Miami Herald* and the *Daily Telegraph*. The wording was identical, so the reports had clearly been taken directly from a wire service: 'Twenty more refugees from Castro's dictatorship escaped from Cuba last night on a fishing boat. Docking in Miami today, the refugees reported the sinking of a yacht by gunfire off the Cuban coast.'

Trent asked to see the postcard. It was the usual beach scene, palm trees, a half-moon of perfect sand and a couple of whitecaps breaking on a reef. The mosquitoes and sandflies had been left out and both poor printing and the cheap quality of card betrayed its Communist origin. The postmark was the capital of Angola, the message basic: 'Sailing for the States next week. How about joining me there for your holidays? – Dad.'

'No letters?' Trent asked Richard.

Richard twisted his shoulders: 'Dad wasn't good at writing. We often wouldn't hear from him for months. Then we'd get two or three cards.'

We, so Richard was recalling his childhood rather than the recent past. 'Did you visit him?'

'When I was at school, a few times, and twice since. He asked me often,' Richard said.

Trent watched a dark, good-looking young man in a brief swimsuit oil himself with narcissistic concentration on one of the sunbeds by the hotel pool. Two maids admired the young man from the upper storey of the hotel. Trent was familiar with the yacht crew social scene and imagined Richard's father scrawling postcards in moments of loneliness in the off-season. Then there would be a new girlfriend and no need to write for a while. But Hewett would have been in his fifties now, and girlfriends increasingly difficult to attract.

Trent tapped the clippings: 'Even if the yacht was the *Beau Belle*, the north coast of Cuba isn't enough to go on. Presumably you've checked with Rogerton-Smithe? What have the Cubans said?'

'The American came ashore in the sailing tender and they have his statement that there were two explosions, but they deny sinking the yacht and haven't found any traces of her.'

'You talked to the American?'

Richard looked even more glum as he shook his head: 'No one's been able to find him since the Cubans put him on a flight to Cancún.'

'And Lloyd's haven't paid up?'

'Not yet.' Richard searched his beer for comfort: 'I mean . . .'

'Rogerton-Smithe's turned out to be a crook,' Auria interrupted, bitter, the despair unmistakable: 'He's holed up in Nassau, living it up. Rik called him on the phone and he said there wasn't a thing he could do the way things were.' She looked across at Richard, then down at her hands held loosely in her lap, short strong fingers, and Trent saw the muscles tighten, drawing the fingers into her palms as if she were trying to crush her thoughts.

Richard made a move to touch her, but his hand lifted only an inch before his confidence expired.

She looked up at Trent, suddenly tired and out of her depth: 'Dad carried his own insurance against anything going wrong. They won't pay up. They think Dad and Rogerton-Smithe were running an insurance scam.'

'What has Rogerton-Smithe done?' Trent asked.

'Rik's the accountant.'

So that was Richard's profession.

'Reinsurance,' Richard said: 'Rogerton-Smithe was using brass plate companies – insurance companies registered in offshore tax havens where there's no control. They pocket the premiums and close down if there's a loss.'

'What's the insurance value of the *Beau Belle*?'

'Quarter of a million in British money.' Auria's brother had finally extricated himself from the group at the bar. Well over six foot tall, he stood smiling down at Trent. In contrast to Auria, his eyes were startlingly blue in a strong, deeply tanned, rectangular face: the crest of cropped hair was bleached almost white by the sun and sea. A white sleeveless vest and faded jeans scissored off an inch below the knees showed off a body that was naturally muscular.

'Hi,' he said: 'Marco Rocco – you must be the man with the cat. Great boat.' His grip was solid, his tone relaxed and friendly – not a man to worry over-much but probably good under pressure, Trent thought. Four or five years older than his sister, he was close to the age limit for a 'yachty' and probably too intelligent, but the charm was there and, with his good looks, there would be many temptations to continue the fun life.

Marco waved over a waiter and ordered a fresh round of drinks. 'Sis and Rik filled you in? We need to find the *Beau Belle* or the old man's going to end up broke.'

'I've told you, my mother won't . . .' Richard began but Marco stopped him. 'What your ma's owed is the least part of it, Riky boy. There's no way Rogerton-Smithe's going to let a half-million dollars blow away in the breeze. We find the *Beau Belle* or we find your Dad. Yeah, I know and I'm sorry, Sis, but we have to face facts,' he said as Auria tried to intervene.

Standing behind Richard's chair, Marco put his hands on the young Englishman's shoulders, kneading gently, sympathy in his voice: 'Rik's bright and he's not a kid, Sis. We know the score so let's have it out in the open where we can kick it around.'

He turned back to Trent. 'Coming up-channel, Rik's dad would have been on watch. The *Beau Belle* carried a sailing tender and a Zodiac, so either he got away or a shell hit the wheel-house – and that's not how the Cubans from the trawler described it, I checked. And the Cubans swear she was inside the reef when they saw her, which is a long way off from where she should have been. According to the coastguard, a couple of beacons were out and it was raining so maybe he got lost. At least she's in shallow water. Finding her's worth ten per cent of whatever the old man would have to pay out.'

'How close a position did the Cubans give you?' Trent asked.

'Ten miles, and even that's a guess.' Marco laughed at Trent's disbelief. 'Meet them and you'll believe me. It's a miracle they hit Florida. All they knew was how to start the engine and turn left once they were out in deep water, but they scraped a chunk out of their keel after they saw the *Beau Belle*, so she has to be inside the reef.'

'Then you're wasting your time.'

There was no pretence in Richard, and Trent read the relief in his eyes. But Auria was already saying: 'Someone has to know.'

Again Trent sensed the fear.

'There must be people you could ask,' she said.

'Easy, Sis,' Marco warned, gentling her with his hands as he had gentled Richard. 'It's like I said. Either Rik's dad is alive and we find him or the old man's run out of luck.'

'He'd die,' Auria said and again turned to Trent, desperate for an opinion to offset her brother's logic. 'Even if Dad could raise the money, the scandal would break him. I mean, who's going to insure the restaurants if they think he was in on a scam? He'd have to close, and he's spent his life building them up.'

'Like they were his kids,' Marco said and Trent, watching the interplay between brother and sister, wondered if there was a bitterness buried deep in Marco. But already the American was back into his stride, smiling easily as he ruffled Auria's hair. 'Sis, if there was a scam, we know the old man wasn't involved, so that leaves Rogerton-Smithe, and he won't let us into the house. A few words with Rik over the phone is all we've got.' And to Richard, who sat silent and miserable: 'Look, I'm not bad-mouthing your dad. For all we know, someone may have been holding a gun to his head, but he was off course and that's what the insurers don't like. If we knew where the *Beau Belle* was, we could go in. I mean, it would be fun, for Chrissakes.' He grinned at Trent: 'Right? Pulling a fast one on Castro? As it is, we know Rik's dad hasn't been on a plane anywhere because the cops are looking for him. So, if he's alive, the best guess is that he's hiding out. Maybe he's met up with the American deckhand. Andros is closest to Cuba. I say we look around. Ask if someone saw a Zodiac. It's not much of a hope, but what else have we got?'

Auria turned to Trent: 'You don't say much.'

Unhurried, Trent reached for his lager. The *Beau Belle* had entered Cuban waters, illegally, true, but by sinking a foreign yacht rather than arresting her, the Cubans risked further alienating the West at a time when, shorn of Russian economic support, they were desperate for foreign investment. So they had to have had an impelling reason for sinking her, or she had been sunk by someone else, someone with reason and sufficient funds to pay the crew to disappear.

Or sufficiently ruthless to commit murder.

No wonder Auria was afraid and Richard anxious to end their search rather than discover whether his father had been victim or perpetrator, while for Marco, the greater the risk, the better the adventure, a philosophy dangerous to his companions and, when hunting a possible killer, lethal.

Trent said to Auria: 'Give me a day to think things over, make a few calls. Where are you staying?'

'The Emerald Palms at Congo Town. Room 22.'

7

Trent dialled O'Brien from the payphone outside the service station. A woman answered and put him on hold while she rerouted his call. When the DEA agent came on the line Trent said, 'Thanks for telling me about this place. Like you said, the fishing's great. How about coming down yourself some time early next week?'

'Let me see, today's Tuesday . . .'

'Right,' Trent said. He pictured the DEA agent meticulously counting out the days and the time on his fingers until he was a hundred per cent sure that he'd calculated their code correctly.

'How about picking me up for a late breakfast Wednesday week?' O'Brien finally suggested: 'Say nine o'clock? You ride north up the track to Mill Town, that's about ten miles. You'll see the school on your left and the teacher's house beside it. Bright yellow door. Get there right on nine so the waffles don't spoil.'

Trent said he'd be there. One o'clock in the morning might be the earliest O'Brien could reach the rendezvous. More probably he'd chosen that hour because anyone tailing Trent would show up on the empty road.

He found a retired fisherman mending nets in the shade. The old man had looked after the *Golden Girl* twice in the past week while Trent fished out on the reef. Trent ran him out to the cat together with two sixpacks of Kalik. While the old man inspected the contents of the icebox, Trent retrieved the 9mm Beretta he kept wrapped in oilskin inside the top of the hollow tube of the aluminium mast. He packed a holdall, slung it into the Zodiac and the fisherman ran him ashore.

'I'm insured so long as there's a watchman on board, so don't get yourself killed,' Trent warned the old man. 'Robbers come, offer them a beer.'

Up at the service station, he wheeled the BMW out of the workshop and filled the gas tank before heading north through Mill Town, where he noted the schoolteacher's house. He rode slowly through the light traffic, enjoying the feel of the big bike, and the cool breeze helped him think.

He was certain that O'Brien had been casting specific bait when he'd mentioned to Pepito his need for a man with a yacht – the files would show Trent and the Mexican's friendship as they recorded that Trent was high on the Cuban DGI's most wanted list. And the *Beau Belle* lay in Cuban waters.

Trent's previous Control had betrayed him and he found himself wondering whether O'Brien could be cast in the same mould – or whether he could be under instructions from Washington. Some sort of exchange? Or perhaps revenge for his having rocked the boat.

He hoped not, because he'd found O'Brien compatible – however, trust in anyone involved with an operation was a suicidal indulgence and his contact in Washington had warned him to take good care of himself. He could walk away from whatever was happening – or sail away from it – but then what? Try again to establish connections or spend the rest of his life hiding and ducking shadows because he hadn't learnt the truth. And there were others to consider. He needed an outside source of information.

Automatically he thought of Charles Benson, who would have been his Control had he remained with the Department. They'd liked each other and Benson had done his best to persuade Trent to stay on. The Bahamas time zone was five hours behind London, so Benson should be on his way home, which was better than the office, where he would be bound by the rules to react according to his departmental hat.

Congo Town was the largest settlement on South Andros, and the airstrip was nearby. Trent booked into the Congo Beach Hotel and called London from his room. A woman answered, gentle-voiced, upper class: 'Patricia Benson.'

'I wonder if I could speak with Charles,' Trent said: 'I'm a friend from out of town.'

Benson came on the line, voice a little cautious: 'Charles Benson speaking.'

'Charles, I'm having a problem with yacht insurance,' Trent began without disguising his voice: 'Apparently the Caribbean is a difficult area. I thought you might have a relative or friend in Lloyd's? I need background on an underwriter called Rogerton-Smithe.'

'Urgent?'

'Very,' Trent said.

'Do you have an address or are you moving around?'

'Moving.'

There was a slight pause while Benson worked out the logistics and how to cover both Trent and himself. 'I've a banker cousin in Nassau. He has a fax in his office. I'll get his number from my book.'

Trent watched the second hand on his watch but Benson was back with a Nassau phone number in under a minute – even had he wished to, insufficient time in which to have the call traced. 'Give him a ring midday tomorrow.'

Trent thanked Benson and had the desk clerk make a reservation with Bahamasair for the morning flight to Nassau. As a field agent, he'd learnt early that fatigue could be as fatal as a bullet. He set the alarm on his watch for eight in the evening.

Rested, he dressed in dark blue slacks and a loose matching shirt that hid the Beretta stuck in his belt and slipped out of the hotel at nine o'clock. He wove the BMW through the streets, watching his back to be sure that no one was following before heading for Mill Town. He parked the BMW off the road a mile short of the settlement and approached the schoolteacher's house through the scrub. The windows were curtained and the only light showed in the front room on the left of the door. He took up position at an angle to the house so that he could watch both the front verandah and the back porch. There was little traffic on the road. A couple of dogs barked intermittently, music played from an open-fronted bar down by the beach, and there were bugs.

At a quarter to ten a blue Ford turned up the lane fifty yards short of the house. The same Ford reappeared ten minutes later and parked a hundred yards in from the main road. A further ten minutes passed before Trent saw O'Brien cross the backyard and enter by the back door. A little before eleven o'clock two cars left the beach bar and drove off towards Congo Town. The bar closed and a half-dozen locals strolled up the beach track, laughing and joking before they split up and headed for home. Shortly after midnight two cars raced south, windows open, music blaring. A half-hour later a Honda 500 cruised by heading south and Trent heard its engine cut on the edge of town. A telephone rang in the schoolteacher's house and a light in the back of the house went on – probably in the kitchen. O'Brien's sentries were in place and Trent now knew that the DEA agent considered trouble to be a possibility.

He entered the house by the back door at exactly one o'clock in the morning. The door opened to a neat kitchen with copper-bottomed pans hanging on the wall by the kerosene stove and sparkling willow pattern china lined up on a wood dresser with brass handles on the drawers and cupboards. A blue and white gingham cloth covered a table set with coffee and a plate of sandwiches. The DEA agent dozed behind a newspaper in a wicker chair to the left of the door. The newspaper hid his hands but didn't cover his eyes. He took his time pushing himself upright out of the chair with his left hand while digging into his jacket pocket for his spectacle case – or slipping a gun back in a shoulder holster. He folded the newspaper neatly and produced one of his little smiles. 'Nice you could make it, Mr Trent.' Pointing Trent to a chair, he locked the back door before sitting down facing him across the table. 'Take milk in your coffee?'

'Please,' Trent said.

O'Brien poured carefully and passed Trent a cup. 'Sugar?'

Trent shook his head and O'Brien pushed the sandwiches across. 'Miss Mary's specials, home-baked bread with fresh tuna and raw onion in lemon juice. With some people, onion affects how they sleep.' This was a statement rather than an apology.

O'Brien stirred a half-spoonful of sugar into his own cup and tapped the spoon against the inside of the rim before replacing it in his saucer. 'Hope there weren't too many mosquitoes outside, Mr Trent,' he said. 'Put your pistol somewhere safe, having it stick in your belly's bad for the digestion.'

Trent eased the Beretta clear of his belt.

'Not on the tablecloth,' O'Brien warned. He munched a sandwich in silence, thinking. Finally he came to a decision. 'You and me, we've learnt to keep our lips buttoned tight, Mr Trent, and that's giving us a problem in communication, which we need to cure. Your Control tried to have you killed and when that went wrong, tried to do the job himself – and some of our people at Langley were behind it, trying to keep you from giving evidence before the House Committee on the wet work you'd done. So I'm not going to waste time telling you you should trust me. That's going to take a while. And I'm not going to pretend that I'm telling you everything I know – you and I both know that doesn't happen in our line of work.

'You have brains as well as muscle or you'd be dead given the things you've done. Those brains should tell you that I've gone to a deal of trouble recruiting you into this operation I'm setting up. You'll also have worked out that the operation is a little outside Agency rules which is why I have you rather than one of my own people in place, and which is why I'd like to stay well in the background for a while.' He sat in silence a moment, grey eyes watchful, trying to gauge whether he was getting his message across: 'What I'm saying is that it's very much in my interest to keep you alive, and that's something I need you to believe, Mr Trent. I set up a meet, it's going to be a safe meet and there's no need for you to hide out in the bushes for a few hours catching yourself malaria.'

He took another sandwich without thinking, looked at it in surprise, then pressed the plate on Trent: 'What we don't eat, I have to hide, Mr Trent, or hurt Miss Mary's feelings.'

Trent watched O'Brien touch a finger to a crumb on the tablecloth and brush it off onto the edge of the plate.

'A neat woman, Miss Mary,' O'Brien said. He sipped coffee, studying Trent over the cup's lip. 'Two Latinos out of Miami picked up your trail when you flew to meet me on Montserrat. US citizens. I had them checked through records and they come up clean, which doesn't mean a whole lot. A friend of mine in the police there held them up a little but they were back on your tail all the way to Santo Domingo. One of them's here now on South Andros, and he may have friends, so I have a man staked out each side of town and a third should have followed you up from Kemp's Bay, except you came from the other direction some time around nine o'clock.

'We pull the Latino off your back now and we never find out why he's following you. Maybe he's seen your photograph without that beard and he's in love, but that's not something I'd bet on, Mr Trent.' He set his cup down and poured fresh coffee for them both. 'I've had my say. Now it's your turn, Mr Trent.'

Trent recounted his meeting and all he'd been told of the *Beau Belle*. 'She sailed from Angola, which is unusual whatever the story, and she sailed up the Great Bahama Channel,' he concluded. 'I'd expect someone to have kept an eye on her.'

O'Brien nodded. 'Drug territory – we had her plotted on the sat screen. We're keeping watch and no one's been within a mile of where she sank.'

'Anyone looking?'

'Not so as you could tell. Cuban Navy sailed a couple of patterns early on but nothing since.'

Proof that he'd been right, Trent thought. 'The Cubans didn't sink her. One of the crew did.'

O'Brien nodded. 'Same conclusion I came to. Any other thoughts?'

'The where must have been deliberate and Cuba's the one place you can't look. So they were hiding something.'

O'Brien nodded again. 'That would be my guess.' He moved his cup and saucer a half-inch back and forward across the table, then a little Irish mischief lit his eyes and he smiled. 'I'd be grateful if you'd take a look, Mr Trent. I don't have the authority to make that even halfway to an official request, but I can bring a good deal of local Bahamian support into play. Come up with something interesting and you and I will be on the way to earning a little gratitude freshly banked in Washington, which wouldn't do either of us any harm. Mess up and you're working for the three kids so I'm safe. It's a one-sided deal, Mr Trent. You should take a couple of days thinking it through. Maybe work out if there's a way you can protect your position like I'm protecting mine.'

8

According to O'Brien, Latinos had been on Trent's tail ever since his meeting with Pepito or ever since he had called Washington. Trent didn't know which and he didn't know what had happened on the *Beau Belle*, but none of his guesses were pleasant. His immediate aim was to be the centre of any unfriendly interest – Marco might be able to take care of himself but Auria and Richard were highly vulnerable.

He booked out of the Congo Beach Hotel at six in the morning and walked round to the Emerald Palms. He wanted his meeting with Auria to be public knowledge, so, although he already knew it, he asked at the desk for her room number, then had the desk clerk call her rather than call himself.

Trent thumbed an old *Time* magazine while he waited for Auria to dress. The staircase led directly off the lobby. Auria hesitated on the landing and held onto the polished mahogany banister as she came down the final flight. Dressed in a white cotton tennis shirt, calf-length culottes in natural linen, and white canvas beach shoes, and with her hair wet from the shower, she looked like a high school senior, a little anxious as she came downstairs to meet her date. But a smile lit her face as Trent stepped out from the shadows and she said : 'Hi, I didn't expect to hear from you so soon.'

Drawing her out to the pool, Trent picked a stone bench above the filter pumps so that their conversation would be masked by the purr. To an observer, they would seem like lovers.

He said, 'I told you I'd make a few calls. There's a slight possibility that I can find out where the *Beau Belle* went down – that is if the yacht was the *Beau Belle*.'

The weight came off her. 'Great!'

'That doesn't mean that I'm prepared to go into Cuban waters. We'll take things one step at a time.'

Auria wasn't in a mood to listen. The brakes were off and her natural enthusiasm shone through. Trent was familiar with the relief she felt. The waiting was always hard to take, the endless waiting in a plane. Finally the green light and the doors opening to the night, wind tearing at the engine roar. The leap into space, waiting for the chute to open, waiting for the ground.

Nobody had trained Auria. Her emotions were strong, impulsive, easy to read. The bridge of her nose wrinkled as she smiled at him: '*Golden Girl*'s something special. I've never sailed on a big cat.'

'You're going to have to post bond,' Trent warned. 'Two hundred thousand dollars.'

She hesitated for only a moment before plunging like a compulsive gambler. 'No problem.'

Trent believed her, but he was sure that the $200,000 wouldn't be hers. She had money, but not that kind of money. 'We'll be based here on South Andros,' he said. 'We can fix the documents in Nassau. Not in the States.'

The wrinkles deepened across the bridge of her nose. 'Tax?'

'Right.' He knelt by the pool, trailing his fingers through the water. With his back to her, he said: 'I'll be away a few days tracking a couple of men and, depending on the depth she's lying at, I may need advice on the diving.' He was musing out loud now, accepting that the *Beau Belle* was there to be found, lulling her fears with confidence. 'I've got dive tanks and a small compressor on the *Golden Girl* but we'll need extra equipment. Proper lights if we dive at night. The Cubans would spot the *Golden Girl* so we'll use the Zodiac for the search. That means portable satellite navigation. There's a

Mexican I know who's an expert on salvage. Nice man, big as a house.' Smiling, he turned to face her: 'It could be fun. Glad someone gave you my name. But, as I said, even if it's possible, it won't be quick. I'd guess a minimum of a month – that's if everything goes right and it probably won't.'

The time scale didn't matter to her. 'I've got my PADI certificate. So has Marco.'

'Good. You'll need to go back to the States to arrange the finance. Give me a number and I'll call you there late tonight.'

'We were going out to the reef . . .' she began, but he cut her short. He wanted her out of the way. 'We need to move fast. The hurricane season's coming.'

Flying into Nassau, Trent called Charles Benson's cousin at his bank and from his secretary collected the faxed report on Rogerton-Smithe prepared by the Lloyd's disciplinary sub-committee. Rogerton-Smithe's Nassau telephone number and address were in the Lloyd's file. Trent dialled and a Bahamian answered by repeating the number. A click told Trent that there was someone else listening. He said, 'The name's Trent. I wish to talk with Mr Rogerton-Smithe about the *Beau Belle*.'

'I'm sorry, but Mr Rogerton-Smithe is not available,' the Bahamian answered.

'Tell him I'm a professional diver and I'm going to dive on the *Beau Belle* whether he sees me or not.' Trent heard the partly muffled start of an interjection before the Bahamian got his hand fully over the mouthpiece. He could imagine the two men signalling to each other. An English voice came on the line, cultured, precise of accent, a little soft: 'Rogerton-Smithe speaking. Is there some way in which I can help?'

'Trent,' Trent said: 'I'm going to be diving on the *Beau Belle* in about four weeks. I thought it would be useful if we talked.'

'I am sorry,' Rogerton-Smithe said: 'I really am awfully busy now. Perhaps next week?'

'I won't be here next week,' Trent said. 'I'm trying to handle this the polite way so we can be friends and co-operate, Mr Rogerton-Smithe. Frankly, you'd be foolish to have it any other way, so why don't I come over and you can have your man mix me a daiquiri?'

Rogerton-Smithe sighed. 'All right. No doubt you know where I live.'

The underwriter had built his house on an opulent beach development. Security men in white sun helmets and starched white uniforms decorated with blue epaulets guarded the entrance. One of the guards took his time calling Rogerton-Smithe's house, getting pleasure from delaying Trent in the heat of the cab in the way that servants of privilege have, when permitted to exercise authority.

The cab driver called the guard a rude name but Trent simply smiled and thanked him when he eventually lifted the barrier. Sprinklers spattered the car as they drove down the palm-shaded private roads with their whitewashed kerbs and borders of clipped lawns, roundabouts planted with cactus and hibiscus, while from behind the hedges came the steady purr of uncountable air conditioners.

Boutiques, a small supermarket and a couple of restaurants and bars formed an artificial village round the marina where big sports fishermen and power yachts lay alongside the docks like force-fed domestic ducks exhausted by the heat. The houses and mansions were Disneyland Spanish in style – white walls, roofs of red tile, arches, patios. An eighteen-hole golf course divided the super rich with beachside properties from the rich rich, whose houses faced seaward across the fairways. Then came the main drive and, further inland, the houses of the merely rich. Rogerton-Smithe was merely rich, but a keen gardener or good with his employees by the look of the beds edging his lawn and the wide variety of flowering shrubs.

The slim young Bahamian who opened the door to Trent tried to pass for a house servant, but the effect was spoilt by a gold bracelet. 'Mr Rogerton-Smithe is on the back terrace,' he said, leading Trent through an open-plan living-room. Trent stepped round a couple of Bokhara rugs on the tiled floor. The pictures were mostly late Victorian with a couple of Edwardian beach scenes of youths wearing striped swimsuits that covered their chests. The furniture was Barcelona chrome with black leather upholstery and heavy glass tables set with *objets d'art* ranging from enamelled and silver boxes to small pieces of good sculpture. It was all good.

'How nice of you to come,' Rogerton-Smithe said, extending a hand as he rose from a cane armchair on the terrace overlooking a small mosaic swimming pool. He was tall and slender with a shaven and almost skull-like face. Although he was in his late fifties, his hair remained dark and without a trace of grey, while a pale blue safari suit accentuated the deep violet of his eyes. The young and shy would have been disconcerted by the directness of his gaze and his grip was firm enough to convince Trent that he did much of the gardening himself. Trent said, 'It's good to see what will grow when you put in the effort.'

Pleased, Rogerton-Smithe said: 'I'm fortunate in having friends who send me plants.'

'A friend sent me a file from Lloyd's.' Trent dropped the big brown envelope onto the cast aluminium copy of a Victorian garden table.

The violet eyes gave nothing away but the underwriter chuckled: '*Touché*, Mr Trent,' and to the hovering Bahamian: 'A daiquiri for our visitor, Robert. Use the blender and lots of ice. Please sit down, Mr Trent, and tell me how I can help.'

Tough, Trent thought. But most people who made money were tough. 'As I told you on the phone, I'm going to dive on the *Beau Belle* in about four weeks.'

'You know where she is?'

'Yes,' Trent said, watching the violet eyes. Not even a flicker, which, in itself, was a kind of evidence. Rogerton-Smithe was very much a prisoner despite all the comforts of his lifestyle, and Trent changed tack as he would have done at the beginning of an interrogation, drawing on the prisoner's isolation, seeking the route to an alliance through common interests and professional experience. 'I understand the *Beau Belle*'s a motor sailor. I sail a big catamaran, no engine except for the outboard on the Zodiac, which I can use if I have to.'

'And if it breaks down, you take it to a mechanic. No

ghastly shore engineers on board spreading grease over everything. Bliss, Mr Trent. Unfortunately, the wind is unreliable and when you have a business to attend to . . .' With a slight shrug, Rogerton-Smithe dismissed the problem as belonging to a past life.

Taking secateurs from his jacket pocket, he crossed the pale clay tiles that surrounded the pool and carefully snipped a white double camellia bloom that the spray from the lawn sprinklers had discoloured.

'Forgive me,' he said as he dropped the bloom into a small wicker basket beside his chair. He swung the chair round so that he faced Trent, preparing the battlefield. As he seated himself, he adjusted his trouser legs to protect the creases; his shoes were hand-made, even the tasselled laces immaculately polished.

'I understand that you were originally thinking of wintering in South Africa,' Trent said.

'I have friend there.'

'But you switched to Newport?'

'The engine broke down. By the time it was repaired, I'd missed the winter season at the Cape and been offered a six-month charter with the possibility of a sale. Fortunate, given my change in circumstances, and sad that it didn't work out.'

The Bahamian appeared with Trent's daiquiri and mint tea for Rogerton-Smithe. Rogerton-Smithe dismissed him with the wave of a hand: 'That will be all, Robert.'

'I don't know Newport.'

'Charming, and a very active social life.' Rogerton-Smithe showed no regrets.

Trent believed in Newport but not in the Cape. 'Don't you get bored?' he asked.

'Robert enjoys the cable TV,' Rogerton-Smithe answered, unembarrassed. 'I read. There's the garden. And a surprising number of invitations, though not always from the nicest people, so one has to be a little careful,' he admitted, with a slight smile at himself rather than for Trent. 'But notoriety does attract. And Nassau is more comfortable than the most open of prisons, Mr Trent. Think of the money one might be tempted to waste on lawyers.' He sipped his tea, watching Trent, trying to sense Trent's opinions, yet not really caring.

He was very much a loner. As he would have done in an interrogation, Trent tempted Rogerton-Smithe with the chance to show off: 'The Lloyd's report is all bones but not much meat, and a lot of it is too technical for an outsider to understand without an interpreter.'

'The language may be technical, the facts could be understood by a child,' Rogerton-Smithe assured him. 'All professions like to wrap themselves in mystery, Mr Trent. I specialised in what we call the "Excess of Loss" market. It would be better described as gambling on total disaster, but gambling and disaster are words financial institutions don't much like.'

Lloyd's, for obvious reasons, was a subject that Rogerton-Smithe's Nassau acquaintances avoided and the underwriter was enjoying himself. A ship suffered damage in a collision; fire destroyed two floors of a tower block; theft, fraud; illness delayed completion of a feature film. 'All common occurrences,' Rogerton-Smithe explained. 'Premiums are calculated accordingly.'

Excess of loss took over where the easily imaginable and calculable became the unimaginable and the incalculable. In the eighties and nineties petrodollars poured in to expand the economy. Tankers 350 metres long were built, vast new office complexes, business after business installed main-frame computers.

Rogerton-Smithe sipped his tea and looked at Trent over the top of his glass: 'You have to understand the explosion in scale of investment brought about by modern technology, Mr Trent. Banks and financial houses won't lend without excess of loss insurance on a project, so without it, there'd be no development.'

And no single syndicate had the capital capacity to cover such giant risks.

'Take a hundred million dollar tanker,' Rogerton-Smithe explained. 'I'd cover and reinsure the risk in excess of five million. The next man would take a further five and pass it on.

A day or two later it would be back on my desk and I'd take a further five. In other words, I'd be reinsuring my own risk and picking up a fresh premium, a delightfully quick and easy route to riches, Mr Trent. We called it the "London spiral". Finally we ran out of believable capacity and turned to the brass plate companies in places like the Cayman Islands. We knew perfectly well that they'd never pay out. That being the case, it seemed sensible to some of us to own our own brass plate companies rather than let other people run off with the premiums. A little naughty perhaps.' He shrugged slim shoulders, dismissing his judgement of himself as unimportant. 'Of course, when I was young, my lifestyle was considered *very* naughty. However I was making people a great deal of money so they didn't care.' Again that slight shrug and the hint of a smile.

It was as if he were a disinterested observer of his own life and, searching the empty violet depths of the underwriter's eyes, Trent found himself reminded of the final page of a book that ended with three dots, then nothing but empty space.

'You warn Names not to treat profits as spendable income,' Rogerton-Smithe continued, 'that there'll be bad years as well as good, so they need to build up an emergency fund. Obviously, you don't press the point or no one would invest in your syndicates.'

'Would they have made a profit?'

'Long term – say twenty years – certainly. As long as they weren't greedy.'

'Or were in your syndicates?'

Rogerton-Smithe felt for his secateurs. He wasn't avoiding the question. He had merely spotted a faded bloom low down on a pink hibiscus. Stooping to cut the flower left him a little breathless and he coughed into a handkerchief. Tucking the handkerchief into his sleeve, he said, 'At the end only the greedy and the very ill-advised were in my syndicates, Mr Trent. Fortunately, the underwriter has advance warning of the crash. I had this house.'

'And the proceeds of your brass plate companies.'

'Precisely, Mr Trent. Although, of course, that would be

impossible to prove, either within the six-year time scale allowed the investigative authorities in the US, or with the funds allowed the British police. Were I to live, in six years I would be a free man, Mr Trent, and a rich one. I have been honest with you. Now perhaps you would be honest with me as to your interest in the *Beau Belle*?'

'Cash,' Trent said. His frank, open smile implied an alliance based on mutual understanding – fellow wolves looking down from the top of a wall at a flock of fattened lambs grazing a spring meadow. 'The *Beau Belle*'s insured for two hundred and fifty thousand pounds with a Cayman Islands company as the registered owners. I thought the owners might pay fifty per cent commission for a report that forced Lloyd's to pay out.'

'Did you indeed.' The tip of the underwriter's tongue was visible for a moment as he moistened his upper lip.

'I'll want a bomb-proof contract,' Trent said. 'Think it over. I'll be back in a week.'

From Rogerton-Smithe's house, Trent returned to Benson's cousin at the bank and opened an account. While waiting for his flight back to Congo Town, he called Auria's number and left a message with her mother that he now knew the *Beau Belle*'s position. Then he called O'Brien for a meeting the following day.

'Is that a positive?' O'Brien asked.

Trent said, 'Yes.'

Back at Kemp's Bay he asked the mechanic at the service station where he could have his compressor serviced and spent an hour in the beach bar discussing diving with the locals. He got through to Auria at midnight from the public phone and repeated that he'd got a definite fix on the sunken yacht. 'We still don't know for sure that she's the *Beau Belle* but I'm prepared to take a look,' he said. Apart from hoisting a banner on the *Golden Girl*, there was nothing more he could do to target himself.

9

Mid-morning and hardly a ripple stirred the sea's surface inside South Andros reef. In these sea conditions, the lightly laden Zodiac made twenty knots with the Mercury running on half-throttle, and the two five-gallon tanks of gas gave Trent a range of 150 miles.

The sea shone glacial green dotted with the dark shadows of coral heads. To port of Trent's course lay the mangrove-bound coast with, inland on the higher ground, strands of thin fir trees, their tops frail and feathery against the bleached blue of the sky. A half-dozen frigate birds floated overhead and out in the dark blue water beyond the reef two dolphins raced parallel with the Zodiac.

Up ahead a pair of open-decked Bahamian fishing cutters tacked clear of Bowen Sound and the crew waved as Trent skittered across their bows. The sun hot on his scalp, he scooped sea water over himself and over the towel covering his icebag. Off the tip of North Andros, two white men and a black guide were casting for bone fish from a Boston whaler anchored on the edge of the mangroves. Trent swung wide and the guide waved his thanks. Out to sea a forty-foot Rybovitch sports fisherman flying the US ensign trolled for marlin. All in all it was as near perfect a day as man could wish for. He eased the helm over and headed across Fresh Creek to the beach below the Chickcharnie Hotel.

Trent found O'Brien sipping a soda in the shade of a palm tree. The DEA agent had changed into a faded green-striped seersucker suit of the usual ancient vintage. The same worn satchel briefcase leant against the leg of his chair, and a pair of antique but powerful binoculars lay on the table. Years in the Caribbean had trained the American to expend the minimum of energy in the midday heat, and he raised a hand less than an inch by way of greeting.

'Birthday present,' Trent said, dropping the icebag beside O'Brien's briefcase. 'Red snapper. Hope you can use them.'

'Kind of you,' O'Brien said, checking his watch. 'Sit yourself down. I ordered us fresh pond crab and rice, pride of Andros.'

A waiter strolled over with a friendly smile. O'Brien asked him to store Trent's fish in the fridge and fetch Trent a Kalik when he brought the crab.

Turning back to Trent, he said, 'The Latino followed you to Nassau. He hasn't come back and, as far as we can tell, no one's taken his place.' Perhaps a little uncomfortable in his thoughts, he watched a small, white sloop tack into the creek. Without looking at Trent, he said: 'Turns out he and his friend had Cuban connections. Probably means they already know what we're planning so you may like to change your mind.'

'DGI?'

O'Brien shrugged: 'I'd have to ask Langley. Let the CIA know and they'll cancel the operation or put their own men in.'

Almost as if it were a personal crusade, Trent thought. He slid the Lloyd's disciplinary committee dossier on Rogerton-Smithe across the table: 'Hewett I know about. What do you have on the other crew on the *Beau Belle*?'

'One of the New Zealanders wrote his folks a postcard before sailing, and mentioned an American, Mac. That fits with the Cuban Navy's report. McKinley Wilson, born Chicago, thirty-three years old, single, professional yacht crew. He may have picked up a job in Cancún because there's no sightings of him any of the places we've looked. I had the New Zealand kids checked. Six months out of college and good jobs waiting back home.' He looked at Trent. There was no mistaking the anger, even if it didn't reach his voice. 'Kids like that don't disappear, Mr Trent. There's a killer loose. You know it. You've been trailing your coat to make sure you're the target. Why?'

Trent said: 'It's what I'm trained for.'

O'Brien's smile was minimal. 'Trying to get yourself killed? Or protecting people?' He tapped a clean blunt fingertip on the tabletop, watching Trent the while, curious. 'Or, having been out a while, were you missing the juice?'

'Does it matter?'

'You're trying to put a new life together. So, yes, Mr Trent, I'd say it's something you need to think about.'

O'Brien slipped wire-rimmed spectacles out of a steel case, gave the lenses a polish, and picked up the Lloyd's dossier. His reading was like everything else he did, a little slow but very thorough. He laid each page on top of the previous one with the occasional tap of a fingernail to keep the edges straight. Finished, he returned the sheets to the file and slid the file back into the envelope. He carefully folded his wire-rim spectacles, replaced them inside their battered steel case and put the case in his breast pocket. He looked across at Trent: 'Forget the paperwork – how did you feel about the Brit?'

Despite having stolen and salted away a great deal of money, the Lloyd's underwriter hadn't struck Trent as greedy, more of a game-player, scoring points against 'straight' society. But Trent's expertise was in international terrorism and political fanaticism. For eighteen years he had infiltrated terrorist groups. He knew their motivation and how their minds worked. And he knew the workings of the agencies that fought against them. Now, looking out over Fresh Creek, he thought that he didn't know much else. 'I'm no judge,' he said.

'A man's a crook, doesn't necessarily make him a killer.' O'Brien gave an almost imperceptible nod of agreement with his own thoughts. 'Let's deal with the yacht first. I have a position that's accurate to two hundred yards. There's a local man you'll meet after we've eaten who has a piece of equipment he says will find her, and he has the *Beau Belle*'s position. Same man has a pair of these new pocket position finders that work off the satellites that I had fetched in. His idea. That brings us to the people you'll have on board.

'The girl first. I've run her six ways and she comes up clean unless you believe getting born in New Jersey is a crime. Binny College, that's a small girls' school in upstate New York; Catholic, which figures with the name. Good grades. Clean driving licence. Amex and Visa with no payment problems. Father has a couple of restaurants, Italian, nothing flash but definitely class – Newport and Oakridge, New Jersey. I even had a friend run the family through with the FBI, which is a thing I don't normally care to do. Not that we're on different sides, but they get a sniff that could mean promotion and they're in on the act faster than a third base steal. A friend with the IRS is still looking. Takes the IRS a while unless they've already got their teeth into a subject but they're tough to fool, which is why the rich spend so much on lawyers who find them tax shelters.'

The big Rybovitch sports fisherman rounded the point and O'Brien raised his binoculars. 'A million and a half cash,' he calculated, binoculars following the Rybovitch upwater towards the Fresh Creek Yacht Club. 'The brother, Marco, is only a half-brother. Mother's son by a first husband who died. Rocco adopted the boy, hence the same family name. Gossip says he's a great lover, rich wives in East Coast ocean racing society. Crews as an amateur for the husbands except he gets paid, probably in cash, which is something the owners can afford and the IRS can't trace, and he's said to be a ruthless helmsman round the buoys. A couple of thousand dollars in his checking account, no credit cards, a mess of parking tickets and three speeding offences back when he was in his late teens which Rocco paid off, but nothing since.

'I checked with the Brits and the Hewett kid comes up straighter than the Pope, and there's nothing on his dad that they know of.'

O'Brien raised his binoculars again to study a couple walking up the Yacht Club dock from the Rybovitch.

'Professional interest?' Trent asked.

'No. Jealousy. Miami cosmetic surgeon. Grossed eight hundred grand last year – restructuring boobs, for Chrissakes, and I'm risking my life for forty-two hundred.' O'Brien laid the binoculars down and shifted his attention back to Trent.

Trent said: 'I'd like you to have another look at Auria Rocco. She's putting up a two hundred thousand dollar bond on the *Golden Girl*.'

O'Brien lifted an eyebrow about a quarter of an inch, which was probably as much surprise as he'd shown in years. 'And I took you for some kind of knight errant, Mr Trent, while all the time you were using your brains. Give me the bank and any lawyers involved and I'll get working.'

The friendly waiter brought their pond crab and a brace of iced Kalik lagers on a tray and O'Brien thanked him with his usual quiet courtesy: 'You like black people, Mr Trent?'

Trent answered truthfully that it wasn't a question he'd ever asked himself. Working undercover, he had judged people by the danger they could place him in rather than by whether he liked them or not.

'Well, that makes you adaptable, which is important if you're going to live out here,' O'Brien said. 'Reason I asked is some of the new people coming into the Agency don't trust the Islanders, and it shows. Fact is there's corruption down here same as there is up in Washington. Maybe down here, being poor, people have more excuse. Pick and choose is the name of the game. I've made a good many close friends over the years. People I'm proud to be allowed to know. All walks of life. Not one of them ever let me down and I never let one of them down. Like I said at Miss Mary's, you got messed up, so I'm not expecting trust for a while yet. I'm going to have to earn it. But I give you a man's name, that's different. You trust him with your life. We're going to work together, I'd like you to bear that in mind.'

'Thank you,' Trent said.

O'Brien chuckled softly: 'You're welcome. We're building a marriage, Mr Trent. That's a difficult relationship.'

10

At three o'clock in the afternoon, excellently fed, Trent cruised the Zodiac along the shoreline. O'Brien had told him to meet the man with the magnetometer ten miles south of Fresh Creek and that he'd be in a red fishing dory: 'You've set yourself up as bait and he's a local cop, Mr Trent. We don't want people frightened off by seeing you together.'

Trent spotted the dory pulled out on a small beach. He dragged the Zodiac up the sand and found the Bahamian police officer lying on his back in the shade. A wide-brimmed straw hat with frayed edges covered his face. Ripped cotton shorts stretched halfway down his thighs. The shorts would have been tight on a child; on the Bahamian they were baggy – Trent had never seen anyone so thin outside of a famine area. In colour, he was deep black and dried sea salt etched his ribs like the shadings of a contour map. He shifted his hat back with a hand whose long bony fingers reminded Trent of dried seaweed and, without further movement, looked him up and down with slow curiosity, large dark eyes set in deep caverns.

'Mr Trent? Skelly. Not original but it's what they call me.' The Bahamian's slow smile showed very white teeth. His accent was establishment English with the vowels marginally softened. He fanned away a fly with his hat and Trent saw that he was either bald or had shaved his skull and, in age, somewhere between eighteen and eighty.

Hands flat on the sand, Skelly pushed himself into a sitting position and kept on pushing. His arms were so long that he was able to swing his feet back under him, knees up higher than his ears. He rose and rose like a genie uncorked from its bottle until, towering over Trent, he stood straight and well over seven foot tall.

'I'm easy to recognise, Mr Trent,' he said with that same slow smile, his eyes warm with self-mockery, 'That's why Mr O'Brien thought we should meet out of town. A nice man, and a very good friend of mine. He was kind enough to show me a few extracts from your file and it made frightening reading. We live off tourism here, Mr Trent, so we don't want too many corpses washed up on the beach.'

'I'll be diving in Cuban waters,' Trent said.

'So Mr O'Brien tells me. I have the position here and a chart we can look at.' A half-dozen slow strides, each a metre and a half long, carried Skelly to his dory and he eased the canvas cover back from the equipment stored in the bows. 'Ever used a magnetometer, Mr Trent?'

Trent said that he hadn't.

Skelly opened the lid of what looked like a large steel lunchbox. A print recorder occupied the right-hand third with, to its left, two sets of four pressure switches, one set of twelve, and a small liquid display screen. The number of switches filled Trent with foreboding. His skills were in destruction. He could strip and reassemble a pistol or automatic rifle with his eyes shut and construct detonators and fuses from the contents of a kitchen cupboard. On the other hand his approach to his Mercury outboard was basic: carry a spare.

'Simple, as long as you don't confuse yourself by reading the manuals,' Skelly told him. 'This is a model G-866 made by EG & G. What it does is register the magnetic field under the sensor but, if you're not technically minded, just think of it as a ferrous metal detector. The background magnetic field round these waters is about fifty-six point eight kilogammas, which I've set up on the machine, so all you need do is switch on and watch the liquid display. If the sensor passes over a piece of iron, you'll get an immediate change in the reading. I've drawn a graph for you that gives the anomaly for different weights of iron at depths up to a hundred feet. At around sixteen thousand dollars, Mr Trent, there aren't that many of these built. If the Cubans look like catching you, get rid of it rather than have it traced back to my office.'

He transferred the magnetometer to Trent's Zodiac together with a coil of cable in a flotation jacket attached to the sensor, and they motored out from the shore, Trent paying the cable out over the stern while Skelly fastened the magnetometer's crocodile clips to the Mercury's twelve-volt battery. A small canvas drogue on the end of the sensor kept the cable taut. 'Tow at five knots,' Skelly told him. 'You'll need to set your depth sounder up beside the magnetometer so you can see it, have the GPS in one hand, and a marker buoy ready to kick overboard.'

Taking the helm, Skelly ran the Zodiac past a floating plank and Trent saw the count jump 3.7 gammas. Skelly circled back a little to the left of the plank and the magnetometer registered an 8.7 gamma anomaly. Circling again and a little further to the left, the anomaly dropped back to 3. Skelly showed Trent the graph: 'We're in twenty feet of water, eight point seven gammas gives you around ten kilograms of iron, which is the weight of the length of chain I dropped. You'll be searching in about the same depth of water. You want an estimate of how much iron the yacht has on board but if she's a big motor sailor it won't be less than a couple of tons so she should be easy to find. I've run successful searches for drug boats smugglers have sunk rather than have caught, but that's in daylight and I've been able to mark the search area. Other than the Cubans, I'd say navigation will be your problem.'

Back on the beach, Skelly unfolded a chart. The sinking of the *Beau Belle* had been well-planned. The yacht had sailed north-west up the Old Bahama Channel to a point where the reef swelled out from the Cuban coast. Instead of rounding the reef, the *Beau Belle* had kept to her heading and now lay in the shallows midway between the shore and the reef edge. The chart warned of strong currents; two of the beacons were out that night, and there'd been heavy rain. If he'd been caught by the Cubans, the skipper would have said that he'd made a mistake as to when to change course. It was a good story, particularly if backed by faulty Loran or Decca navigation equipment.

Trent said, 'Diving at night, it would help to know how reliable the Cuban lights are. Is that something you could ask the US coastguard without their getting excited? Say over the past six months?'

'No problem. These days they keep that sort of information on computer.' Skelly unlocked the bow locker on his dory and dug out a plastic wrapped package containing two hand-held Magellan GPS and a manual. Next came a short-barrelled Smith & Wesson hammerless Police Special, three boxes of cartridges, and a gun permit in a waterproof bag. Grim, he looked down at Trent: 'Mr O'Brien believes there's a killer loose, Mr Trent. I don't want to know what guns you've got hidden on your boat but if you have to shoot anybody here in the Bahamas, I'd rather you did it with a legal weapon. That happens, call Headquarters and ask for Superintendent Skelly. Give Archibald as your name if it's just normally bad and Victor if it's a massacre. I'll be out within a couple of hours. If necessary, we can fix up a story between us.'

Handing Trent the revolver, he smiled as if taking the decision had lifted a weight off his shoulders: 'Carry it at all times, Mr Trent. If that means wearing socks so you've got somewhere to hide it, sweaty feet are a small sacrifice compared with losing your life.'

Back on board the *Golden Girl*, Trent brewed coffee before sitting down at the chart table with a blank sheet of paper. He marked the centre as the provisional position of the *Beau Belle*. Given this position as accurate within 600 feet, the search area was approximately a quarter-mile square. Adding the turning distance at the end of each sweep made four and a half minutes for each traverse.

He would be in a fifteen-foot inflatable at night, and even a torch might alert the Cubans, so the search pattern had to be simple to carry out. Steering across either wind or current would push the sensor off-course, so he checked the Admiralty Pilot. Both were onshore, which gave him a latitudinal base line for the pattern. On a clear night, Lobos Cay Light would be visible twenty-five miles north across the Old Bahama Channel. If he steered for the lighthouse on each sweep, the convergence would be negligible.

If possible, he wanted to do the search by himself. He waited till one o'clock in the morning before slipping away quietly from the *Golden Girl* in the Zodiac. With an extension tube over the Mercury's tiller, he could steer while crouched over the magnetometer. A beacon twenty miles north across the Tongue of the Ocean served as target. Two hours' practice and he knew, for certain, that he needed a second pair of eyes. Marco had to sail the *Golden Girl*, which left Auria or Richard.

Stowing the magnetometer cable, Trent sat in the gently rocking inflatable. The heat of the day had left the horizon softened by a slight haze of evaporation but the sky overhead was clear and Trent could see the dark markings on the almost full moon. A hint of swamp air reached him from the cut dividing North from South Andros. He could feel it now, the familiar lightness of mind as the first faint traces of pattern developed. It was always the same, this concentration on the facts, on what had actually happened. Then came the slow unravelling of the whys, and lastly the motivation. Looking towards the shore, he pictured how the operation would play. Cuba.

11

As an officer in the Cuban Navy, Roddy de Sanchez was perhaps disloyal in sweating through the US Air Force exercises each weekly morning before breakfast. Weekends, he jogged. The alarm clock by his bed showed 07.06 and he had his head between his knees when his mother shouted up the stairs that he was wanted on the phone. Struggling into his bathrobe and down the stairs to the extension in the front hall took a couple of minutes, by which time the caller had been disconnected or had rung off.

Roddy poured himself a cup of coffee in the kitchen, sat at the breakfast bar, and watched his mother knead wholemeal dough. Roddy's mother had baked their bread as far back as Roddy could remember. Therapeutic, she claimed, and she liked to darn socks. The washing and ironing, all other cooking, and the housework she left to a maid, and to the cousin who had lived with them since being deserted by her husband.

Roddy's mother was a small woman with fine bone structure. A series of nips and tucks over recent years seemed to have pulled away the gentleness that early photographs showed, as if the gentleness had been surface camouflage for the martyr crucified within.

The phone rang again at a quarter past seven and yet again at twenty-five minutes past seven, only a couple of double rings each time so that Roddy hardly had time to reach the receiver even had he wished to do so. But the time between the calls contained the information – the Englishman, Trent, had agreed to charter his yacht. The second time it happened Roddy called the exchange to report a possible fault. His mother looked up from her bread-making and waited for him to finish.

She said, 'Roddy, I implore you, be careful.' She held her arms out to him, then remembered the flour on her hands and stood there a moment, lost in indecision and misery.

Roddy said, 'It's all right, Mama. Nothing's happening. Truly, I promise.'

The child of civil war, Roddy's mother hoarded shattered promises, relishing the fragments as other women of her age repossess past lovers in their daydreams. The only lovers in her dreams were those her husband enjoyed when his duties forced him to sleep at his headquarters. She sighed and turned back to the dough while Roddy returned to his room to shower and dress.

He breakfasted on fresh yogurt with raw oat flakes and a second cup of coffee made with freshly roasted beans. He called Estoban Tur before leaving the house and set up a meeting for later that morning.

Roddy's father's generation had created the Cuban Revolution. Roddy's age group were more interested in designer clothes, the latest dance tune, how to get their hands on American dollars. They were embarrassed by the fervour of the foreigners from the continental mainland of Latin America with whom Bureau Three plotted insurrection. Roddy had forsaken his normal wardrobe for a pair of khaki slacks, a cheap T-shirt, and sandals. He parked his MG at some distance from the port district where a tumbledown block housed the Bureau. The dozen or so entrances from crowded alleys enabled visitors to come and go unnoticed.

Estoban's office on the first floor was ill-lit, grubby, and stank of stale tobacco and sweat. Though the room was over twenty feet square, the only furnishings were a dozen directors' chairs with patched seats set round a plywood conference table. Ringed stains left by coffee cups formed a continual border a foot in from the table edge which, in turn, had been charred by countless cigarettes.

Unshaven and wearing his other brown polyester suit, Estoban looked equally shoddy. 'What brings you slumming?' he asked as he waved Roddy to a chair at the table, and slumped down facing him.

'The man you want. Trent,' Roddy said.

A membrane seemed to drop over Estoban's eyes so that they were suddenly without expression, and without any depth.

Unnerved, Roddy said: 'I think I've got him for you.'

He had brought a chart of the north coast of Cuba. Unfolding the chart on the table, he repeated Marco Rocco's account of the sinking of the *Beau Belle*. A Naval Intelligence interest had been established by his interview of the American crewman and he had requested the Department of External Affairs to forward to his office copies of all correspondence relating to the yacht.

Press reports that the yacht had been sunk by gunfire had produced a steady stream of letters from both the British and New Zealand governments. There were also requests for information from the insurers at Lloyd's.

'She's insured for two hundred and fifty thousand pounds sterling and Lloyd's won't pay out without evidence of why she sank.' Roddy slid a file containing copies of the correspondence across the table to Estoban. 'Those involved were looking for someone to uncover the evidence. Our field agent put Trent's name into play and he's been hired.'

Slouched back from the table, Estoban turned the pages in the file with one finger. He seemed disdainful of the contents, or disinterested. Finally he looked up. 'The yacht is in Cuban waters?'

'Or close enough. That's our guess,' Roddy said. 'I'd like to put homing devices on Trent's equipment so we don't lose him.'

'From the Bureau's technical department? So you have my fingerprints on the operation?' Estoban pressed the fingertips of both hands flat on the letter he'd been scanning, nodded, and smiled at Roddy. It wasn't much of a smile and it didn't pass within a mile of his eyes. He flipped the file shut and sped it back so that it slid off the tabletop onto Roddy's lap: 'I want him alive, Roddy. Drive him ashore.'

Trent spent the day ordering supplies and equipment, checking gear, and refilling the dive bottles with fresh air. The fisherman who acted as watchman rowed out in the late afternoon with a brown envelope containing what a police constable had told him were the *Golden Girl*'s ship's papers.

Trent waited for the old man to leave before opening the envelope. Skelly had put the faxed report from the US coastguard between two pieces of card so it felt right. The fax catalogued malfunctions of one or other of the relevant beacons on the Cuban coast with a start date three weeks before the *Beau Belle* sailed from Angola. The shortest malfunction lasted twenty minutes and the longest three hours. At no time were both lights out at the same time, but the frequency of malfunctions increased. Finally the International Maritime Agency issued a warning that both beacons would be out of service for repairs over a period of not less than forty-eight hours. The *Beau Belle* sank on the second night of the repair period and no further malfunctions were recorded.

An official with access to the beacons had planned the sinking of the *Beau Belle*. According to O'Brien, a Latino with Cuban connections had tailed him from his meeting with Pepito until he had told Rogerton-Smithe that he intended diving on the yacht. Trent could have written a dozen scenarios on the basis of those two facts, which was why he didn't bother.

Instead, he took the Zodiac into the beach and called Auria from the payphone.

Auria and Marco Rocco flew in with Richard Hewett from New York to Paradise Island Airport. Marco, his easy charm infallible, was first through customs and immigration. He wore bleached cotton slacks, T-shirt, sneakers, and a planter's hat, and carried a big blue nylon holdall slung over his shoulder, pro dive fins strung to the handles. He waved a pair of wraparound sunglasses at Trent, yelling, 'Hey there, skip, how's it going?' as he charged across the terminal, embracing Trent in a bear hug, slapping him on the back. 'Great to see you.'

The warmth, however superficial, was natural and hard to resist. Considerate of his sister, he dropped his holdall at Trent's feet and shouldered his way back through the holiday-makers to grab Auria's bag.

Richard trailed in Auria's wake, awkward, as ever, dressed in clothes too hot for the climate. Slim and tall, with a beak of a nose, only his lack of confidence stopped him from being handsome. Lack of confidence and that he felt himself to be out of place. In contrast Auria, with her stocky, muscular body and short hair, might easily have been a tennis pro or a diving instructor at one of Nassau's up-market resorts. But Trent sensed that she had changed in her few days away. She seemed wary of their relationship; there was no spontaneous smile, no more belief that what they intended could be fun. Strictly business, Trent thought as he watched her, and he was certain that she was under orders. Reluctantly under orders, and angry at being trapped. And ashamed.

She asked Richard to help Marco find a cab and get their bags loaded, and then told Trent in private that she had consulted a lawyer; the charter contract, banker's draft, and $200,000 bond were prepared. All they required was a witness to their signatures and a bank of deposit.

They took the cab over the bridge into Nassau, Marco up front beside the driver commenting with his usual enthusiasm about whatever caught his fancy, women, boats, architecture. Life and everything in it pleased him.

Sandwiched between Auria and Trent, Richard rode in silence, hands clasped between his knees. Trent suspected that he and Auria had been arguing, Richard keen to give up the search and, if he knew of it, disapproving of Auria putting her money at risk. Now the time for argument was over and, as they crossed the bridge, Richard gloomily looked out of the cab window.

Trent gave Marco the address of a ship's chandler together with a list of supplies he'd ordered earlier and Auria suggested that Richard accompany her brother – they would all gather in an hour at Captain Nemo's waterfront restaurant.

The bank was an air-conditioned glass cube. The British Intelligence officer's cousin had his office on the fifth floor and met Auria and Trent at the elevator. Tall, slim, brown eyes and hair, aged in his mid-forties, he shared that attribute of the British upper class of appearing casually dressed despite wearing a perfectly cut suit and cricket club tie. A forelock falling over his right eye made him seem diffident as he shook Auria's hand.

'Good of you to come,' he said, as if they had made a long detour through country lanes for afternoon tea. 'Trent, isn't it? And Miss Rocco? Peter Benson. Do sit down, won't you?' The banker steered Auria to a comfortable armchair set at an angle to his desk: 'Dreadfully hot outside. A cold drink?'

He spoke into the desktop intercom: 'Sybil, I wonder if you would be terribly kind? Two lime juices with plenty of ice.' Switching off the intercom, he straightened a silver-framed photograph on his desk as if it were a talisman connecting him to the real world outside. Then he looked across at Auria, polite, questioning, a little out of his depth but determined to be of help. 'Mr Trent mentioned some papers, Miss Rocco, connected with a bond.'

Auria took a thick white lawyer's envelope from her nylon sports bag.

A soft knock on the door heralded a middle-aged Bahamian woman with a silver tray – white blouse, black skirt, spectacles hanging on a gold chain. The banker rose quickly to his feet, thanking her profusely for her trouble, and taking the tray so that he could pass Auria a tall frosted crystal tumbler, fussing that the lime might be too sweet or not sweet enough.

Trent would have expected Auria to be irritated by the banker. Instead, she played to him, flirtatious, anxious to please.

Slipping spectacles onto his nose, the banker studied the documents, shuffling them clumsily, as if unused to such things, and appearing to skim the pages without expecting to fully understand their contents. Tinted lenses hid his eyes and he took them off before saying to Auria: 'Yes, well that seems all very fair. Unusual, of course.' A slight movement of his hands suggested that he found unusual everything that crossed his desk and that the fault was his.

Auria laughed in response, leaning forward in her chair: 'I'm great on a tennis court but this stuff . . .' She held her hands open so that he could see the racket callous: 'I mean, all I did was tell the lawyer what I wanted. One page, I thought, and he came up with this. The fee he charged, I just hope it makes sense.'

The banker chuckled and said that he was sure it did. His body language implied that he and Auria were already friends and equals – after all, the funds were hers. His role as banker placed him at her service, while Trent was an employee.

Turning to Trent, he said: 'Miss Rocco is depositing a bond with the bank against your yacht, while on charter to Miss Rocco, being seized or lost at sea while under conditions unsatisfactory to your insurers, Mr Trent. The bond is supported by Miss Rocco's bankers. It seems a most satisfactory arrangement.'

He handed Trent the charter contract. Sub-clauses attended on sub-clauses in lawyers' English. To have understood all the contract's implications would have required an interpreter, who, in turn, would have had to be a lawyer, but the bond was real enough: $200,000 to be drawn on a New Jersey bank and a draft on the same bank for $10,000 to cover the cost of the expedition.

'We need to sign,' Auria said, suddenly anxious to have the meeting over.

'Yes, of course.' The banker's hands fluttered over his desktop, apologetic for any delay. 'I'm sure you're quite satisfied, Mr Trent?' He spoke into the intercom, telling his assistant that he required her as a witness.

Trent turned back through the pages. The delay increased

Auria's anxiety and Trent felt the fear in her again and an unspoken plea, not to Trent, but to whichever deity she believed in, that nothing would go amiss. He tossed the charter agreement onto the banker's desk: 'Fine by me.'

They had a two-hour wait before the late afternoon flight to South Andros left from Nassau Airport. Trent left Auria to wait for Marco and Richard at Captain Nemo's and telephoned the banker. There were four clauses in the contract which the banker disliked. The clauses were deliberately separated but, put together, the meaning was clear: if Trent died before claiming the money, the bond went back to Auria Rocco.

'Pity we don't know who her lawyers are, but frankly, if you lose your yacht, you'd better watch your back,' the banker warned, no hint of the amateur in his voice: 'If you want to trace the source of the funds, the IRS are your best bet. I can't help there. The IRS don't care for Bahamian banks.'

Trent then called O'Brien and gave him the bank details on the bond and draft. 'Keep checking on the girl. She's been told the next steps in whatever's happening and she doesn't like it.'

An hour's flight in a six-seater took them to Congo Town on South Andros and they found a cab to drive them on to Kemp's Bay. Trent showed them over the *Golden Girl*, explaining the galley and how the marine toilet and shower worked. The two guest cabins in the starboard hull he gave to Richard and Marco, his own cabin to Auria, apologising that his clothes remained in the bottom two drawers and that she would have to share her shower and head.

He left the charter party to settle in, and ran ashore in the Zodiac to pick up supplies and a spare twelve-volt battery for the magnetometer. When he returned to the catamaran, he found the threesome drinking beer in the cockpit, Marco keen to run ashore in the Zodiac for dinner.

Grateful to be left alone on the *Golden Girl*, Trent ate a bowl of cereal before laying out his sleeping bag on the nylon webbing connecting the two hulls forward of the saloon. Soon after ten o'clock Auria and Richard returned. Marco ran the

Zodiac back to shore. It was almost first light before Trent heard him ease the tender alongside, stumbling a little as he made for his bunk.

Barefoot and silent, Trent lifted the anchor at first light, raised the mainsail, and bore away from Kemp's Town on the gentle offshore breeze. He set the catamaran to sail herself with a rubber bungee holding the tiller arm and made his way forward to the sail locker.

The catamaran had three jibs, two genoas, two feather-weight ghosters, and a vast balloon spinnaker in her headsail wardrobe. Trent kept the sails rolled and lashed with strong sewing cotton in their separate bags. He selected the largest of the two ghosters, hanked the spring shackles to the forestay and shackled a halyard to the head of the sail. Leading the sheets aft, he looped them round the winches port and starboard of the cockpit and raised the sail so that it hung in its cotton lashings like a long white sausage. A jerk on the port-side sheet snapped the lashings and the breeze pried the sail open. Trent winched in the sheet as the sail filled and the bows lifted a fraction, rustling over the smooth sea with the sound of stiff writing paper being ripped.

With the sun low, the dangerous coral heads were almost impossible to see. Trent settled his back against the bar that connected the twin tillers and eased the big cat out into deeper water beyond the edge of the reef and parallel to the coast.

Auria stuck her head out of the saloon and looked over at the coast before ducking back. In a few minutes she returned with two mugs of coffee and a bowl of muesli. Barefoot, she wore her white bikini and had draped a towel over her shoulders. She handed Trent the muesli and offered to take the helm while he ate, but he was already slipping the bungee rubber over the tiller arm.

Auria sat on the leeward cockpit locker. Now that they were under way, she seemed more sure of herself. She said: 'You don't like to share. Is that because you live alone? Or do you live alone because you don't like to share?'

When he ignored her question, Auria asked: 'What did the Weather Bureau forecast?'

'Calm for the next forty-eight hours.'

'Great, he can speak.'

Her lips were slightly parted, red marking her cheekbones, her determination clear. 'Richard and me, we're not a couple. We're in this thing together,' she said, watching Trent. 'I want to find the *Beau Belle*, that's all.'

Everything seemed easy, when you were young and attractive and had a comfortable home: summer vacations sailing off Newport; loving parents with funds to pay your Access, Amex, and Visa accounts; when you were sufficiently intelligent not to have to worry too much over graduating. And now it had all gone wrong.

And Richard? Probably awake in his bunk but shy of coming on deck. A lot of sadness and insecurity there. There hadn't been much fun in the young man's life, and mastering his accountancy exams must have been a tough grind.

Watching the coast, Trent sipped his coffee. Sniffing the rich scent of mangrove swamp on the breeze, his thoughts turned to Marco, the handsome, happy-go-lucky lover with a fresh pennant tacked to his mast. Trent had suspected bitterness in Marco when Auria had referred to her father's love for his restaurants, and he found difficulty in imagining such a free spirit waiting table. He asked about it and Auria said: 'He worked there the year he left high school. It didn't work out.'

She took Trent's mug and bowl to the galley. After a while Trent heard her talking to Richard and the clatter of china on the saloon table. They returned to the cockpit together. Auria had donned shorts and a T-shirt. She took a book forward and lay in the webbing between the two hulls. Richard remained in the cockpit. He wore his usual grey flannel trousers and long-sleeved shirt, a Panama hat shading his face.

'I'll change course in over the reef once we're clear of the sandbanks south of Andros,' Trent said. 'I thought we'd drop anchor and do a practice dive. Then run down to the edge of Old Bahama Channel. I'd like to be off Lobos Cay Light before dark.'

Richard said, 'I'm not good in the water.'

Trent wondered if that was why Richard had been reluctant to search for the *Beau Belle*. He thought that Richard would hate having to wear a lifejacket, but it was either that or a safety line whenever he came on deck. But he had misjudged Richard. Pulling on the lifejacket over his shirt, Richard said: 'I handled a motor yacht with my father years ago but I don't know about sails.'

Trent explained and demonstrated how the cat responded to the wind and sails, then gave Richard the compass course and left him at the helm, telling him to play around a few degrees each way so that he got the feel of the *Golden Girl*.

He left Richard in command on deck for a while, to increase the young man's self-confidence. Fetching a Magellan GPS, he took a reading and entered it on the chart more for practice than from necessity. Then he dropped down into the galley and prepared a salad. As the daughter of a restaurateur, Auria must be used to good food.

As he mixed the salad dressing in a jar – sweet basil, white wine vinegar, first pressing of Lucca olive oil from a gallon can – he cursed himself for a fool. He had read the dossier on Rogerton-Smithe briefly before visiting the underwriter, and Rogerton-Smithe's account of his actions agreed with the disciplinary sub-committee's findings. Now he wished that he had taken more interest in the appendix which listed the Names who had invested in Rogerton-Smithe's syndicates. He was sure now that, had he looked, he would have found Rocco listed. Rogerton-Smithe must have patronised Rocco's Newport restaurant; rich, sophisticated, his yacht lying in the marina, Lloyd's clearly a sound investment.

If he had missed such an obvious connection, what else had he missed, Trent wondered. A picture formed of the *Beau Belle*, waiting untouched, bait on the sea floor.

12

Marco stretched and yawned as he came out of his cabin into the galley. He looked up at Trent seated at the chart table and grinned: 'Hey there, skip, how's it going? I guess I'm a little late.' He yawned again and scratched his chest: 'Party time in Kemp's Bay – wow, what a night. Coffee?'

Trent said, 'Please.' He glanced out at Richard in the cockpit. With the sun well up now, the accountant's face ran with sweat under his hat and dark patches marked his thick shirt. Trent fetched a pair of lightweight cotton pants and a smock from his cabin and put them on the saloon table before taking a fresh reading with the Magellan. Suggesting Richard come below, he slipped the bungee rubber over the tiller arm and showed him how to enter latitude and longitude from the Magellan onto the chart.

Marco brought mugs of coffee from the galley and laughed when Trent waved him to leave them on the saloon table. 'Yeah, I know,' he said, 'cats sail on an even keel so the coffee won't spill. Just don't come on with the missionary act, skip. I've heard the arguments. I want to convert, I'll convert.' On his way out to the cockpit, he gave Richard's shoulders a squeeze: 'How's it going, Riky Boy? Learning a new trade?'

A yacht is no place for privacy and Trent heard Marco make his way forward to bid good morning to his sister, and his protest as she told him to leave her alone. 'Hey, come on Sis, all I had was a little fun.'

'That's all you ever have,' Auria said. Silence followed. The soft pad of Marco's footsteps eased back along the side deck followed by a thump as he dropped into the cockpit. He grinned at Trent, man to man, shameless: 'OK if I take the helm?'

'Keep her a little out from the reef,' Trent said.

Richard asked if he could look at the large-scale chart of the Old Bahama Channel and the Cuban coast and Trent slid it out of the drawer. While Richard studied the chart, Trent found the relevant chapters of navigational instructions in Volume I of the Admiralty's West Indies Pilot. 'There's a strong onshore current and the prevailing wind's from the north-east,' he said, passing the book to Richard.

Richard read fast and with obvious intelligence, referring back to the chart repeatedly.

'The Pilot's useful as a general guide but it's written for big ships, so much of it doesn't apply,' Trent said. 'The current could be difficult, particularly getting back to the *Golden Girl*.'

Using Trent's brass dividers, Richard measured the distance from the edge of the Great Bahama Bank to the Cuban coast. 'Twenty miles.'

'Calm seas and a reasonable wind, two hours,' Trent said. 'The Cubans will be watching the channel. We need to be back and clear of Lobos Cay before dawn.'

Richard said: 'It makes better sense for me to stay with Marco on the *Golden Girl*.' He looked up from the chart. 'I wouldn't be much help if something happened to you while you were underwater.' Again he studied the chart. 'I never thought this was sensible.'

'How did you meet Auria?' Trent asked, a casual question.

'She got my mother's address from the insurers. It seemed sensible for me to fly out . . .'

And now he found himself both in love and facing the possibility of his father having sunk the *Beau Belle*, or worse, much worse. Trent said, 'There are clothes on the saloon table. You'll find them more comfortable in this heat.'

Marco stood relaxed, his back to the tiller arm, accustoming himself to the feel of the big cat. The breeze had moved round further towards the north and Trent eased the sheets before going forward. Squatting beside Auria on the trampoline, he watched the sea curl back from the bows along the smooth white of the port hull.

Trent said: 'It will take two of us to man the Zodiac tonight. Richard can't dive and Marco has to sail the *Golden Girl*.'

Auria looked up from her book, meeting Trent's eyes for a moment: 'I thought I was along just to sign the cheques.'

'Don't be a fool. I'm going to drop anchor in about an hour so we can make a dive and practise with the magnetometer.'

Trent and Auria dived from the Zodiac. Seated on the round fabric tube, they held their masks firmly in place and tumbled backwards into the clear water. Trent watched while Auria trickled air from her buoyancy jacket to balance the lead weights on her dive belt. As soon as she had achieved negative buoyancy, she ghosted down, drifting through coral valleys forested with fans of white lace. Trent caught her and held her a moment, signalling that she should stay still and use her eyes rather than her fins. Fish small and bright as sapphires darted through the fans; miniature clouds of white powder puffed where parrot fish butted the coral with their beaks; red snapper fluttered like falling leaves; a small ray ghosted across the sand; from a rock fissure, the spiny antennae of a lobster waved.

Trent grabbed the lobster in his gloved hand and slipped it into his dive net. Already Auria was on the other side of a coral head. Beyond her a steel grey barracuda hung motionless, a foot below the surface.

He watched the bubbles trickle from Auria's mouthpiece. At this depth she was a confident and accomplished diver, her use of air neither miserly nor spendthrift. If diving on the *Beau Belle* proved trickier than he expected, he would take her down the cliff edge and see how she fared at greater depths, but for now he was satisfied.

He spotted a second lobster in a crack and a nurse shark

stirred sluggishly in the shade of an overhang as he coasted past. Finding two more lobster, he signalled Auria back to the Zodiac. He strapped his air tank to the Zodiac's carrying handle, rolled over the tube into the tender, and took her equipment.

Clasping his wrists, she ducked down, then used the sea's buoyancy and the thrust of her fins to drive up out of the water. She dragged her jacket off, tanned body shimmering in the brilliant sunlight, her smile back in place, radiating youth and energy and enthusiasm.

'That was so great,' she said, fingers combing the salt sea out of her short dark hair.

'You dive well,' he said.

He left her to start the Mercury and watched as she steered them back to the catamaran. Loading the magnetometer and sensor cable, he explained the search pattern to her, sketching it on paper. They practised for an hour, Auria at the helm while Trent watched the latitude and longitude on the Magellan GPS. Trent heard Marco call instructions to Richard as he tacked the *Golden Girl*.

They lunched underway, Richard at the helm. Marco and Trent watched for coral heads as they slipped over the smooth shallow waters covering the vast coral bank, Marco right forward in the bows and Trent up on the saloon coach roof. They wore Polaroid sunglasses but, even with the sun high, only the shallowest heads showed pale brown beneath the mirror surface.

Grey and low in outline, the Cuban patrol boat lay at anchor in the lee of an islet ringed by mangrove. The few palm trees on the crest of the islet cloaked the boat from the open sea and she was almost invisible in the gathering dusk. The young Commander yawned and stretched as he pulled himself up the companionway into the wheel-house. Naval Intelligence had fitted a direction finder beside the chart table. Hands on the controls, a radio operator sat crouched over the screen. His headset rendered him deaf to outside noise and he started as the Commander tapped him on the shoulder. He looked up, then back to the screen, and pointed to a dot of light. 'They're on the move, Commander, passing Lobos Cay.'

One hundred and forty feet high and twenty miles from the nearest land, Lobos Cay Light stood on a scrap of white coral. Directly beyond the lighthouse lay the Old Bahama Channel, three thousand feet deep, the sea dark and lumpy as the *Golden Girl* slipped by in the dusk.

The *Golden Girl* was Trent's home and his only possession. In the eighteen months that Trent had owned the catamaran, he had never entrusted her command to anyone else. Now he left Marco to sail and navigate across the busy sea lanes. The American was in his element, relaxed, confident, his feet spread wide as he stood with his back to the tiller bar, tough, muscular body united with the rhythm of the waves. Richard supported himself against the saloon bulkhead, binoculars up, hand compass ready to take bearings when Marco asked him.

Rather than risk interfering, Trent joint Auria in the bows. The night closed round them as they watched a huge tanker power up-channel. Foam burst along the line of her hull like surf on the foot of a black cliff the crest of which was commanded by the bridge and accommodation. Trent felt Marco ease the helm over a few degrees to meet the charge of the tanker's wake. The catamaran's bows lifted high and the jib slapped as the wind emptied from the canvas. Then came a sharp crack like a gunshot as the catamaran slid down the wave and the sail snapped taut.

Trent checked his watch. 'Let's get some coffee inside us.' He sat at the chart table, checking one last time. The Magellans gave positions accurate to fifty feet and he had chosen a rendezvous three miles outside Cuban territorial waters. Marco would tack up-channel, returning after two hours, then each hour on the hour. If they weren't back in five hours, he would sail the *Golden Girl* to Lobos Cay and wait there till the following night, pick-up time 3.00 am and 4.00 am. If they failed to rendezvous on the second night, he would return to Andros and report to the authorities that Trent and Auria had gone fishing in the Zodiac along the edge of the Great Bahama Bank and that the outboard must have broken down.

'Ten minutes,' Marco called softly.

Trent and Auria stood by the lines holding the Zodiac in the stern davits. Richard crouched over the port sheet winch.

'Ready about,' Marco warned, and pushed the helm over. Richard let go the sheets and the sails emptied as the *Golden Girl* turned up into the wind.

'Let go,' Trent told Auria, and the bottom of the Zodiac slapped the sea. 'In you get.'

Marco called, 'Good luck!' but already the *Golden Girl*'s sails were filling as he bore away.

Ten minutes to the search area and the sea became suddenly ragged as they crossed the lip of the reef. Ahead lay a pale curl of surf while away to the east the moon's loom dyed the horizon with a first streak of faded silver. Trent could see now, lying low on the water, the darker shadows of the sand spits a mile off the coast, and he checked the Magellan, easing the helm a degree to starboard.

They crossed the latitude marking the Cuban side of the search area and he cut the throttle, swinging the bows to starboard. As Auria took the helm, Trent fed the sensor and magnetometer cable over the stern. Holding the Magellan in his left hand, he signalled their course to Auria with his right. They reached the longitudinal line of the first search run. Auria pushed the helm over and headed the Zodiac towards Lobos Cay Light.

Trent counted the seconds as he concentrated on the two liquid displays, magnetic and depth. He had calculated each traverse at 240 seconds and he checked on the Magellan that they were clear of the area before signalling Auria to swing the Zodiac to starboard through 180 degrees. They recrossed the southern boundary, picked up the second longitudinal mark and headed again for Lobos Cay Light. Each complete circle took eleven minutes, the sea smooth, breeze negligible. Easy as eating pie.

The moon rose, a pale yellow disc, and Trent could see

now, as they headed back towards the Cuban coast, Auria's mouth drawn tight in concentration.

Halfway into the seventh traverse, the magnetometer reading suddenly leapt five gammas. Trent pressed the button on the Magellan, storing their position in memory, slapped the side of the Zodiac for Auria to shut the Mercury, and shot the small Danforth anchor overboard. Already the magnetometer reading was back to normal. Five gammas at a depth of eighteen feet – if it were the *Beau Belle*, she lay at least seventy metres to port of the sensor. Pulling mask and fins on, he grabbed a light and slipped into the sea. The cable lay just below the surface like a giant sea serpent. He followed it back, switched on the light, and played the wide beam over the sand below. Nothing showed on the bottom and he circled towards a flat head of coral. Fish slipped grey out of its shadow, dancing in the lamp's pale rays. Beyond the coral head lay a long dark shape and Trent piked and dived, the excitement strong in him so that nothing mattered but the chase.

The sand lifted in pale green puffs as he drove across the sea bed. The shape rose at him, dark and smooth. Then he was on it, the light playing up the side of a worn granite ridge that lay like a dead whale, half buried in the sand. Disappointment thickened in his throat as he rose over the rock flank. Beyond, the sea bed stretched pale in the cone of light, empty as the desert. Trent surfaced and turned back towards the sensor. Looking down, as he swam towards the flat coral head, he saw something curled in its shadow that had been hidden from him by the overhang when he had approached from the opposite direction. He dived and found a mound of snapped anchor chain shackled to a big flat-fluked fisherman's anchor embedded deep under the lip of the coral.

He turned onto his back and rose again towards the surface, and for a moment saw the long bullet shape of a shark against the pale shimmer of moonlight on the surface. He rolled immediately, swimming down and towards the Zodiac, counting the beat of his fins. The air fought to escape through his lips clamped tight on the mouthpiece of his breathing tube as he flashed the lamp upwards, searching as he rose stiff and still as a stick so as not to swirl the surface. The air exploded the water out of his breathing tube and he filled his lungs, immediately diving again. Twice more he surfaced. At last the Zodiac rocked above. He drove up at its port hull, hands grasping for the carrying handle. One heave and his right leg swung up and over the tube. He lay for a moment, steadying his breathing. Then he looked up at Auria crouched in the stern. 'Sorry, an old anchor.'

Circle and circle again, the moon high and the night air muggy and thick with the fetid scent of mud-flats, and always the navigation beacons lanced their spears of light over the grey hulls.

They had lost time while he dived and he told Auria to increase speed on the shoreward legs of the search. She opened the throttle too much and the Zodiac leapt ahead only to be braked by the drag of the sensor cable. As Trent pitched forward, he saw the depth reading plunge to 300 feet with an anomaly of twenty gammas on the magnetometer. He pressed the Magellan's memory button as he fell against the instruments. The readings didn't make sense. He steadied himself, studying the liquid displays as he waved Auria to shut the throttle. The depth was back to twenty feet but the magnetometer continued to show an anomaly of six gammas, in twenty feet of water not even a quarter of the reading he expected from the *Beau Belle*, and he had already made a mistake in diving on the anchor rather than trust Skelly's graph. The sudden surge in speed across the sensors must have affected the readings. Three hundred feet was ridiculous.

He motioned Auria to circle back. 'Slowly . . .'

13

Sheltered from the breeze and the slight swell, the patrol boat waited still as a barracuda in the lee of the islet. The duty operator sat at an angle to the direction finder so that the Commander could see the screen. Frozen like voyeurs at a bedroom window, they watched the light circle in an ever tightening pattern. The operator had been on watch for six hours and he stretched now, easing the stiffness out of his shoulders, and turned to the officer: 'Looks as if they think they've found something.'

Trent studied the readings as he guided Auria. The depth pattern showed a formation that reminded him of a can of beans with the lid pushed in while still hinged on one side. The can was about two hundred feet in diameter and dipped thirty feet. At one point at the bottom of the slope the recorder plunged off the scale, as if there were a plug hole in the ocean floor.

Signalling Auria to cut the motor, Trent dropped the anchor and coiled the sensor cable into the Zodiac. Auria crouched beside him. 'We've found it?'

The anomaly was less than he had expected. He said: 'I'm not sure. There's a dip in the sea bed. Whatever it is, it's down fifty feet. I'll take a bottle.'

He'd be gone only a few minutes so he didn't bother with a

buoyancy jacket. He fastened his weight belt and tank harness and pulled on his fins. Seated on the round hull, he spat into his mask and adjusted his mouthpiece before slipping overboard with a lamp.

He equalised the pressure in his ears and reached the bottom at twenty feet. The lip of what he'd thought of as a can lay just ahead. He glided forward and looked over the jagged edge down a sheer wall, greeny-white in the lamplight. It was very much as he had imagined it up in the Zodiac. He was looking down in to a phenomenon of the Caribbean known as a 'blue hole'. There were hundreds of them. One weekend he and Pepito had dived on one of the most famous, off the coast of Belize, over a half-mile in radius and eight hundred feet deep. The holes were formed by freshwater springs, deep underground, slowly eating away the soft limestone until finally the roof collapsed. Judging by the jagged edge, this roof must have fallen comparatively recently.

He followed the wall down, equalising again, and found the lower section of a wooden mast floating upright but upside down. A rope held it to a tangle of steel rigging and canvas bunched at the bottom of the 'V' so that he couldn't see the yacht. He swam to the side and shone the light underneath the mess. For a moment he didn't understand, then he realised that the shattered timbers he could see were the bows of the yacht mashed between the roof edge and a ledge that jutted out from the sheer wall. The rest of the yacht was underneath the roof, which presumably explained the anomaly being less than he had expected. He wondered whether the weight of the yacht or an earth tremor had brought the roof down. He recalled hearing that a tremor shook this area of the Caribbean every thirty hours.

Following the wall round, he found what he had thought of as a plug hole. The roof had struck an outcrop as it fell and a chunk of the roof had snapped off, leaving a hole about five feet square. He left the lamp there as a guide.

Auria was leaning out over the side of the Zodiac. It would have been cruel to delay telling her for even a second and he raised a thumb as he surfaced and spat out his mouthpiece.

'She's there.' The moonlight seemed very bright and he read her excitement as he pushed up his mask. He said: 'I can't see much because of the rigging and the sails. I'll need the other lamps and gear.'

She took his tank and he kicked himself up into the boat. Although he had been underwater for only five minutes, he changed to a fresh tank and wore his buoyancy jacket. He strapped the Phoenix dive computer to his wrist and loaded a bang stick. Crowbar, flashlight, underwater Nikon, a coil of light line.

Auria was preparing her equipment but he stopped her. She had to stay in the boat – at least till he knew what was under the roof. To keep her there, he attached lines to the two spare lamps and lowered them overboard. He said, 'I'll give one tug when I need slack, multiple when I want them lifted. I'm going to clear some of the mess. Once that's done, you can come down.'

He was gone before she could answer. He set the dive computer and adjusted his buoyancy, then piked and swam to the sea floor. He took his time, already pacing himself. A single tug on each line, and he drew the two lamps down with him over the lip.

He lowered two lamps through the plug hole and made the third fast to a knob of lime directly above the hole as a guide back to his exit. The limestone scraped his air tank as he drew himself head first down into the hole, and his shoulders brushed the rock, then he was through, but holding onto the edge of his escape channel as he steadied himself, counting slowly to calm his breathing as he checked the dive computer – seventy-three feet, twenty-three minutes of dive time remaining before decompression became necessary.

Unwrapping the line round his waist, he made one end fast beside the lamp marking the cavern entrance. The other end he made fast to his dive belt, looping the slack over his left wrist. He swam close to the wall and with the roof only a couple of metres above him. He swam slowly, the bang stick in his right hand, the two lamps and the crowbar hanging from his wrist. In his other hand he carried the flashlight. The beam alternately carved into the darkness ahead then circled as he dropped off coils of line. Finally the beam struck the *Beau Belle.*

Trapped in limestone jaws, the yacht projected out and down from the wall at an angle of forty degrees so that, though the cave roof pressed on the forward deck section, the wheelhouse and deck saloon remained unscathed. She seemed incredibly vulnerable, suspended above the void by her crushed bow timbers. She had been a beautiful yacht, old-fashioned in her varnished teak superstructure and brass deck fittings that were now dim with verdigris. Shattered sections of her two wooden masts floated against the roof and the rigging hung down like strands of a torn spider's web.

Trent swam carefully at deck level. He made his guide line fast to a deck cleat and hung one lamp over an awning stanchion at the after end of the saloon coach roof. Brass jaws held a short boom with a neatly furled sail of heavy canvas to the stump of the mizzen mast. Hanging the second lamp on the boom tip, he swung the boom out, spread the rigging, and glided down over the far side deck and rail. The flashlight swept the hull and he saw what he had suspected: two holes had been torn in the planking six feet apart and a foot below the water-line. Spikes of teak knifed outwards from the holes. Trent played the torch beam through the holes over the big diesel. The engine was hardly marked. It would have been shattered if the holes had been made by gunfire, and the spikes of splintered teak would have pointed inward.

He photographed the holes, then rose to the side deck outside the wheel-house door and checked the dive computer: fourteen minutes left to decompression.

The flashlight swept over the interior of the wheel-house. A big brass compass stood in heavy gimbals forward of a varnished wheel with the engine controls and dials all heavy brass. The chart table was to port of the wheel with the radar screen above. To starboard a companionway led below to the forward accommodation. A settee bunk ran athwartship against the after bulkhead of the wheel-house with a door on each side, one leading down to the engine room, the other to the galley that separated the wheel-house from the deck saloon.

The forward accommodation would contain the crew's quarters and would have been used by Richard's father, if only to stow his gear during the voyage – he would have slept in the wheel-house. So if Hewett had carried anything bulky he would have packed it into the owner's stateroom lying aft of the engine room below the saloon.

Trent tried the wheel-house door. The brass handle turned easily but the door refused to budge. Rather than use force, Trent floated aft to the glass-panelled doors to the after deck. He broke the glass with the crowbar, taking time to chip out the shards so that they wouldn't catch or slice his wet-suit. Each piece of glass that fell to the saloon deck stirred silt into tiny cloud puffs that drifted upward through the water held immobile by the cabin bulkheads.

Taking the lamp from the awning cleat, Trent drifted through the door, moving carefully so as not to further cloud the water. The upholstery on the chairs and settees had crumbled, as had the carpet. There were worm casts everywhere and a sprinkling of tiny crustaceans danced in the lamp glow. He fastened the lamp at the head of the companionway that led down to the owner's stateroom. The stairs spiralled through 160 degrees with a tiny lobby at their foot. He sank down the stairs head first, using handgrips to steady himself in a vain attempt to keep the water still.

He turned the brass door handle to the owner's stateroom and pulled gently. He tugged harder but the door timbers had swollen, locking the door tight in their grip. In these small movements the water became more clouded and fear of sightlessness within the enclosed space pried at his confidence as he dug the crowbar into the teak edge of the door. He levered with one hand and pulled hard on the handle with the other. The door burst open into his face. Huge gas bubbles imprisoned within the stateroom blasted over his mask and hurled him back against the foot of the stairs while the doorway spewed thick green tendrils into the lobby.

Something grabbed him from above, cold and slippery. It

was on his shoulders, invisible. It cloaked his mask with slime, crushed his upper arms, dragged at his air hose. Trent fought its embrace, dropping the crowbar as he snatched the bang stick from his belt. In struggling, his fins beat the fine detritus so that the water in the narrow passage became, in seconds, a thick soup.

The soup blinded him and whatever monster held him tightened its grip, writhing down his chest and over his air bottle so that his upper body was entirely enveloped within its slimy folds. He lurched backwards, turning within the animal's grasp in a desperate lunge for the companionway. And there in the torchlight wide-open jaws snarled a foot from his face. Dagger teeth glowed green, so close that he could see the chipped point of one tooth.

Trent fought his right arm up and rammed the bang stick into the jaws. He fired and the head disintegrated. Blood exploded into the soup and the thick body of a huge headless green moray eel spilled slitheringly slow from a locker behind the stairs to the saloon. The edge of the invisible tentacle cut at Trent's wrist. Suddenly recognition came to him through the fear, and he fought his breathing back under control, counting as he brought his heartbeat down, keeping very still. Then, carefully, he prised up the edge of the plastic sheet that had enwrapped him.

He wanted to get out. To be in the open. To be safe above the cavern roof, in clear water with the stars and the moon silvering the surface and the shadow of the Zodiac beckoning: that he wanted more than he had wanted anything in his entire life. But the plastic sheet was only a hint, as was the thick green soup. He must have evidence.

He reloaded the bang stick and checked the dive computer. Three minutes to decompression . . .

He pushed his way into the liquefied spinach, fingers nervous as he felt blindly along the cabin panelling. He found the first porthole and unscrewed the brass clamp. One more porthole on that side of the cabin, then he crossed to starboard and found the remaining two. The clear water beyond the portholes immediately clouded as he swung the heavy portholes open. He found the door again and gasped as the eel's body rolled under his fin.

He rose up the companionway, dragging behind him a trail of vegetable pulp. Great pools of trapped gas quivered against the white paint of the saloon cabintop and the dive computer moved into decompression mode as he swam for the door out onto the after deck. Quickly he worked his way up the side deck, smashing the glass out of each window with the crowbar – saloon, galley, what remained in the wheel-house, then back to the other side so that the currents would clear the inside of the yacht.

Switching off the two lamps, he drew himself fast along the safety line leading to the cavern entrance. The green-blue glow of the third lamp beckoned as Trent's fins churned the blackness. He switched off the lamp in the cavern entrance and rose slowly up the slope of the broken roof. He swam in faint moonlight reflected off the pale limestone.

With visibility and open water the fear seeped away in trickles. For a moment he had to hold the mouthpiece in place with his hand because of the weakness of his jaw muscles. He lay against the limestone and watched the dive computer tick away the minutes of his decompression period, then rose a further ten feet and saw a crack running across the cave roof a third of the way down from its top edge. The crack ran across the full thirty feet of his visibility. The cave roof buckled slightly at the crack to form a shallow angle, the roof remaining in one piece through the pressure of its own weight. He imagined an earth tremor opening the crack: the roof would collapse inwards on itself like a book before sinking slowly to the cavern floor, the *Beau Belle* crushed beneath it.

Three more minutes to wait. He lay against the limestone, thinking about the *Beau Belle*, flashlight off, the silvered chain of bubbles floating up into the moonlight. Marco would be at the rendezvous in twenty minutes. They had time enough.

The computer released him and he surfaced beside the Zodiac. Auria knelt on the floorboards, leaning out over the hull. The water held by the rim of his mask warped her face. He pushed the mask up but kept his mouthpiece between his teeth. He needed time before committing himself to speech.

Auria grasped his dive tank and heaved it into the boat. Trent drove himself high out of the water and flung a leg over the tube.

Seated astride the tube, he said, 'There's a sort of drop below us, the beginnings of a blue hole. The *Beau Belle*'s caught on a ledge. We need to get back to the *Golden Girl* for a couple of anchor warps to make her fast before she slips any deeper.'

There was anger in her and suspicion as she said: 'So I pay the bills but I don't get to look?'

'Let's make her safe first,' Trent said as he stowed his equipment into his dive bag. The Mercury started easily. Lifting the anchor, Trent rammed the Zodiac onto the plane, then throttled back till he heard the high speed injector shut off. They were making twenty knots as they headed out towards the Old Bahama Channel.

14

Roddy de Sanchez had been in the temporary radio room at the coastguard station on the north coast for twelve hours. He had taped a chart to the wall above the table on which he'd set the radio. A black button marked the dive spot, red pins the patrol boats. He logged every communication. Calculations he made on separate sheets of paper. These sheets he laid singly on a plastic chopping board he'd brought from the kitchen so that the pressure of his pencil wouldn't leave a trace and he set a match to each sheet the moment it was full.

According to the chart the Englishman had dived at twenty-five feet, which gave two hours on the bottom without need for decompression. Most divers would have stayed down the full time but Trent had surfaced after thirty-two minutes which didn't make sense to Roddy. There must be a great deal to investigate on the *Beau Belle*. So the wreck wasn't the *Beau Belle* or Trent needed extra equipment from his own yacht. Almost certainly the latter. Either way, Roddy didn't want the patrol boats moving yet. He had jammed a tiny piece of sharp gravel under the door. Warned by the screech on the tiles, he turned.

Estoban Tur stood in the doorway and for the first time Roddy admitted to himself that he was frightened of the plump, olive-skinned Director of Bureau Three. They were too different. Roddy wasn't a hater. There were women who accused him of not being a lover either, more of a playmate, lightweight. He supposed they were right. Had he cared more, he would have refused to become involved in his father's schemes. He wasn't greedy for wealth or power, which marked him as unique in three hundred years of family history. But he hadn't refused, and now it was too late.

Drawing the Englishman's course on the chart, he said: 'Trent's heading back to his catamaran.'

First they saw the sails, two silvery fins swooping above the water. Then came the hiss of the twin hulls. Trent signalled with his flashlight and canvas slapped as the *Golden Girl* spun up into the wind in a cloud of spray.

Auria cried, 'We've found her!' as Trent docked the Zodiac broadside between the transoms.

Marco grabbed the painters and Trent told him: 'We've got to get back. She's on a ledge. I need the mooring ropes and the storm sail in its bag.' Marco was too much the sailor to waste time asking questions, but Richard leant over the rail, anxious. Trent thrust a dive tank into his hands. 'Quick, we've got to lighten the Zodiac . . . and I want the spare belt weights from the dive locker.'

With the Zodiac travelling at speed, Trent hadn't noticed the wind, but he could feel it now in his face, stronger than when they'd first headed for Cuba. He passed Richard the second tank he'd used – that left three in the Zodiac – and grabbed the coils of rope, weights, and sail bag.

'Give me an hour,' he told Marco, and bore away.

They dropped anchor in the same place. Speech had been impossible with the Mercury running but now, as Trent slipped back into his harness, Auria said: 'I'm coming with you.'

'You can't,' he told her. 'One of us has to be in the boat to handle the lines. Get this done without an argument and you can dive yourself sick.'

He shoved the spare weights and crowbar deep into the sail bag, leaving the mouth of the bag partly open so the air could escape easily. Then he tied the end of one rope to the bag and lowered it overboard. He had a clear picture of what he had to do. 'Remember, pay the rope out slowly,' he warned as he tied the two mooring ropes together. Clamping the mask to his face, he tipped backwards into the sea.

He checked the dive computer, followed the rope down, and retrieved the crowbar. The sail bag he left at the lip of the blue hole, then he swam down the wall to the plug hole with the rope end and switched on the first lamp. The *Beau Belle* lay fifty feet away under the roof and he fed sixty feet of rope into the hole, measuring with his spread arms. Briefly he looked towards the surface, moonlight almost indiscernible. Then he gripped the edge of the plug hole and drew himself through.

Once beneath the roof, he turned onto his back and pulled the rope up between his legs. Gaining a little slack, he kicked towards the yacht, then drew up more slack, the rope end dangling into the depth of the blue hole so that a loop couldn't catch on a projection. The drag became less as the rope shortened till finally he rolled over and saw the yacht in the beam of the flashlight. He swam the last few feet and made the rope fast to a deck cleat before switching on the lamp he'd left at the end of the boom. With the lamp on, he saw that the water had clouded at the after end of the yacht and shoals of small fish darted in and out of the soup dribbling from the portholes.

Returning to the plug hole, he swam to the top of the wall and searched the sea floor. The coral head he found was thirty feet back from the lip. He signalled Auria for more slack. When the join reached him, he untied the two ends and looped the first rope in a clove hitch over the coral. Then he swam back to the plug hole and repeated the whole process with the second rope. The dive computer allowed him fourteen minutes more.

He jemmied the wheel-house door open with the crowbar and pulled open the door down to the engine room. A body hung upside down, blocking the companionway. The flashlight struck a brass bell push jerry rigged to the top of the companionway and two cables snaking down. Trent pictured the trawler ploughing out of the night and the sudden change of course, and the bow wave that must have made the man strike the bell by accident as he slipped. The explosion would have ruptured his eardrums, stunned him, and smashed the air out of his lungs.

Trent had intended making the second rope fast to the diesel engine but, faced with the corpse, he swam on across the wheel-house and led the rope down and round the underside of the hull so that the yacht was held in a loop which he made fast with a bowline back inside the wheel-house. Eleven minutes . . .

The doors to the port and starboard cabins were open, the cabins empty. The forecastle door was shut and wouldn't budge. Four parallel cracks ran down the panelling, a brass bolt at the top of the door had been shot home, and the key was absent from the lock. Trent took two photographs, then slid the bolt, and jammed the crowbar into the frame beside the door knob. Feet braced against the frame, he heaved and the lock burst. The shattered bows had enabled the water to circulate freely and fish and crabs had dined well so, apart from bones, there wasn't much left. Three photographs of the interior and one of the door lock were enough.

He shoved himself back, turned, and swam fast up the companionway and through the wheel-house to the galley, where he paused for a moment, flashlight searching the shelves. A cut-glass salt cellar would do and he grabbed it. Six minutes.

The big pro fins drove him into the saloon and down the companionway into the soup welling from the owner's state-room. He unscrewed the top of the salt cellar and scooped it full. Only four minutes remained as he flipped over and drove up through the saloon and out onto the deck.

Despite the need for haste, Trent had to be careful of the rigging as he swam up the sloping foredeck. The after section of the forecastle hatch blocked the angle between the crushed bows and the cavern roof. Trent lay flat on the deck to photograph the brass hasp and padlock that had held the hatch shut. One minute.

He switched off the lamp on the boom and raced for the exit. The computer signalled that he was into compression time as he slid out through the hole and he had to decompress for two minutes halfway up the wall, with a further three minutes at fourteen feet. A coral head lay a little to the right of the one to which he'd anchored the first rope. He looped the second rope over it, swam back to the lip of the blue hole, and lashed the sail bag round both ropes where they crossed the edge, so that the rock wouldn't cut the ropes if the *Beau Belle* slipped free.

With four minutes to wait at seven feet, he hung on the Zodiac's anchor rope. The rope jerked frantically – Auria signalling. She grabbed his tank as he slipped free of the harness and he heaved a leg over the side tube. The surface seemed light as day and the sea and wind tumultuous after the dark silent stillness of the cavern. Auria held a finger to her lips and pointed.

They sat, holding their breath as they listened. It was there, over to starboard, towards Cuba, the low grumble of big turbo-charged diesels idling; Russian diesels, a Cuban patrol boat. Trent sensed the ship's radar and sonar, two forks of a snake's tongue, flick at them. He waited for the searchlights.

The light came, but from far away, so that the beams flickered over the matt grey of the Zodiac, soft as candlelight. Around them the soft lap of the sea against the gently rocking hulls, the stench of mangrove swamp, and the moon softened by the haze of the night's humidity.

'What do we do?' Auria whispered.

'Run for it,' Trent said as he listened to the patrol boat easing eastward against the current, twin searchlights knitting an intricate pattern of light across the sea.

Starting the outboard, he drove fast for the reef edge and open water. A mile away the patrol boat turned and the grumble mounted to a roar as the big diesels hurled her onto the plane. The wake of the Zodiac and the sound of the Mercury would give them away. Trent shut the motor and waited.

The patrol boat crossed their stern and immediately Trent raced the engine. Three minutes gained, but the Cuban ship was already curving into her turn, quartering the shallows.

Trent cut power and pressed Auria flat to the floorboards as

III

the searchlights licked at them. The distance remained too great. Race and wait, race and wait . . .

The patrol boat spun on her tracks, her course closer. The next turn brought her closer still. There was nothing casual in the search. The Zodiac rose to the chop marking the edge of the reef. Less than three miles to their rendezvous point with the *Golden Girl*. Fifteen minutes to the first rendezvous time, and Marco would have already turned down-channel to pick them up. Would the Cubans come after them? Cut them off from the sanctuary of the Great Bahama Bank?

To starboard a container ship steamed down-channel, moonlight ghostly on the white of her hull. The container ship's wake came at them and Trent opened the throttle full, racing the Zodiac along the curling break of the wave so that his own wake would be lost in the foam. He must follow the container ship down-channel, then break back along the far wake to the rendezvous. He urged the Zodiac on as if he were riding a steeplechase. The high square stern of the container ship loomed a hundred metres from them, the black letters of her name and port of registry tall as a man: FRUHLINGS-MORGEN, BREMEN.

Behind them, the Cuban patrol boat quartered the edge of the channel, same speed, same long sweeps, each a little further from the coast. But the Zodiac was well away from its pursuer's searchlights and the container ship's wake and engines cloaked the craft from Cuban radar and sonar.

Trent brought the helm over five degrees, the blunt bows of the Zodiac butting up the steep foaming slope. They sped across the boiling froth spewed by the ship's propellers. Then they were beyond the spray and running fast along the curl of the wave with the rendezvous only a mile away. Nothing to do but wait for the *Golden Girl*.

Wiping the salt water from his eyes, Trent checked their position on the Magellan. Then he saw, outlined against the light, the dark silhouettes of the Cuban patrol boat's two sister ships, waiting. He cut the engine but knew, as the searchlights lanced towards them, that they had little hope of escape.

Alone, he would have raced for Lobos Cay, but one sweep

of a machine-gun would chop Auria into chunks of meat. Loosening the screws holding the Mercury, he said : 'I'm going to drop the engine overboard and all the search gear. They'll pick you up. Tell them you were out snorkelling. You tried to start the engine. You hadn't screwed it down tightly so it spun off the transom. It happens all the time.'

He looped the sensor cable to the outboard and dropped it overboard. 'You've been drifting all night,' he told her. 'They'll believe there were two boats and that they've lost the one they were chasing. With a bit of luck they'll return you to the *Golden Girl*. At worst they'll take you into Cuba and put you on a plane. We'll meet in Nassau.' He opened the gas tanks and forced them under the surface, letting the sea pour in so they'd sink.

'What will you do ?'

'Swim for it.'

The searchlight beam slid over them.

She said, 'If I tell them about the *Golden Girl*, they'll be watching for her. It will be the end, won't it ?'

'Of the diving ? Yes.'

'So I have to swim.'

'Two miles . . .' But Auria was already slipping into the water. He wrapped the Magellan into a plastic bag, thrust it inside his wetsuit, sliced the bow line, and frayed the rope end on the serrated edge of his dive knife so that it would look as if it had parted against a rock. Quickly he hefted Auria's dive tank onto her back, taking its weight as she slipped into the harness. He let out sufficient air from both hulls to make the Zodiac look as if it had been adrift for weeks. Fins and mask on, he slipped into his own harness and rolled over the side. Tying the spare half of the painter as a leash between them, he signalled Auria to use her snorkel and pointed towards the rendezvous point.

He could feel the throb of the patrol boat's diesels. He motioned Auria down and they slipped their regulators between their teeth, sinking into absolute darkness. Twenty feet, thirty, forty, fifty.

Levelling, Trent swam slowly, his hand on Auria's arm. He

breathed slowly, careful of his air. The propellers shook the water, then came sudden thunder as the coxswain thrust the patrol boat's engines into reverse. The searchlights had found the Zodiac.

Trent felt Auria tremble against him as he watched the compass and the depth on his dive computer by the light of his pen torch. The water magnified every sound from the patrol boat as her coxswain manoeuvred her alongside the Zodiac. Trent wondered what equipment they had. Sonar sufficiently sensitive to reflect their presence? Easy to drop a charge over the side . . .

Five consecutive reports followed fast on each other as the heavy wood treads of a rope ladder clattered against the patrol boat's hull. Trent put his arm round Auria, holding her still, and raised his watch close to his mask, flashing the torch on the dial. Five minutes had passed and they had sunk to sixty feet. But they were clear of the patrol boat. He signalled Auria up with a slight pressure of his hand, forty feet, thirty, twenty, steady at twenty, the slow beat of their fins pushing them forward.

The patrol boat drew away, propellers churning. Trent had no means of communicating with Auria other than with the pressure of his hand but already the patrol boat's engines were muffled by distance and he felt her relax . . . too soon, because the boat turned hard, sweeping back towards them, not creeping as it had in its search but driving at them like a beast charging its prey. The thunder roared at them, all round them, and on top of them, the current ripping at their mouthpieces as the patrol boat carved through the sea directly above their heads. They hung there in the water, waiting. Waiting.

The patrol boat drove on fast towards port, and the danger was past. Trent drew Auria up through the blackness to ten feet and waited, watching the dive computer tick away the minutes as they decompressed. Six minutes. Starlight flickered over the blue-steel surface of the sea and danced with the air bubbles trickling from their lips. They lay flat on the surface, the swell rocking them. Safe.

Trent felt for the button on Auria's buoyancy jacket and

filled it with air before loosening the buckles and rolling her dive tank free, letting it sink away under the weight of lead on her belt, then his own tank, and Auria grabbed at him, dragging the snorkel from her mouth. 'God, I was scared.'

'Nonsense, you're brave as a lion,' he told her.

A mile, perhaps two, to the rendezvous; his own buoyancy jacket full, he dug the Magellan out of his wetsuit, holding it clear of the water as he checked their position and calculated the course they must swim.

'Don't hurry,' he warned Auria: 'It's no harder than taking a snorkel trip along the reef.'

A snorkel trip into the light breeze that had gentled them across the channel the previous day from South Andros, but Trent felt, as he took his bearings, that the breeze had freshened with the approaching dawn, not yet enough to physically slow them, but sufficient to seed a fresh anxiety, and the Admiralty Pilot had warned of an onshore current.

They swam for twenty minutes before Trent read the Magellan. Their course directly into the wind and waves, he was disappointed by their progress. With less than thirty minutes to the final rendezvous time, he urged Auria on, the seas already a little steeper.

A further twenty minutes and once more he sought their position. Auria grasped his hand, freeing her mouth of the snorkel: 'The wind . . .' she began.

Confidence mattered. He freed his own mouthpiece: 'Keep at it. You're doing well.'

Twenty minutes more and they were at the rendezvous, the wind so strong now that they had to keep swimming to hold their position. With a hard thrust of his fins, he forced himself high out of the water, but there was no sign of the *Golden Girl* and the first pale signs of day showed in the east.

Again and again he raised himself high on a wave in his search. Marco was a half-hour overdue and all the time the wind and seas and current gathered in strength to drive them back from the rendezvous to the Cuban coast, twelve miles away, fourteen at the most.

He freed his mouthpiece. 'We're turning back, Auria.'

15

Roddy fetched a fresh can of black coffee up from the mess. Estoban sat slouched in a chair facing the chart. There was nothing he could do here and Roddy wished that he would go home. The Bureau Three Director had hardly moved in hours. He didn't say anything, just watched the chart and read the radio traffic from the patrol boats as Roddy logged it. But there had been nothing to report for hours now, nor would there be.

Roddy poured the coffee and passed Estoban a mug: 'Stop worrying. They found the Zodiac so he's in the water and he'll be wearing a buoyancy vest. He may have waited for the catamaran for an hour or two, but in the end he's got to come ashore.' He laid a ruler on the chart to show the onshore current and the wind, then indicated the stretch of coast where the Englishman would be washed ashore and where Estoban had set his trap. Like a spider, a plump spider, Roddy thought, and shivered as he felt a surge of sympathy for the man in the water. Estoban Tur would get his man and Roddy's father had what he wanted, the position of the *Beau Belle*. All Roddy wanted was to be free of it all – free to play tennis and make love in the moonlight.

The sun was the enemy. It squatted directly over their heads, a throbbing blinding brilliance. Auria slept or was unconscious. After nine hours in the water, Trent couldn't tell which. He had lashed their forearms together so that she floated beside him and had modelled a hat from the legs of her wetsuit to protect her face and neck. For the hundredth or thousandth time, he turned her face away from the sun. The combination of wind and sea and sun had split his own lips so that gripping the snorkel had become one more part of the pain and he was tired, desperately tired. But once again, he raised the tiny sail he had cut from the front of his own wetsuit, a bib that he supported against the backs of his forearms.

The next wave lifted them and he kicked, keeping them in the surf for an extra few seconds as they rode the wave shorewards: six waves to the minute at four metres gained per wave, twenty kilometres to the shore, fourteen hours – then subtract twenty per cent to allow for the onshore current that pushed them down-channel. He had repeated the arithmetic again and again, the discipline giving his legs the strength to drive the heavy fins. Salt caked his eyes beneath the glass of his mask and he had given up trying to read his watch.

He closed his eyes for a moment, resting them against the glare. Close to him a train roared into a tunnel, the harsh thunder deafening. The train roared into another tunnel, longer. And now the train swayed violently, tossing Trent from side to side. On and on the train charged.

Suddenly Trent was awake and struggling as the surf thundered over his head. His shoulder struck coral and he felt the cold as his wetsuit ripped. He grabbed Auria in his arms, rolling to protect her with his own body as he fought for the surface. But it had been an isolated coral head. They were past it. And the surf drove them in towards a steep lip of sand shaded by palm trees at the foot of a jungle-clad mountainside.

Trent kicked his fins off. A breaker smashed him down as he scrabbled for purchase. He held Auria's face clear of the water and dragged her forward. Again the sea slammed into his back and he stumbled as he gouged his toes into the sand. The next wave lifted him. For a moment he was on his feet and he drove forward those last few yards, then he was falling to his knees again, but safe, Auria clasped in his arms.

He carried her up into the shade and knelt over her, pumping her arms until she gagged, then rolled her onto her side. Water dribbled from her mouth. She tried to open her eyes but the effort was too great.

Cuba was dangerous territory and Trent swept their footprints from the beach with a fallen palm frond. A coconut tree leant out towards the sea. He sliced two strips from his wetsuit and bound his feet eighteen inches apart with one strip, looping the second strip round the tree trunk. He caterpillared up the trunk and knocked a half-dozen nuts free. He chose a young nut with water in it and chopped the top off with his dive knife. Kneeling beside Auria, he raised her head and held the rim of the nut to her lips. She swallowed a little and he rested her head back on the dry leaves, squatting beside her as he watched the life seep back. Her eyes opened.

He said: 'I have to look for a boat, will you be all right?'

He climbed, searching for a path. Finding none, he returned to the shore and headed east, keeping to the shade, careful not to leave tracks, and he moved slowly to husband his strength. The beach ended at a steep bluff and he climbed, only to find a second empty beach and beyond it another bluff but, beyond the bluff, threads of smoke rose through the trees.

He climbed higher, searching for a point from where he could survey what lay beyond. He could hear water cascading and the smoke was there. Perhaps a small fire of green wood, he thought, as a curl of the wind fetched the scent to his nostrils. The cascade was close, and he stepped cautiously between the trees, steadying himself against their trunks as he checked the ground for loose stones and dry sticks. He found the stream and knelt beside it, drinking deeply before he followed it down to a rock outcrop over which the water plunged. He lay flat and crawled through the trees to the edge of the drop.

The water plunged to a tidal pool some thirty yards wide and a hundred long. The pool lay between the steep sides of the two short promontories and was sheltered from the surf by a bar that the sea had built into a small strip of beach below the point of the far bank. A path led back from the beach to a small house built on a natural terrace that had been widened to encompass a vegetable patch at the rear.

The house was built of planks and roofed with corrugated sheets that extended forward over the open door to shade a narrow verandah. Earth steps, banked with split logs, led down from the verandah to the pool. An open hard chine dory lay at anchor below the steps with a line from her stern looped round a tree-stump so that she could be hauled into the bank. The dory was around eighteen foot long and painted grey. Her transom supported an outboard motor, tilted clear of the water and covered by a piece of old green canvas. Oars rested in rowlocks along the gunwales and a mast, with a sail rolled round it, lay along the floorboards. The red-painted fuel tank for the outboard was on the verandah. The dory was perfect for Trent's purpose. She was perfect for anyone fleeing Cuba. Too perfect.

He shifted his attention back to the house. There were no windows at the front nor at the side open to his view. He guessed that there would be a door at the back to match the front and possibly a window facing out to sea. A clay water pot stood on a wooden stool close to the front door, an aluminium ladle on the wooden lid, and an upright chair with a cane seat stood against the wall the other side of the door. Either the water pot or the chair would force an attacker out from the protection of the wall. And the left of the house was protected by a chicken run penning a dozen hens while, to the right, where it would be most open to the breeze, a rack supported fish drying in the sun.

Trent watched and waited for twenty minutes. Finally a pale-skinned mulatta woman dressed in a loose off-white skirt and a halter top came out of the house. She stood looking up at the mountainside above the cascade for a while, then she walked along the terrace to the chicken pen and threw in a handful of grain from a can nailed to one of the posts. She looked back at the house, up at the chimney which rose a metre above the roof line, then she went into the house and reappeared with a plastic bowl and a string bag of potatoes. Taking a smaller aluminium bowl out of the plastic one, she filled it with water from the clay pot before sitting down on the edge of the terrace with her skirt pulled up and her legs in the sun.

Trent judged that she was in her early thirties. She wore her hair long and combed back loose down her back, and she sat with her legs a little apart. She made a great piece of bait. There was more smoke coming out of the chimney, so she must have added green wood to the coals.

Trent counted as she peeled nineteen potatoes, dropping the peel into the plastic bowl and the potatoes into the aluminium bowl of water. The potatoes were of reasonable size and Trent thought she would eat two, three at the most; three each for her companions with perhaps one over in case one of them had a large appetite – so there were six of them altogether, and probably the other five would be men.

Anyone falling for the trap would attack the house from the rear, so there would be a sentry in the bushes to the rear of the vegetable patch and one in the house with the woman. For insurance, there'd be a third man by the sand bar. Not above the strip of beach, because that was too obvious. But on Trent's side of the stream, hidden in the trees. The last two would be a half-mile back each side of the house, watching for movement from the mountainside.

The sentry on the mountain would have signalled. Not with a radio, because the slightest crackle of atmospherics would have given him away, nor a flag, but by releasing or pulling down a branch that could be seen from the house. The woman had looked up the mountain before checking the smoke. Having signalled, the sentry would search back along the coast for other intruders. He would find Auria. He would threaten to kill her or her companion if she shouted a warning. Then he would hide close by with a view of the beach.

There was something wrong with the scenario and Trent struggled to think through his fatigue. Who wanted to escape from Cuba? Criminals, officials who'd had their hand in the till, dissidents refused an exit visa. But mostly kids fleeing consumer abstinence in search of the American way of life; designer labels the image, rather than the fifty thousand homeless in New York City.

So why so complex a trap? Unless they were expecting a professional with his expertise. The patrol boats had cut him off and must have stopped Marco on his way back to the rendezvous. And the prevailing wind and current from the seach area would wash a swimmer up on this stretch of coast.

But a falseness in the picture nagged at him as he watched the woman throw the potato peelings to the chickens and carry the bowls into the house. It was too pat. Deliberately pat. As if every detail had been rehearsed.

He played the scenario again. The woman had come out of the house, looked up the mountainside, seen the signal. She had put fresh wood on the fire so that Trent would see the smoke. Then she had come out onto the terrace and peeled the potatoes. Nineteen potatoes. So careful a trap and so obvious a mistake.

Edging back from the cliff edge, he turned and headed for the beach where he had left Auria. He snaked down through the trees on toe tips and elbows, belly flat to the ground. Auria lay below as he had left her, apparently alone, and Trent waited, resting and listening, as he searched for the wrong stir of a branch or leaf. Finally he spotted the Cuban, not the whole man or even part of him, but a patch of matted shrubbery that remained still while the rest of the bush trembled beneath a gust of wind.

The Cuban was a little to the right and ten yards uphill from Auria. He had cut the heart out of the bush and sat within the cave of greenery with the cut branches replaced to camouflage him from the beach. The live thickness of the bush protected his back and sides and he would be armed with an automatic rifle and a pistol.

Already above the man, Trent inched his way higher, searching for a boulder, round and big enough for his purpose. He prised the soil away from its downside with his dive knife. Ready, he stood hidden by a tree while he gauged the slope.

One shove of his foot and the boulder tumbled down to the Cuban's left. The Cuban exploded out of the bush, swinging to confront the charge, Kalashnikov up, finger already tightening on the trigger. Surprise held him for only a second as he realised his mistake; only a second, but five bounds had carried Trent to the Cuban's right, each footfall rehearsed and exact – pivot downhill, two more bounds, and dive – his shoulder smashed into the Cuban's ribs, blasting the air out of his lungs. The Kalashnikov spilled from the Cuban's hands as he tried to protect his face from the fall and Trent was on top of him, throwing knife held to his throat. 'Don't even breathe,' Trent warned as he felt for the man's pistol holster and found it empty.

'Stretch your arms out in front of you,' he ordered, and to Auria: 'Find his pistol. It should be in the bush.'

He knelt, a knee on the Cuban's spine. 'I'm going to tie you up.'

Auria had found the pistol. 'You're all right?' Trent asked and she nodded. He told her to take his dive knife and slice the Cuban's trouser legs into strips.

He tied the man's hands behind his back and strapped his knees together and his feet. Then he hauled him back up the slope further into the trees and finally looked at him properly. The Cuban was in his early twenties, slim, and fine-featured, hair cut a little longer than his Sergeant probably approved – good on the dance floor, Trent thought as he recognised the shame in the young man's dark eyes and in the line of his mouth. He was scared – but the fear wouldn't be for himself; trussed, he was safely out of the battle – so the fear was for his companions and his shame for having let them down. Trent said, 'No one's going to get killed. But I need your boots.'

Auria watched him as he laced the jungle boots. He supposed that he must look a villain, scarred body covered in mud, blood caked on his left shoulder torn by the coral, cracked lips, hair and beard matted. He stood up, wrapped the young Cuban's pistol belt round his waist, and picked up the Kalashnikov. He would have smiled encouragement but his lips were too dry and stiff. 'I've found a boat,' he said. 'Stay here and I'll pick you up before dark.'

Trent plotted his attack as he jogged back towards the house. The backstop at the end of the near peninsula overlooking the sand bar came first. The Cuban should have rigged trip-wires or threaded strings through the scrub. In his search, Trent parted the bushes slowly and with painful delicacy but found none. The sentry sat in deep bush dangerously close to the edge of the bluff above the sea. Surprised, he might lunge forward in terror and fall head first to the rocks twenty feet below.

Trent was oblivious of the bite of sharp stones and thorns as he snaked forward inch by inch. He was within six feet of the sentry when the Cuban fumbled at his waist and Trent thought for a moment that the man had sensed his presence. But the Cuban took tobacco and papers from his pocket, and it was easy for Trent as the Cuban concentrated on rolling his cigarette. Trent laid the rifle aside. Much of his weight supported on his fingertips, he edged his feet forward until he squatted like a frog about to spring. He filled his lungs and eased forward an extra foot, waiting. The sentry struck a match and Trent leapt. His left arm slammed round the man's face to silence his scream while the fingers of his right hand dug at the man's neck. The blood cut off from his brain, the Cuban slid sideways, unconscious.

Trent sliced the legs from the Cuban's trousers as he had with the young man on the beach, gagged and strapped him, then dragged him back by the heels to where his thrashing would be out of sight and sound of the house.

Trent had known in which direction the first two Cubans would be facing. The sentry guarding the rear of the house from beyond the vegetable plot might be watching the back door or the mountainside, or looking back towards the distant *pueblo*. The one direction in which he would be unlikely to face was towards the sea, where the backstop whom Trent had already silenced had been on guard, and which could be viewed from the house. Trent watched the house from above the sand bar. The fire smoked well. After a while the woman came out and leant against the post at the far corner of the verandah. She raised her left arm and scratched her side beneath her halter top with an indolence and casual sensuality that would have assured a watcher that she presumed herself unobserved. She yawned, stretched, and rubbed the back of her arm across her face before going back into the house. To sleep, a watcher would have presumed.

Trent looped the rifle sling over his shoulder, collected the Cuban's belt, and swung down the bluff into the sea. He waded out beyond the sand bar before turning for the far bank. He held the rifle now in front of his face with only his head above the surface as he rounded the tip of the far promontory. Climbing the rocks, he snaked into the scrub that cloaked the edge of the slope behind the vegetable plot and waited while he regained his breath. He rubbed fresh earth into his skin as camouflage. As he inched forward, he searched and cleared the ground ahead of brittle sticks and dry leaves. It was a skill honed over the years by an unforgiving teacher, Death. That he was alive proved his skill and the rules were simple: total concentration, absolute silence, breathing controlled, each movement rehearsed and so slow as to be imperceptible.

He was almost on the sentry before he saw him. The Cuban lay in a slight dip that widened at the edge of the vegetable plot to give him a direct view to the back door of the house. His automatic rifle lay to hand but he was reading a paperback.

Trent laid his Kalashnikov aside. He needed to be a little further back to be hidden from the Cuban's peripheral vision and the distance must be exact. In position, he rose to his feet, immobile against the broken background of mixed scrub and trees.

The shadow of a big man appeared well back from the doorway so that he would be unseen except by someone in direct line with the sentry. The faint glint at waist height would be a rifle. Trent stood frozen, defenceless. A mosquito whined across his face and settled on his cheek but he didn't blink, no part of him moved.

The man in the house tapped a foot twice on the floorboards

and the sentry looked up from his book and raised a hand. The shadow of the man moved clear of the doorway as a fat bead of sweat dribbled down through the dirt on Trent's face. Trent took one step forward and dived. His forearm hit bar-hard with his full weight behind it midway down the sentry's back and blasted the air out of the man's lungs.

Trent found the man's carotid artery and cut off the blood for less than five seconds. The tail of the unconscious sentry's shirt served as a gag, the first two men's belts lashed his feet and hands. Trent sliced the man's trousers, replacing the belts with the strips. Speed was essential. At any moment the man in the house might reappear, but Trent needed all three belts and a gag ready.

Abandoning the Kalashnikov, he raced forty yards along the scrub edge, then angled back across the vegetable plot to the chicken run. The hens cackled madly as he leapt the wire. He grabbed a hen, kicked a corner of the wire loose, and rammed the hen's head through the gap. The hen screeched and beat its wings.

The Cuban inside the house came to the door and cursed as he saw the trapped hen. As he ran past the corner of the house, Trent dropped him with a single chop to the side of his neck. He slammed the gag into the man's mouth, belted his limbs and grabbed for the chickens, three in each hand. Out of the run, he lay flat by the door.

He had to know which side of the door she was on. He heard her, not a footstep but a slight squeak of a floorboard to his right and on his side of the hut. He swung the chickens through the door at head height and followed them in a low charge. The woman was still trying to get the flapping chickens out of her face as Trent hit her legs low down with his shoulder. She dropped her rifle and tried to get her hands back to save herself as she struck the floor. Trent got a hand on the rifle and swung it over to the far wall before flipping her over onto her stomach. She kicked hard and screamed names at him that he wouldn't have found in a school dictionary. He got the third belt looped round her wrists and pulled it tight while telling her not to panic.

She wasn't panicking. She was trying to kick or bite any part of him that came within reach, preferably a part that would hurt the hell out of him. To bind her legs, he used the sling from her rifle. He rolled her onto her back so that she would be more comfortable with her face off the floorboards. Her skirt was rucked up to show her thighs and her halter top had ridden up over one breast. He tried to pull the halter top down but she kicked at him again and he jumped clear.

She screamed at him and spat and found more names and bucked and heaved at her bonds as if keen to hold his attention while either the sentry from behind the vegetable plot or the backstop by the sea came to her rescue. It was all very theatrical.

'I tied them up. No one's hurt,' Trent said.

He went out to check the big man's bonds and drag him into the shade.

He knew that he ought to get down to the boat but he went into the house first. She watched him, the fight gone out of her. Trent said, 'I'm taking your boat. Are you in charge?'

'You are,' she said.

He said: 'You know what I mean.'

'I was.'

With the ebb of adrenalin, he had to force himself to think. He wanted to be angry for himself. Angry at being used. But he thought instead of the cracks in the *Beau Belle*'s forecastle door. The New Zealanders would have screamed as they hurled themselves against the panelling.

Exhausted, he looked out through the door at the dory anchored below the steps. He felt the woman waiting. He knew that she would report every detail of the action, every word, but he had nothing to say.

126

16

Estoban Tur had left the coastguard station soon after dawn to supervise his trap. Roddy waited all day for confirmation of the Englishman's capture. To be close to the telephone, he had strung a hammock between the pillars outside the coastguard sergeant's office. The wind had strengthened steadily since soon before dawn and now, in the late evening, blew Force Six out of the north. The wind kept the mosquitoes at bay and Roddy slept fitfully.

Perhaps it was the squeal of car brakes waking him that made Roddy think of a wild boar as Estoban, unshaven and in his shapeless suit, charged out of the darkness. Sweat dripped from Estoban's face and stained his jacket at the armpits. He had undone the top three buttons of his shirt and dragged the knot of his tie halfway down his chest. He breathed heavily and, as he reached the terrace, seemed to shoulder the air between them out of the way.

'The son of a pig Gringo's escaped,' he shouted. Fingers crushing emptiness, he beat the air. 'We had him. We had the son of a pig.'

He shook Roddy, spilling him out of the hammock and, unable to contain himself, kicked Roddy's coffee mug across the tiles. The mug shattered against the wall.

'Jesus, Jesus, Jesus,' Estoban swore, thumping his fists on his thighs. He hauled Roddy to his feet then smashed a fist into a pillar. 'Can you imagine? Ten years I've waited. Ten years to get my hands on the pig and those incompetent idiots let him steal the bait.'

Drained by his rage, Estoban collapsed into the hammock and lay there glowering, his voice thick with disappointment. 'Two of them, Trent and a girl. Imagine the shame of it.' He pawed at Roddy's arm: 'No one must know. Promise me.'

Promises were Roddy's stock-in-trade; promises of faithfulness and of love, promises that eased the moment of parting. He thought of the Englishman more than of the girl, Marco's sister. The Englishman had inhabited his mind for days now, and he could feel him, like a hunted animal, twist and turn, and suffer the shattering swing from relief to despair with each fresh run for shelter smashed. 'We need a drink,' he said to Estoban. 'I'll see what I can find.'

A corporal had a bottle of rum in his locker and Roddy poured quadruple measures both for Estoban and himself. He waited for Estoban to fall asleep before using the telephone in the sergant's office. The phone rang only once before his father answered.

'He's got away,' Roddy said. His father asked how and where Trent would make for. Roddy hesitated but his father was already studying a chart.

The Admiral said: 'We're all right till dawn, no chance of a ship picking them up. Once it's light, I'll have a radar watch on the channel. That leaves Lobos Cay.'

'Probably,' Roddy agreed. There wasn't anywhere else. He said. 'There's half a gale blowing and they're in an open dory. They'll be lucky to survive the crossing.'

'I'll have a squad put ashore,' his father said.

Roddy briefly considered asking whether the squad was necessary, but there was no point to the question. The Englishman had served his purpose. He and the girl knew where the *Beau Belle* lay and how she'd been sunk. They had to be stopped. Replacing the receiver, he walked outside and down the short wooden jetty. Away from the protection of the building, he raised his face to the wind, feeling for the strength of it and its direction as he imagined the hunted couple in the tiny sail boat.

The big swell lifted the dory ten feet into the full force of the north wind. For a moment the small boat lay pinned to the wave's crest as Trent fought her bows up. Then the wind released the little boat and he eased the helm as she plunged down the slope. The boat shook as the flat 'V' of her bottom slammed into the trough and spray cascaded over her bows. For a few seconds she lay becalmed. Then came the next swell to offer her up to the wind. The pattern had remain unchanged for fourteen hours.

To avoid Cuban patrol boats, Trent had sailed down-channel for the first two hours before turning north. As the sky lightened, he saw, half a mile away, the pale line that marked the edge of the Great Bahama Bank. He glanced down at Auria, curled on the drenched floorboards like a rock awash. For hours now, they had been too exhausted to waste energy on words or even a smile. The dory dipped and slammed, Auria awoke and bailed, then dozed again.

The tip of the sun rose from the sea as Trent shot the dory through the tangle of waves and spray that surged over the reef's edge. Immediately they were into calmer water. Trent held to his course for fifteen minutes before dropping anchor. They slept shaded by the sail spread like a ridge tent across the oars lashed to the mast. It was nearly noon when Trent was wakened by Auria, restless in her sleep and muttering. They lay against each other in the narrow hull, Auria using his arm as a pillow, their clothes wet and beginning to steam in the heat beneath the canvas. Trent couldn't move without risk of wakening her so he lay thinking of the day ahead, his arm numb and uncomfortable under the weight of her head.

South Andros lay forty-eight hours to windward while they were within three hours of Lobos Cay. There'd be a radio in the lighthouse, he thought, as he pictured the scrap of coral. The Cubans would know about the radio. Either the *Beau Belle* or something on her had to very valuable for the Cubans to put a landing party ashore on foreign soil, but the possibility had to be considered.

He felt his way into the thoughts of the leader of such a party. The Cubans would come ashore and be picked up under cover of darkness. They would expect Trent and Auria to reach land soon after dawn. By noon they would give up unless they knew that Trent was a professional, in which case they might suspect that he was waiting for nightfall.

If this scenario was right, the Cubans would stand down around noon, make themselves something to eat, smoke a cigarette, and sleep for a few hours with a sentry up in the lighthouse keeping watch. Trent remembered the walkway that circled the top of the tower as narrow; the sentry would stay inside unless he was used to heights; he might notice even a small sail miles away but the glass panels would muffle the purr of an outboard motor.

Auria stirred again and her hip dug into one of the scrapes on his thigh. Trent tried to ease his arm free but she held onto his hand. Then she woke and looked at the hand she was holding. She groaned and tried to move away, striking her knee on one of the dory's ribs. She sat up with her back to him and rubbed the spot.

'God,' she said after a while.

She drew the sail back and shifted onto her knees so that she could see where they had anchored. Reaching for the water pot stowed beneath the stern, she drank abstemiously and wiped her lips on her arm. She handed the pot back to Trent without turning to look at him. But she inspected the boat as if to reassure herself of its size as she sorted her memories: 'We sailed this thing through a gale, right? Where are we?'

'Great Bahama Bank. About half a mile in from the channel. We need to get going,' Trent said.

First they sailed for an hour. Then, with the mast lowered and the sail stowed in the bows, Trent motored a half-circle that kept him a good two miles off Lobos Cay. In explanation of their course, he told Auria that he wanted to approach the lighthouse out of the sun.

She thought a moment, then laughed nervously: 'Like a fighter plane in the movies. Who are you expecting?'

'Nobody, but nothing's gone right so far,' he said.

He dropped anchor a half-mile off the Cay and slipped overboard. He held to the gunwale a moment and she said, 'Yeah, don't tell me. I'm not to move from here till you yell or get back.'

'I may be quite a while. Hours, possibly all night.'

He swam breaststroke rather than raise his arms out of the water. Lobos Cay was an oval one hundred and fifty yards long by fifty yards wide. At its summit the Cay was perhaps twelve feet above sea level while the light soared a hundred and fifty feet in height. Painted in black and white bands, the metal tower sprouted through the roof of a colonial-style bungalow shaded by verandahs. There were two small huts, a concrete house with radio aerials and a flag mast, and two palm trees that leant with the prevailing northerlies.

Frigate birds and gulls screamed at each other as they swooped at a patch of foam a few yards off the beach. Swimming closer, Trent saw that the foam was made by shoals of small fish nibbling at the body of a black man dressed in a white short-sleeved shirt and white shorts floating belly up in the shallows.

He wondered why the dead man had been left so close to the shore. Perhaps the killers had dumped the body out at sea only for the tide or current to wash it back. Or perhaps they had re-embarked and didn't give a damn that the corpse was a warning. Or perhaps they wanted him to think that they had already gone.

Trent crouched low in the water so that only the top of his head showed. There were no signs of life on the Cay but the top of the lighthouse was a splash of reflected sunlight that could hide a dozen men, as could any of the buildings. He thought how silly it was to feel more vulnerable in a swimsuit than when normally dressed.

Thirty yards of flat dirt separated the water's edge from the first hut. A single window overlooked the beach where he lay.

131

The door would face south away from the prevailing wind. It was a further forty yards to the lighthouse building.

Surprise was his only hope. Every hundredth of a second counted. He slipped his swimsuit down over his feet and, naked, slithered forward out of the water. Flat on his belly, he first scooped sand over his hair as camouflage.

Only his toes and his fingertips worked as he edged himself towards the hut, inch by inch across the baked powdering of fine sand that covered the coral islet. In seconds his body ran with sweat saltier than the sea. The sweat stung his eyes and the criss-cross of scratches and raw patches on his body.

He advanced, face buried in the sand, blind, slowly. He could sense the hut now, a slight change in the sound of the sea rebounding off the wall and of the touch of the breeze deflected.

The tips of his fingers touched the sill of the concrete foundations. Now only his toes dug into the sand as he worked his body round until he lay full length against the side of the hut. He raised his head carefully and immediately smelt the thick slaughterhouse scent of fresh blood. Nobody ahead of him. He looked back over his shoulder. Nobody.

He rose to his feet a little to the left of the window so that he could see at an angle across the interior of the hut to the open door. The furniture comprised a couple of canvas beds, a table, and two benches nailed together from driftwood. Fishing nets were piled against the wall facing him and bamboo marker poles for the nets lay across the rafters. The floor was coated in fine dust and he saw footprints in the doorway, and something about the size of a full sack of corn had been dragged across from the door to the corner which was out of his view to the left of the window.

Back on his stomach, Trent slithered round the corner of the hut. The open door masked him from the lighthouse building and he moved faster than he had across the open ground. Head at ground level, he looked in through the door. The sack in the corner was a Bahamian fisherman. He had dragged himself into the corner like a hunted animal, or a child trying to make itself small, and whoever had stood in the doorway had shot him a dozen or more times in the head and chest. One bullet would have sufficed.

Trent crossed to the window. The sea slapped and sucked and he heard, through the screech of the gulls and frigate birds, the scuffling scratch of palm fronds as they slithered over each other in the breeze. Nothing else moved. Only an hour of daylight remained, but he took his time, studying first every inch of ground that separated the hut from the light-house bungalow, then the windows opening onto the verandahs.

One corner of the concrete building from which the radio aerials sprouted was visible beyond the lighthouse. Trent presumed that it was a coastguard or customs post. The radio operator would make contact at fixed hours three or four times a day. If he failed to do so, a helicopter or a patrol boat would run out to the Cay, so the killers would have kept the operator alive so that he could make his reports. Most of the killers would be in the lighthouse, and they would have kept alive one of the lighthouse staff to man the light. But they wouldn't leave witnesses when they re-embarked.

Covered by the hut, Trent crawled back to the sea and, with only his nose and eyes above water, circled south. A twenty-foot lobster boat had been sunk alongside a small stone jetty below the lighthouse. The two bundles with gulls picking at them at the shore end of the jetty would be Bahamians who had come down to welcome the squad of killers. The jetty forced Trent out into deeper water but, beyond it, he was hidden from the lighthouse. He followed the coast round until the second hut gave him cover. The hut was without windows and less substantial than the first.

Trent sprinted the twenty yards up from the beach. Close against the wall, he squatted and scooped fresh dirt over his hair and wet skin, rubbing it in. Then he crawled to the corner of the hut on his belly and inspected the guard post. It was a single-storey square building topped by a tin roof sloping four ways to form a low pyramid. A flat-roofed extension stuck out to the south, probably a storeroom. Two windows in the main building overlooked the twenty yards of open ground that separated the guard post from the end of the hut. Judged by the aerials, the radio was in the corner of the building to his right while the main entrance probably faced the lighthouse.

Trent crawled along the other side of the hut towards the storeroom extension and crossed the first ten yards of open ground on his stomach doing his toes and fingertips routine. Once past the halfway point he was covered by the storeroom from both the windows and from the lighthouse. He crept forward into the protection of the wall and along to the first window.

The window opened outward. Wood-framed, it was divided into six panes and protected on the inside by a framed mosquito screen. Trent looked in from the left first, ducked down, and looked in from the right. The room was about ten feet by ten, and furnished with one upright chair, a ply table, cheap wardrobe, and a government-issue iron bed. Given the mess, a full magazine must have been emptied into the man under the sheet. The door to the corridor or central hall was shut.

Creeping forward, Trent looked in through the next window. A second window faced him across the angle. A Kalashnikov and two spare magazines lay on a table between the two windows. A fair-skinned Latino dozed in a canvas chair. The pistol in his lap was a 9mm Czech automatic.

Across from Trent a Bahamian sat at an old-fashioned communications set on a wooden workbench fixed to the dividing wall. The radio log lay open on the bench with a ballpoint lying in its spine. The Bahamian had his back to Trent. He hadn't made a dive for the Kalashnikov because his legs had been broken and strapped to the chair so that the pain was bearable only as long as he didn't move.

The Latino was little older and had probably seen military service in Angola so was used to killing in action. But he was half asleep, which gave Trent a slight edge. In the end it would come down to the mosquito screen and how well he landed.

An open door to the left of the radio bench gave on to what looked like a central passage leading to the main entrance. Trent would have preferred the door shut in case there were other members of the shore party in the building. Opening a door took a couple of seconds, and even fractions of a second were vital. Trent calculated that he had eight seconds, ten at the most. He had a chance if the mosquito screen gave instantly. If it held, he was dead.

He wrote the latitude and the longitude of the *Beau Belle* in the whitewash below the window with the point of his knife and put the knife back in the sheath held against the nape of his neck by his coral beads. He had a last look at the table and the Kalashnikov, then took ten steps backwards and dropped into a crouch facing the window at an angle. He didn't think about the window. He didn't even see it. And he didn't see the Cuban. He saw the spot on the floor which he had to hit.

He had a habit of counting when under pressure. He counted to five. Then he was up and racing. He hit the window with his left shoulder. The frame shattered and the mosquito screen flew across the room. Head tucked, he hit the floor with his left forearm and somersaulted onto his feet, but he was off-balance and falling as he crashed into the table. He grabbed the Kalashnikov with his right hand and pivoted as he pitched forward so that he fell on the right side of his back. His nudity saved him. It was a trick he had been taught by a Yugoslav Scot in the SAS: 'Doesn't matter who they are, they'll look down at your perishables,' the Yugoslav had guaranteed.

The Cuban looked down for less than a second, but it was enough. 'Don't even breathe!' Trent screamed in Spanish. Kalashnikov rock steady, he got to his feet and ordered the Cuban to hold his pistol by the barrel and place it on the floor.

Over in the lighthouse they might have heard the breaking window and Trent hadn't much time. To the radio operator, he said quickly: 'Get a message through to Superintendent Skelly that Victor called. He needs to fly out here at first light.' Pain had dyed the Bahamian's face flaky grey but there had been hope in his eyes for a moment.

'A helicopter can't reach us by nightfall and they'll get massacred if they try landing in the dark,' Trent explained.

He needed to know how many men he was up against. The Bahamian had counted six.

Trent said to the Cuban: 'I'm the Gringo with the catamaran. Maybe your *Jefe* warned you, I kill for a living.' He touched the muzzle of the Kalashnikov to the Cuban's throat: 'Some careers, luck is important. With killing you are good or you get killed. To own a large yacht, you have to be very good.'

The Cuban said, '*Si, Señor*,' and Trent lowered the gun muzzle.

He could see the stages now, how it would work. He asked the man his name and the Cuban said: 'Juan Bordes, Señor.'

Trent said: 'Juan, you are going to walk out of the front door and shout at the lighthouse. One or two of your friends will come to the edge of the verandah, maybe closer. You shout, "Hey man, would you believe it, a gull big as an aeroplane smashed the window."

'You take one pace forward and say: "Come and see for yourself." Then you say that you have tethered the radio operator by his neck and that you must get back before the fool hangs himself. It is very easy, a part even a bad actor could play.' Trent scooped up the Cuban's pistol, ejected the shell from the breach, emptied the magazine, and handed it to him: 'Carry it so your friends can see.'

Trent closed the door to the radio room behind them and Juan walked ahead down the short corridor to the main entrance. He was a slim man, of medium height, with a high forehead and short swept-back hair. He wore loose fitting khaki drill without markings and dun-coloured trainers. Hand on the door, he hesitated, some sort of a clerk dressed for a weekend picnic in the country and nervous that the weather might break.

Trent prodded him in the back with the Kalashnikov: 'Move, and make it good. You're acting to save your life.'

Juan pulled the door open and they heard the squeal of gulls down by the jetty. He took a step outside and yelled for attention a couple of times before one of his friends appeared at a window on the ground floor of the lighthouse. Then he shouted: '*Oyez, hombre, que creis? Un galeo grande com un avión, buff contra la ventana. Si, muerto, hombre, claro . . .*'

His friend came out onto the verandah and then onto the open ground and a second man appeared at the door. A nerve in the rear of Juan's neck twitched. Trent knew he was about to dive left or right. 'Don't try it,' he whispered harshly.

Juan's shoulders sagged a little and he shouted: 'Hey, come over and look.'

The man who'd come outside said something over his shoulder and the second man came out.

'The radio operator,' Trent prompted.

The Cuban called. 'I've got a rope round the radio operator's neck. He'll hang himself if he falls off his chair.' His friends laughed. The one on the right wore a Zapata moustache. The other man was tall and fat and wore his hair swarmed forward to cover a bald pate. The Zapata wore a shoulder holster. The butt of the fat one's pistol stuck up behind the brass buckle fastening his leather belt. They both carried Russian machine pistols but not as if they expected to have to use them in a hurry.

Juan turned and walked back into the guard post and passed where Trent lay shadowed against the corridor wall. The other two Cubans were halfway between the guard post and the lighthouse. Trent was sandwiched and Juan calculated that he wouldn't shoot for fear of warning the two men outside. He grabbed the door handle and was halfway through into the safety of the radio room when Trent's knife hit him below the left ear.

Trent slithered back and retrieved his knife. Then he rolled clear of the wall so that the Zapata and the fat man could see him and see the Kalashnikov. The two Latinos were caught out in the open with nowhere to go except back to the lighthouse. The fat one tripped his companion and ran for it. Trent shot him through the right shoulder. The Cuban dropped his machine pistol, pitched to his knees, and held his injured arm, a steady stream of biological expletives blending with the screeches of the startled gulls.

137

'On your feet or the other arm goes,' Trent shouted. 'Drop your guns and get over here, both of you.'

He manoeuvred them close so that they shielded him from the lighthouse. One arm or two, the fat man remained dangerous because he was too full of hate to care whether he lived or died. The Zapata was less fanatical and the fear showed in him. Trent ordered him to slide his shoulder holster in through the door and take the pistol out of the fat man's belt and throw it away.

'Now back up, both of you,' Trent ordered. He followed in a low shuffling crouch and close to them as they backed across the open ground and he kept checking between their shoulders the walkway that circled the top of the lighthouse as well as the windows opening onto the verandah.

There were six windows and a set of double doors dead centre that stood open. The windows were low and screened while the verandah itself was stone and about thirty inches higher than the surrounding sand. Four wooden pillars supported the verandah roof. At least one man would be up in the tower so there could be two down below. They would wait till he was up close and open to a shot from the walkway. Then they'd attack from opposite corners of the verandah and from the walkway at the same time. He thought that if he dived across the verandah and through the doors he might find cover inside the building. He was wrong on all counts. The attack came from straight ahead.

One of the Cuban landing party stood well back in the shadows behind the doorway and hosed the Zapata and the fat man out of the way with a machine pistol. A bullet hit the outside of Trent's left thigh as he dived and rolled for the edge of the verandah. He lay flat on his back hard against the verandah and scarcely breathed as a stream of bullets sliced away the edge of the paving inches above his body. Stone chippings spattered him and he could feel the blood wet on his leg, but he was already on the move. Of the half-dozen Cubans who had landed, three were dead. The verandah protected him from the lookout up on the lighthouse walkway. The man shooting at him was inside the bungalow by the double doors. And there was a sixth man somewhere, the leader.

Trent thought of the radio operator's broken legs and the two dead Bahamians he'd seen in the hut and in bed at the guard post. The unnecessary violence indicated a man who enjoyed killing and inflicting pain. A man who, given the opportunity, would gloat and take his time.

Trent let go the Kalashnikov and slid the pistol holster off his shoulder. For the Cuban killer to feel secure, Trent needed to be at least three feet from the weapons. Hands folded behind his neck, he moved in inches, his weight supported on heels, buttocks, elbows, and shoulders. He could picture the killer and already the scenario was forming. First he reached down with his left hand to the wound in his thigh and spread the blood. Then he drew his knife and slid the blade in a deep 'V' from the centre of his scalp to the edge of his hairline.

17

Search parties had been ordered out at first light and Roddy waited with Estoban most of the day at the coastguard station for the expected report of the dory being washed ashore. None came, and in the late afternoon Roddy drove down the coast to his father's headquarters. As he drove, Roddy tried unsuccessfully to rid himself of his preoccupation with the Englishman. Trent had survived the crossing and if he had sailed for Lobos Cay, he would have come ashore well before midday, so he had evaded that trap too, and must be safe now, easing north towards Andros over the calm waters of the Great Bahama Bank. Roddy imagined the Englishman at the dory's tiller and wondered whether or not he and the girl were lovers. Marco Rocco's sister. It seemed fitting.

The road climbed over a spur and he pulled the MG onto the verge and parked to enjoy the sunset which painted the horizon in layers of yellow and pink and red and orange. The wind had dropped to a whisper so that the colours of the sunset spilled like fine oil across the glossy surface of the swells that rolled in across the channel. Roddy could see, between the trees, a slither of beach dyed a deep rose-gold. He doubted whether he could exist in any other country.

Admiral de Sanchez kept an apartment on the top floor of his headquarters with large windows that opened to a roof terrace with views to the sea. Unembarrassed, a young female rating in a cotton bathrobe opened the door to Roddy, handed him a glass, and pointed him to the bathroom where the Admiral kept his orchids. The Admiral had installed a big old-fashioned cast iron tub with claw feet and brass taps in the centre of the room, leaving the walls clear for the wooden steps laden with blooms.

Roddy found his father soaking, the water halfway up his chest. He held a cigar in one hand, a wineglass in the other, and wore a pink bath cap to protect the dye in his hair.

The Admiral raised his glass to Roddy and pointed his cigar at the ice bucket beside the bath: 'Serve yourself, my son. The Gringo's on Lobos Cay. We've got him.'

Roddy checked the label on the bottle, a 1982 Chilean chardonnay. Filling his glass, he towelled the condensation from a white-painted cane chair between large terracotta pots of orchids by the window. He thought that his father, in a photograph, would have looked grotesque and foolish. As had other powerful men.

'Trent, is he dead?' he asked.

Roddy's interest seemed to amuse his father. 'The last report said our men were closing in. He has no place to hide. The incident is over, Roddy.'

Condensation streamed down the tiled walls and had collected in trembling droplets on the underside of the ceiling beams. Roddy mopped the sweat from his face. 'Estoban Tur won't forget,' he said, and had the satisfaction of seeing a momentary deepening of the lines that surrounded his father's eyes.

But the Admiral spoke calmly: 'Tur let the Gringo escape, Rodrigo. He will be fortunate to retain his directorship of Bureau Three.' Carefully dropping the ash from his cigar into a flowerpot, the Admiral gave a small nod of agreement with his own thoughts: 'Yes, my son, extremely fortunate.'

Roddy imagined the lethal rumours already fed through the appropriate channels. He said, 'What's happened to the Bahamians on Lobos Cay?'

His father waved the question away: 'Rodrigo, concern yourself with your duties and not with mine.'

141

Duties were always familial. The Holy Family! Pushing himself out of his chair, Roddy opened the fogged-up window so that he could watch the last of the sun melt into the ocean. The Admiral never permitted an open window in the bathroom and, rebellious for once, Roddy said: 'There were eight Bahamians, plus Trent and the girl.' Ten dead.

He shivered as he turned to face his father. The Admiral had set down his glass and the light tattoo of his fingers on the edge of the bath was a warning that Roddy and his sister had learnt as children to heed as the first signs of an impending storm. The Admiral said: 'The Bahamian authorities will believe the Cay was taken over by drug smugglers for a big transshipment, Roddy. That's how it will be reported in the press.'

Roddy supposed that all admirals and generals viewed the broad perspective, the battle rather than the body count, let alone the individual dead. But with his father this distancing was more fundamental. Perhaps because he remained in his beliefs an outsider to the Revolution in whose service he had built so successful a career. Fear of accidental betrayal had made him hold his children at a distance when they were young: his love was somehow abstract, Roddy thought now, the hurt no less because of his understanding of it. Caught on a roller coaster of his father's design, he said: 'We *are* drug smugglers.' And murderers, he wanted to add as he pictured the Bahamians already dead on Lobos Cay and his father's killers closing in now on the Englishman and the girl.

Three men remained of the six who had landed on Lobos Cay: Tony, Raphael Segundo, and Jorge the basketball player. Tony was the leader; Tony Munoz, nicknamed the Judge. He was the Judge because he always listened with apparent sympathy to the pleadings of those he had been ordered to kill. His looks were nondescript, middle-aged, reasonably clean and neat, complexion off-white, hair off-black, brown eyes, mid-height, mid-weight. He got his pleasure from subjugating his victims to humiliation and from inflicting pain. His men were frightened of him.

Watching the Zapata and the fat man shield the Gringo as they backed away from the guard post had excited the Judge. He should have blasted them out of the way when they were in the middle of the open ground, but he liked to be close so that he could listen for the smack of the bullets and watch them strike. He was certain that he had hit the Gringo but he took no chances.

Jorge guarded the bungalow from the main entrance and the Judge had posted Raphael Segundo up on the walkway circling the light chamber, so the Gringo would be dead meat if he broke from cover. The Judge licked his lips as he slipped out through a rear window. He carried a machine pistol at the ready.

Light on his feet and silent, he rounded the second corner and saw the Gringo sprawled naked on his side, one arm thrown back as if reaching for the Kalashnikov or pistol holster which lay a metre away, and his other arm folded under him at an odd angle so that it looked like the broken wing of a bird. The Gringo had been hit in the head, and blood masked his face and had flowed down into the sand. There was a second wound in his thigh and clearly a third bullet had shattered his arm. His eyes were wide open and stared emptily towards the sea.

'Dead,' the Judge called to Jorge, hidden in the shadows within the bungalow. The Judge had hoped to find the Gringo alive. Disappointed, he walked forward and kicked the dead man over onto his back. His eyes were drawn down to the Gringo's privates.

Then there was a terrible burning in his throat as he choked on his own blood. The gun slipped from his hands as he tried to get his hands up, but he hadn't the strength and his knees gave.

Trent grabbed the machine pistol as it fell. Three bounds took him across the verandah. He hit the window with his shoulder and charged across the room with a spray of bullets cutting his wake. Seven steps and he dived flat so that the man by the door would swing his gun on past him and above his head.

Two seconds for the gunman to swing his weapon back and down but he didn't have two seconds. Trent's first shot killed him.

Trent rolled to his feet. He snatched the revolver from the gunman's belt, grabbed a wooden chair, and sprinted for the stairs that spiralled up the tower. Bare feet silent on the metal treads, he climbed fast, round and round the inside of the narrowing metal tube. Two hundred and sixteen steps up into deepening gloom.

As he climbed, Trent studied the girders that supported the light chamber and the iron braces that fanned out from the centre like the spokes of a bicycle wheel.

At the top of the stairs a steel trapdoor barred entrance to the light chamber. Trent slid the machine pistol as far out along the underflat of an I-beam as he could reach. He checked that there was a bullet in the breach of the revolver he'd grabbed, snapped the hammer back, and dropped the pistol down the stairwell. The revolver hit the floor and fired. The steel tower trapped and magnified the explosion so that it echoed round and round for what seemed like minutes.

Trent screamed and shoved the chair ricocheting down the stairs. Grabbing one of the floor braces in both hands, he swung himself out over the 140-foot drop. The clatter and crash of the chair masked any sound he made as he hooked his legs up over the brace and edged his way out to where the rods were sufficiently close to each other for him to lie across them. He retrieved the machine pistol and waited. He was good at waiting and he imagined the Cuban isolated above him in the light chamber picturing what could have happened below. The last of the day faded and now the only light in the tower came from a small glass panel in the trapdoor.

Half an hour passed before the hinges screeched and light flooded in as someone raised the trap. Next came a burst of automatic fire which would have cleared the top of the stairs. It left Trent's ears ringing. A pair of white trousers knotted into a sack followed. The sack was stuffed with a mixture of books and tools so that it thumped and banged as it bounced down the metal steps. The trousers hit the chair way below and broke it loose, the combined crash and clatter echoing up to add veracity to Trent's scenario.

Black legs appeared. The Bahamian light keeper. The gunman followed a step behind, an arm round the Bahamian's throat and a pistol held at his head.

The gunman shouted down: *'Oyez, Jorge! Tony! Que pasa abajo?'* What's happening below?

He edged down another step and another step, then shouted again and waited for the echo to abate before forcing the Bahamian down a further step. Again he shouted, the beginnings of hysteria breaking his voice high: 'For Jesus' sake, answer! What's happening? Where are you?'

Two more steps down and the angle was right. Trent's first shot smashed the gunman's right wrist and sent his pistol into the void. He shouted in English to the light keeper: 'Hold on!' and put a second bullet through the side of the gunman's skull.

Released, the light keeper grabbed at the banisters as he fell on his back. The gunman pitched over him and rolled on down, thudding and thudding against the metal treads.

Four o'clock in the morning and Roddy de Sanchez watched a tennis match played on a slow clay court somewhere in Europe and broadcast over satellite TV. The game was too one-sided to hold Roddy's attention and he had trouble staying awake. He had waited all night for the duty radio officer to confirm the Englishman's death so that he could order the embarkation of the squad on Lobos Cay. The confirmation should have come in a three-word code repeated three times at fifteen-minute intervals for a period of one hour, but they'd heard nothing since the initial report of the Englishman's arrival. A decision on whether to send the boat in had to be taken well before first light.

In his late teens and early twenties Roddy had been flattered at being party to his father's habitual philandering, but over the past months he had grown uneasy and now, having made coffee, he knocked on the Admiral's door rather than take the tray into the bedroom.

'Well?' the Admiral asked as he stalked into the living-room.

'Nothing,' Roddy said.

Dressed in a towelling bathrobe and slippers, the Admiral stood at the windows that faced across the roof terrace to the sea. His fingers beat out the familiar little tattoo of irritation on the plate glass, but he'd made his decision.

Trent injected the radio operator with morphine from the guard post medical kit. He attended to his own wounds while waiting for the drug to take hold, then strapped the radio operator's legs in splints and, with the light keeper's help, put him to bed. He found a barrow in the fishermen's hut and wheeled the murdered Bahamians up to the lighthouse and the six dead invaders down to the end of the quay, where he propped them against each other so that their faces were visible.

He had searched the dead and found no identification of any kind, not even a coin, and their armoury would have been the choice of professional gunmen from either side of the law.

Armed with a Kalashnikov and dressed in an old pair of jeans from the guard post, he walked up from the jetty and waited with the light keeper on the far side of the storeroom, where they remained in shadow as the fierce beam of the light swept the ocean.

The keeper was middle-aged and overweight but service on a gale-swept scrap of coral had given him unusual composure and resilience. Drug-related piracy and murder were common-place in the Bahamas and he believed the invaders were either setting up a transshipment from Colombia into Florida or preparing to ambush a transshipment. Trent he presumed to be with a British or US government agency and attached to the Bahamian authorities.

'Scaring the birds away from the corn?' he suggested with a nod at the pyramid of corpses on the jetty.

Trent said: 'Something like that.'

The keeper followed the beam from the lighthouse with his

146

binoculars as he searched the sea for a boat which he didn't expect would come.

'Whoever they are, they'll be waiting for a message over the radio,' he argued.

Had Trent been as certain, he would have fetched Auria and called Skelly to send in a helicopter immediately rather than wait for daybreak.

As well as a major freight route, the Old Bahama Channel was a rich fishing ground, and twin white mast lights, one above the other, signalled where a half-dozen boats trawled the edge of the reef. The fishermen approached closer to Lobos Cay over the next two hours until finally Trent and the keeper could see the nearest of the boats in the beam from the lighthouse.

The boat was stubby and square-countered. She motored past at a distance of about two hundred metres from the shore. She continued on her course for at least a mile before she turned and motored slowly back. Tuna rods fanned out aft of her chunky wheel-house and the mast lights showed the figure of a lookout in the tower. The lighthouse beam swept the boat and flashed on the lenses of the lookout's binoculars. No question that he was studying the Cay.

The keeper scuttled away across the sand to the lighthouse while Trent crawled to the beach and waded out alongside the jetty. He waited in the 'V' between the bows of the sunken lobsterman and the stonework, head and shoulders clear of the water, Kalashnikov hidden by the lobster boat's gunwale.

The tuna boat turned back again and Trent, listening to the slow powerful rumble of her diesels, was sure that they were Caterpillars. She was only fifty metres off the shore as she came abreast of the jetty. A searchlight on top of her wheel-house flicked out and lingered over the corpses. The note of her engines dropped as the skipper put her throttles to idle, then down to a gentle tick-over as her bows swung shoreward and she drifted towards Trent's hiding place.

Her prow crunched gently into the lobsterman as the skipper used the sunken boat as a fender. The lighthouse beam lit her. For a moment she seemed suspended motionless in the water, so close that Trent could have stroked her bow and counted the nailheads that showed like pockmarks in her white paint. He waited for a sailor to make the leap ashore over his head and for lines to drop to the jetty. Instead the skipper suddenly rammed the controls full astern. The diesels roared and the big propellers blasted sand and phosphorescence the under-water length of the hull so that the current surfaced at her bows and boiled into Trent's face. The boat turned away. Neither name nor port of registry marked her counter and, as she slipped into the darkness, her navigation lights flicked out.

Trent waded ashore and limped up towards the lighthouse. The keeper met him on the verandah. They sat on the steps and watched the lights of the other tuna boats for a while without need of speech and grateful for the first traces of dawn that touched the horizon. Trent thought of Auria marooned half a mile away, but he hadn't the strength for the swim. Better to wait for Skelly.

18

The Bahamian coastguard helicopter lowered Trent into the water beside the dory. Auria had heard the shooting, and the fear that had been her companion as she had lain in the bottom of the small boat through the night turned to rage which exploded over Trent as he scrambled on board.

Not having slept since leaving the *Golden Girl*, his eyes were sunk in deep caverns. He had shaved the forward half of his scalp at the crown and bandaged with two strips of sticking plaster the 'V' he had cut. And he had strapped the bullet wound in his thigh.

She shouted at him, demanding to be told where he'd been all night.

He said, 'On the Cay.'

'For Christ's sake, I know that.'

Trent said: 'I'm sorry.'

In response to her inquisition, the bare bones of his story came out in dribs and drabs: he had been hit on the head on landing and had little idea of what had gone on other than that there had been a fight between a party of smugglers and Bahamian customs officers.

He had been fuelled by adrenalin for the past two days. The danger behind him, exhaustion made him clumsy and he flooded the outboard motor when he tried to start it and nearly lost one of the oars as he rowed the dory. He brought them ashore on the far side of the Cay from the jetty so that Auria wouldn't see the dead, and he sheltered with Skelly in the lee of the guard post as the helicopter lifted away with the radio operator and Auria on board.

Skelly had taken a statement from the lighthouse keeper. With the helicopter gone, he walked out to the end of the jetty. At their first meeting on the beach, he had been offering a helping hand to big brother Washington in the shape of O'Brien. Now he wore khaki, pressed and starched, badges of rank, and his police hat with silver braid on the peak.

Skelly had put on more than an official persona with his uniform. His fellow countrymen had been brutally killed and it was personal. He studied the corpses of the murderers for a while, prying them apart with the toe cap of a well-polished brown shoe as Trent limped down to join him.

'Cubans.' Skelly was certain. 'Dominicans, on average, there'd be more black blood. Latin Americans, there'd be less. I can't tell whether they come from Florida or the home island, but you'll help me there, Mr Trent.'

'The tuna boat wasn't Cuban. She had twin Caterpillar diesels.'

Skelly nodded. He glanced up at the gulls circling overhead and beckoned his two constables to cover the bodies before leading the way up to the lighthouse bungalow. He crossed the ground in long strides and Trent, with his wounded thigh, had to hurry to keep up.

Trent had laid out the Bahamian dead under bedsheets in the front room. Skelly lifted the sheets back so that they could see the men's faces: 'They had families, Mr Trent, wives and children.' Trent stayed silent and Skelly continued in a soft conversational tone: 'I should have had you off the islands the moment O'Brien showed me your file. These people were innocent bystanders. I'm not blaming you, Mr Trent. I'm blaming myself for allowing O'Brien to mount an operation from the Bahamas that required a man like you.'

'You mean a killer,' Trent said. He walked out into the sunlight and down to the beach below the lighthouse. He needed sleep more than anything else. He lay down with his heels in the water and watched the puffs of white cloud. He heard Skelly giving orders and, after a while, the crunch of the police officer's shoes approached across the sand. Trent thought that it would be very easy to sail away to somewhere where he wasn't known. But that was an illusion. He said: 'Mr O'Brien wanted me to find the *Beau Belle*, Superintendent. And Miss Rocco paid me to find the *Beau Belle*. That's what I've done.'

By way of answer Skelly sent a flat stone skittering across the surface of the sea. He threw a second stone. The third failed to skip and he sat down, knees gripped in his arms, and far enough away from Trent not to encroach on his territory. He sat in silence for a while. Eventually he said: 'Last time I was in England a survey of some inner-city housing estates showed sixty-eight per cent of women frightened to go out of their homes after dark. Your government had agreed to spend eighty billion pounds on Trident submarines but claimed they couldn't find the funds for a dozen extra policemen on the beat. I find that obscene, Mr Trent, and now the drug culture is doing the same thing to the Bahamas. As a Bahamian police officer, I fight that, Mr Trent.'

He rattled a handful of pebbles, then flicked them one by one at a head of seaweed floating ten metres out from the beach. He hit the seaweed each time and his tone of voice, whatever the words, remained calm as a vicar's tea party.

'Mr O'Brien heads the Caribbean section of the American DEA. Neither of us are on the take, Mr Trent, so we help each other where possible. Usually that means that O'Brien helps me because he has greater resources. Sometimes he exerts a little pressure which I have to accept because the US controls our economy.

This is one of those times. I have instructions to co-operate but I don't have the facts and don't know what the operation entails, and that makes me nervous, Mr Trent.'

While speaking, Skelly had been watching a distant freighter push up-channel. Now he looked over at Trent and added: 'Perhaps irritable as well as nervous. The Cubans would have murdered the lighthouse keeper and the radio operator.'

It was all the apology Trent imagined he was going to get so he said: 'That's all right.'

'Thank you,' Skelly said.

The Bahamian made as if to shake Trent's hand as a seal on his apology but Trent didn't move so he changed his mind. He took off his bush jacket with the embroidered crowns sewn to the shoulders. He folded the jacket carefully and laid it on the dry sand behind him. Then he took off his peaked hat and set it on the jacket, top side down to protect it from the sun. A sheen of sweat glistened on his shaven skull and his ribs showed through his white cotton singlet. He smiled as he looked down at Trent, not exactly a practised smile, but nevertheless a smile that said to Trent that Skelly was used to getting his own way when he used it.

The Bahamian said: 'My wife claims I'm an awkward man to live with, Mr Trent, but she's an intelligent woman and we're still married, so I can't be that bad. Why don't you and I try co-operating?'

Trent almost laughed: 'Superintendent, people like you and O'Brien use people like me. You don't co-operate with us.'

'Bitter . . .'

'Experienced,' Trent corrected. 'As far as you're concerned the difference between me and those men on the jetty is that I was employed by what you think of as the right side.'

Skelly took off his shoes and socks and stood up to drop his trousers. He tucked the bottoms under his chin while he straightened the creases, then folded the legs neatly and laid the trousers on top of his hat. He pulled his singlet over his head, dropped it on the rest of his clothes, and walked into the sea. Ten yards out he turned and stood on one leg, the other foot tucked behind his knee, and his arms spread like wings. Head poked forward, he pouted his lower lip: 'You get four guesses, Mr Trent. Black? Chief Superintendent of Police? A heron? Someone you should reserve judgement on? Think about it while I take a swim.'

He swam out a hundred yards and back, then stood beside Trent, drying himself in the breeze.

152

A gust spattered Trent's face with sea water. He said: 'We might begin in a small way.'

'Like a blind date?' Skelly chuckled as he sat down. 'How about telling me how the dive went.'

Trent described the search and the two dives and he watched the lines in Skelly's face deepen as he recounted discovering the New Zealanders. Skelly's questions were painstaking in their thoroughness and at first concerned only with the minutiae as he constructed a policeman's picture that was all evidence and no conjecture. But his questioning widened as Trent related how they had been hunted by the patrol boats and forced to swim for the shore.

'They knew you were there? You were the bird-dog, Mr Trent.'

Trent considered the description apt. The difficulty lay in recognising which of the hunters ran the hunt, who were the hounds and who the jackals, and whether the *Beau Belle* was the quarry or a Judas goat.

He listened to Skelly feeling his way into the scenario: 'They wanted you alive, Mr Trent. Or they didn't want to kill you. But you got away from them. Then they had to silence you. What did you find out? Murder? A few sticks of dynamite and the evidence disappears. So it has to be something of value. Drug-related, because O'Brien's involved. Something more important than a cabin of marijuana soup. And if it's that important, why didn't they search for the yacht themselves?' He looked down at Trent. 'You don't say much.'

'We don't know much.' But Trent scented that Skelly had come close with his last question. According to O'Brien, the Cuban Navy's search for the *Beau Belle* had been cursory in the extreme. Perhaps because they didn't want to draw attention to themselves. And, given the use of explosives, whatever was hidden on the *Beau Belle* had to be bomb-proof.

He said: 'Angola's a good place to buy illicit diamonds.' He hadn't been thinking of diamonds, they had popped into his head. And immediately the jump came. Lateral thinking.

Once the connection was made it was so obvious that he was nervous as he asked what effect the cavern roof would have had on the magnetometer readings.

Skelly sensed it. 'None at all.'

Trent lay there on his back, feeling the sun on his face. The sun had been the enemy the previous day. Now it felt friendly and healing. He got to his feet and limped to the lighthouse. A Navy cutter had sailed from Nassau to pick up the corpses but it wasn't due for another six hours and one of Skelly's men had thrown water over the sheets to keep the bodies cool. Skelly's bare feet padded across the wooden floorboards and halted behind Trent. Trent said: 'The fourth crew member – I want him. And I want the man behind this whole thing. Whoever he is, whatever the politics.'

He faced Skelly. He had led the Bahamian onto foreign territory and he gave him time, not pushing yet, but determined to have the police officer's commitment or walk away from him. The Bahamian looked from Trent to the dead, then out through the window to the sea. Reflected off the sand, sunlight lit the underside of his jaw so that his skull-like head seemed to hang disembodied up near the rafters.

'You've studied my file,' Trent said.

He heard the brush of Skelly's hands one against the other as the Bahamian wiped the sand from his palms.

'You're a police officer,' Trent said quietly: 'I don't want you reading me the law halfway through whatever I do.'

Skelly looked back at the dead covered by the wet sheets: 'What the Americans call a piss or get off the pot situation. What do you want?'

'*Whatever the politics* – I want you to say that so that I believe you,' Trent said, 'then I want a Zodiac and a dive tank flown in.'

'You're sure you don't want me to kneel and lay my hand on the dead?'

'That might help,' Trent said. 'And check with the Americans what boats were fishing the channel last night. Have one of your fisheries people run the inquiry so we don't hit a nerve. An inquiry that includes Caterpillar diesels.'

'Cutting out O'Brien.'

'Cutting out the politics,' Trent corrected.

Roddy de Sanchez had driven back to Havana with the dawn. 'Act naturally,' his father had ordered, and Roddy sorted files in Archives for eight hours then played six sets at the club and dropped off a girlfriend on the way home. He drove at a steady forty kilometres an hour to conserve fuel and parked the car in the front driveway beside his father's official Volga. He carried his sports bag round to the rear of the house. Lights shone in his father's study and Roddy hesitated, then entered by the kitchen door.

Roddy's mother sat at the pine table, hands folded as if in prayer to the marble pestle and mortar in which she had pounded garlic and chilies. The astringent perfume stung Roddy's eyes as he stopped to kiss her cheek. He held her a moment, hand on her shoulder. He needed to feel her presence as something special, but they were strangers, her cheek cool and smooth and impersonal as paper, wrapping paper, he thought.

She said: 'Your father's waiting for you,' and he replied that he would be down in a minute. He carried his bag upstairs to his room, unpacked the soiled sports clothes, and powdered the inside of his tennis shoes. He wanted to scream and leap up and down and crash through the floor and on through into . . . into darkness, he realised.

Even a month ago he had been able to fantasise his freedom to be what he had thought of as the true Roddy: fun to be with, kind, reasonably thoughtful of others, able to laugh at himself; not a great thinker, perhaps, but competent at his job; loyal from habit or through laziness, or perhaps because he was easily satisfied. Uninvolved.

He washed his hands and went down the stairs to his father's study. The Admiral sat at his desk. Roddy's sister, Maria, sprawled in one of the two leather easy chairs. An inch taller than Roddy, she had swum in the national team. Square shoulders and long strong legs gave evidence of her training and she wore her hair cropped. In contrast to her athleticism, there was an almost aggressive sensuality in her lips and the curve of breast and in the way she carried herself that made Roddy imagine often, as he watched her, a cartoon interbreeding of the New Woman of a 1930s Communist poster with Hollywood's sultry Latin seductress.

Roddy said, 'Hi,' and to his father, 'You told me to act naturally so I stopped off at the club.'

The Admiral closed the Morocco-bound desk blotter on the letter he'd been writing and slid the cap onto his gold Parker pen. His expression and voice were calm as he related the report of the captain of the tuna boat, who had found the landing party dead, their corpses arranged in a pyramid at the end of the jetty on Lobos Cay. The Bahamians must have flown in reinforcements without using lights and low enough to escape radar surveillance.

'How would they have known?' Roddy asked.

'The radio operator, a word code we didn't know about.' The Admiral dismissed the question as unimportant. It had happened. 'We'll hear from Rocco when he gets to Nassau if the Englishman is alive.'

'And Rocco's sister,' Roddy said. The deaths were too much for him. 'Why don't we forget the *Beau Belle*?' he said and, looking to his sister for support, read the contempt in her eyes.

The Admiral put his pen into the centre drawer of the desk and closed it. Freed, his fingers began their dance on the gold leather only to be stilled as he interlocked his hands.

Roddy remembered one of the few games his father had played with him in early childhood: here is the church and here is the steeple, open the door and here are the people. Now there were liver spots on the backs of his father's hands and Roddy longed to feel sympathy for him and to be supportive in his feelings as well as in his actions, but he felt only an empty distance through which they looked at each other, strangers, as with his mother. He shrugged wearily. 'What do you want me to do?'

'Set up the deal with your American, Rodrigo.'

19

The sky was clear and the stars bright. In two hours the moon would rise. The Zodiac rode the crest of a swell that rolled in towards the reef. High on the wave, Trent searched the foam. A dark patch showed to starboard and he leant on the steering arm, then drew it back and, opening the throttle wide, shot the Zodiac through the gap.

Once inside the reef, Trent steered a long curve to the *Beau Belle*. The lightly laden Zodiac skittered over the protected waters, the hum of the 100-horse outboard sure and powerful. Trent dropped anchor and wriggled into the tank harness. Safety underwater demanded foresight and he had planned the dive in detail as he crossed the channel. Skelly had equipped him well: buoyancy jacket, Normalair regulator, dive computer, bang stick, underwater flashlight, crowbar, forty metres of lightweight line, spare tank.

Trent lowered the spare tank to the bottom. Setting the dive computer, he bled the air out of the buoyancy jacket, piked, and slid down the Zodiac's anchor rope. Touching bottom, he jammed the small Danforth anchor under a rock lip and looped the spare line over a coral head. Sure of the Zodiac, he checked the two ropes with which he had anchored the *Beau Belle* back from the edge of the blue hole to the anchor points. Satisfied, he lowered the spare tank to the plug hole, followed it down, and lashed it to a limestone spur a metre above the cavern roof.

He turned on the lamp he had left at the exit, slipped head first through the plug hole, and followed the guideline to the yacht. He circled the yacht before swimming slowly up the side deck to switch on the remaining two lights. The water had cleared round the yacht and tiny fish darted in and out of the open portholes to the owner's cabin. With the glass smashed out of the windows, fish cruised the saloon and a lobster's antennae waved from under the cocktail cabinet.

The marine life made the yacht less of a tomb and Trent felt more at ease than on the previous dives as, lamp in hand, he dipped over the wheel-house and down the far side of the yacht. He had hoped to avoid Hewett by entering the engine room via one of the jagged holes torn in the hull by the explosives, but even with the worst of the splinters chopped away he was unable to get more than one arm and his head through. The deck boards remained well beyond his reach.

He rose up the side of the hull, into the wheel-house, and opened the door down to the engine room. Hewett's body blocked the head of the companionway. Trent gripped the dead skipper's feet and pulled tentatively, nervous that the limbs would separate from Hewett's trunk. A mist of thread-thin sea worms and minute crustaceans rose from the disturbed clothing which crumbled and fell away so that Trent saw the key strung on a cord round Hewett's neck and a leather pouch. He pulled a little harder and the corpse moved, slowly at first, then with a rush so that Trent had to fend it away from his own body.

The pouch contained an Australian passport in the name of William Green and travellers' cheques. The key had been made for a Chubb security lock, probably a safe. If so, it would be in the owner's stateroom. He guided the corpse into the galley and closed the connecting door back to the wheel-house before swimming on through into the saloon and then sinking down the circular stairs. Only scraps remained of the big eel.

Trent glided hand over hand through to the stateroom. He

kept his fins still so as not to disturb the sludge of vegetable matter that covered every surface. A large double bed took up much of the cabin while narrow couches port and starboard served as sea bunks. A dressing-table that shared duties as a desk ran along the forward bulkhead. Trent found the small Chubb safe built into the bulkhead behind the dressing-table drawers. The ship's papers, crew list, and three passports were wrapped in a traditional oilskin wallet. Two of the passports belonged to the New Zealanders, one to Hewett in his own name. And there was a canvas bag fastened with a drawstring.

Trent loosened the string. The small pebbles looked dull and uninteresting. Stowing both packages inside his wetsuit, he glided back and dug into the sludge between the port-side couch and the bed. A second and third layer of compressed vegetable matter sealed in plastic wrapping had been protected from the explosion by the upper layer. Trent took one of the slabs and kicked back through the thickening soup to the stairs and up through the saloon to the wheel-house. He checked the computer. Twenty-eight minutes to fly.

The engine room companionway was cramped and his dive tank scraped along the bulkhead as he drew himself down head first. The engine room deck boards were patterned steel. Trent lifted a board close to the Gardner diesel and flashed the lamp into the bilges. As to specification, internal ballast in twelve-inch ingots lay between the timbers on top of the keel box. The gross weight in the specifications amounted to one ton. The ingots were pig iron, primed with red lead, and painted in Admiralty grey.

To gain purchase, Trent held onto the engine while he prised out two of the top layer of ingots and dug the tip of his knife into the first of the lower level. The paint came away easily and gold glowed dully in the lamplight. He tested the two ingots from the top layer and they were the same.

He had checked half the length of the engine room when he felt a tingle as if he were swimming in a stream of aerated water that carried a small electric charge. The sensation enveloped his body and his eyes seemed at fault, his view of the ingots fuzzy rather than out of focus. The feeling passed and, as his vision cleared, he saw the two ingots that he had prised loose slide slowly towards him across the deck. He glanced towards the companionway and saw that the handles of the tools hanging on nails above the workbench now pointed at him.

He thought he was hallucinating, that there was something wrong with the air in his tank. The tingling came again, and the fuzziness of vision, now followed by a heavy scraping above him and beneath his feet, then a deep crunch as the earthquake collapsed the roof of the blue hole and ten thousand tons of limestone drove the *Beau Belle* down into the depth of the cavern.

Then water in the cavern acted as a hydraulic brake on the collapsed roof so that the movement down was slow but relentless. Cocooned within the engine room, there was no sense of sinking and Trent watched the depth meter on his wrist as he waited for the *Beau Belle* to come to the end of the two lines he had made fast to the coral heads on the sea floor. Twenty-three metres, twenty-four, -five, -six . . . thirty, thirty-five, then a jolt as the line to the deck cleat held.

Blocked on one side by the *Beau Belle*, the cavern roof buckled at the crack across its centre. A projection caught in the rigging. The larger section of the roof broke free and, no longer braked by the water, gathered speed as it sank away to leave the *Beau Belle* sandwiched between the smaller section and the cliff wall.

Trent clung to the engine as the massive limestone pestle crushed and ground the superstructure. He felt the first line snap and the vast weight tear the rigging bolts out of the hull. Released, the roof section side-slipped clear of the hull like a plate dropped into a pond, and the line made fast round the hull sprang taut. Depth forty-six metres, and the computer gave its first warning.

Trent kicked across the engine room to the foot of the companionway. He flashed the lamp up and saw the companionway blocked with enough crushed timber and twisted steel to halt a wrecking crew armed with power tools. Trapped.

He turned smoothly and glided over to the workbench. An oiled teak chest under the bench contained woodworking tools. He took a saw and chisel from the chest, a steel-hafted hammer from hooks on the bulkhead, and the cable that had connected the battery to the dynamite.

Three kicks took him to the larger of the two holes blown in the hull only for the lamp to show him that the *Beau Belle* had swung on her tether and now rested port-side against the limestone wall. He looped the cable round his waist and made the ends fast either side of the hole so that he was held steady while he worked the saw. He had trimmed away the splinters before trying to reach the floorboards from outside the hull. Now he cut with the grain along the planking towards the first rib. He knew the dive tables by heart and the increasing dangers of losing mental control below forty metres. He knew that he had less than twenty minutes of air available at his present depth and he knew that he already required a minimum of ten minutes decompression time.

The equation was quite simple. He was going to saw wood for the last twenty minutes of his life. He laughed and water crept round his mouthpiece so that he coughed. He was about to take the mouthpiece out but a splinter caught his knuckles and the sight of the blood trailing away to his right snapped him back from the edge of narcosis. He began a second cut two inches down from the first and sawed three inches deep along the plank parallel to the first cut. He hammered the chisel into the cut, took it out, and forced the crowbar into the gap. He heaved back and the short length of wood snapped free. The second piece was easier.

As he sawed, he built up a picture of where the *Beau Belle* rested in relation to the now-vanished plug hole. Both the yacht and the coral head to which she was now anchored had been to the south of the entrance, with the coral head perhaps ten or twelve metres farthest south. The yacht must now lie directly below the closest point on the cavern lip in relation to the anchor point. The edge was jagged, and must have cut into the rope, and it would cut deeper with any further movement of the yacht.

He crowbarred a fourth section of planking free and glanced at the computer. He had to be free of the yacht in eight minutes, but he would die of the bends if he surfaced. He pictured the *Beau Belle* hanging on the single rope. One hundred and seventy feet down to the bottom of the cavern. One hundred and thirty feet up to the sea floor. And the spare tank seventy feet to his right and sixty feet up. With five minutes of air left he snapped a fifth piece of planking free of the hole. One piece more and he might be able to wriggle through without his air tank.

The top side of the yacht lay almost flat against the cliff but, below the hole, the hull curved away towards the keel. He would have to squirm down and swim under the hull. He pictured each action and saw that he would need both hands free to force a way between the planking and the limestone. There'd be no room for his tank, no way of dragging it after him. He would have to get his escape absolutely right.

The last section of plank gave under the crowbar. He looped the flashlight over his wrist and loosened the dive tank harness. He dug the crowbar between the hull and the cliff and hooked one leg round it, pulling back as he breathed deeply, in and out, using the last of the air in the tank to charge his lungs.

He laid the tank on the deck right up against the hole and, with the regulator between his teeth, thrust both arms and his head through the hole, and shoved until the gap widened a few extra inches. He thought of counting as he usually did, or saying a prayer, but he hadn't time. Now or never. He switched on the flashlight, took a last deep breath, and spat the mouthpiece out.

He twisted from side to side, using elbows and shoulders and hips to maintain the space between the *Beau Belle* and the cliff. His arms and shoulders and his head broke through into clear water. For a moment the weight of the yacht threatened to squeeze the air out of his lungs. He fought his knees down the cliff and thrust his backside against the planking. The weight eased and he shot down the curve of the yacht's bottom past the keel and along the cliff face. The falling roof had clouded the water with sand and lime. Eighty feet to swim along the cliff and up sixty feet to the spare dive tank.

He drove along the cliff with long easy beats of his fins. His lungs contained four times as much air as they could hold on the surface. The air was held at two times the pressure in a car tyre by the counter pressure of the water. The outside pressure would lessen as he rose towards the surface. If he failed to breathe out as he rose, his lungs would explode. If he breathed out too quickly he would run out of air and drown.

With visibility less than an arm's length, his chances of finding the spare dive tank were zero, but somewhere up ahead floated the snapped guideline he had rigged between the plug hole and the yacht. The sand suspended in the water defused the flashlight beam into a pale cloud that guided him up and along the cliff. The air trickled from his lips and he counted now the sweep of his fins and checked his depth on the computer. It had to be there, the dark line of rope against the pale cliff. Unless it had snapped at the plug hole, or broken away from the stump of rock to which he'd made it fast. Fifty beats of his fins, sixty . . .

He could go on swimming along the cliff face until he had exhausted the oxygen in his lungs. He could rise to the surface and die in the agony of the bends. He could open his mouth to the water. Or turn back towards the *Beau Belle*. It had to be there.

His eyes threatened to burst out of their sockets under the pressure of the air trapped in his nose. His lungs burnt. The strength in his legs seeped away with the burnt oxygen. Twenty seconds, he thought. Twenty seconds of life left to him and he counted slowly in his head to control his fear. Eighty beats of his fins, ninety, and his lips rammed shut as he fought to maintain his level. Then he saw it, below him, the tail end of rope.

He piked down, not grabbing at it for fear that it would tear away from the rock and still not certain that it was attached. As he swam down, the increased pressure squeezed him as if he were a tube of toothpaste. He saw the regulator hose first. CALM, he screamed in his head. STAY CALM.

He seized the harness in his left hand first to be sure of the tank, then grabbed the hose and ran his hand down to the regulator. He pressed the valve with his thumb to blast the water out of the tube and rammed the mouthpiece between his teeth. DOWN, he screamed at himself. DOWN into the safety offered by greater pressure, pressure that would compress the bubbles of nitrogen that had collected already in his joints and in his blood. Down to where he could relax and get his breath and strength back and his nerves under control. Down in obedience to the dive computer.

Five minutes at fifty feet, then up to thirty-five. He recovered the length of guideline and swam south to the anchor rope supporting the *Beau Belle*. Rising to the edge of the blue hole, he cut the legs off his wetsuit and used the knife handle to stuff the neoprene under the anchor rope where it dipped over the cavern lip. He unravelled a short length of the guideline and bound the neoprene in place. Then he backed up the frayed section of the anchor rope with a doubled length of the guideline. In all sixty-five minutes passed before the computer brought him to the surface beside the Zodiac.

A gentle breeze caressed his face as he pushed his mask up. The coastal perfume almost choked him, perfume blended from the scents of palm and mangrove, and of drying salt on the mud-flats, and a trace of rotting leaves and pine gum from the mountainside. He slipped the harness off his shoulders and let the dive tank sink away. His weight belt followed. He tried twice to drive up out of the water into the Zodiac but there was insufficient power left in his thighs. With the side of one fin he prised the other loose, then toed off the first. The outboard propeller guard served as a step and he clambered over the transom.

Lighthouses swept the sea with their beams blindingly brilliant while, away to the east, the moon surfaced. The soft slap and lick of the sea against the Zodiac beat like a drum and the surf out on the reef thundered in his head. A gull cried, startled off the mud-flats, the thud of a distant diesel pushed a fishing boat out to sea. A truck driver missed his gear change at a bend on the coast road.

Trent's role in the Cold War had been as simple as driving a truck for a big transport corporation. The good guys drove on the right side of the road. The bad guys drove on the left. The Department had told him where to go and what to carry. He had delivered on time so he had been permitted to choose his own route. Now he was unsure of what direction to take.

For a while he watched the Cuban coast. He felt a little envious of the DGI. Cold War or no Cold War, for Cuban Intelligence the enemy remained the United States and its trade embargo and its support of the oligarchies and military dictatorships that made Latin America a hell for the great majority of the population.

He thought about the ease of his escape from Cuba, and about the ton of gold on the *Beau Belle* that had a money value in the region of $13 million, and of the two New Zealanders and the Bahamians on Lobos Cay who had been murdered for it. Thirteen million in gold ingeniously hidden in Cuban waters.

The owner of the gold had to be very certain of his ability to recover it. But then what? To bank that quantity of gold required government co-operation pretty much anywhere in the world. So the owner of the gold had something of political value to trade in return for government aid, and something of sufficient value to have the dead buried in a closed file. Stopping the owner of the gold made a good destination. Trent started the outboard and motored out along the reef in search of a hiding place for the *Golden Girl*.

20

Lobos Cay Light beckoned Trent back across the Old Bahama Channel. From a hundred yards out he could see the tall, sapling-thin figure of Skelly outlined against the whitewashed wall of the guard post. He slewed the Zodiac into the jetty. Skelly made the bow line fast and held out a helping hand as Trent clambered ashore.

'The *Golden Girl* reached Andros a couple of hours ago,' Skelly reported. 'Rocco told the authorities that you and his sister failed to return from a diving expedition along the edge of the reef. We told him his sister was safe and that you'd had a bang on the head. He seemed pleased.'

'Good,' Trent said, and Skelly guided him by the elbow up to the guard post.

'There's conch soup on the stove and fresh bread,' Skelly said. Two of his police constables were in the kitchen and he pointed them to the door. Seating Trent at the table, he sliced bread and ladled soup into a bowl.

They faced each other across the table, Skelly waiting, Trent unsure of how much to tell him. The spoon rattled against the edge of the plate as he tried to eat. Embarrassed, he crumbled bread and put a piece in his mouth but it was too dry and stuck in his throat.

Skelly poured him a glass of water and asked: 'What happened?'

'The dive wasn't as easy as I'd hoped,' Trent said. 'I left your dive tanks on the bottom.'

'No problem.' Skelly fetched a bottle of rum from another room. He poured a couple of inches into a tumbler for Trent, a small one for himself. He touched his glass to Trent's. 'Cheers.'

'Cheers,' Trent said. Hands on the table, he warmed the rum.

Skelly said: 'You must be tired out. Steering a big outboard for any length of time puts the devil of a strain on your hands and wrists.'

'I suppose it does,' Trent said. He raised the glass in both hands and swallowed a little. The warmth exploded in his belly.

Skelly took the soup bowl back to the stove to reheat. He sat on the countertop, waiting, feet on the floor. Trent thought that being that tall must have a lot more disadvantages than advantages – except for a basketball player. He said, 'You must hit your head a lot.'

Skelly smiled. 'You learn to be careful, Mr Trent.'

'Just Trent,' Trent said. He unzipped his wetsuit and dropped the passports and the bag and the packet of compressed vegetable matter on the table. He undid the plastic wrapping on the vegetable matter and pried the leaves apart. Nudging the opened package across the table, he said: 'There's about half a ton on the *Beau Belle*.'

Skelly gave Trent back his soup before examining the leaves. A little surprised, he said: 'Some sort of grass . . .'

'As in hay? Not what you smoke?'

'Not what I'd smoke. Eat, you'll feel better.' Skelly spread the passports apart so that he could read the names: 'William Hewett, William Green.'

'And the New Zealanders. That leaves the fourth member of the crew, let's call him X,' Trent said. He knew the scenario as well as if he had written it himself.

Hewett had never saved and he was getting to an age where jobs were less easy to come by. He had wanted retirement money and along came X with a foolproof and risk-free proposition. X borrowed money to buy Angolan marijuana.

In fact they bought uncut diamonds with the cash and half a ton of horse feed wrapped in seranwrap. Hewett was an expert in explosives. According to the plan, he would blow up the *Beau Belle* in Cuban waters at night with the uninvolved members of the crew in their bunks. He and X would get away on one tender, sell the diamonds, and vanish, presumed lost at sea. The New Zealanders would get away on the other tender and report that the yacht had been sunk by gunfire.

The lenders of the money were given photographs of the cargo being loaded and a sample of first-class Angolan marijuana. They were criminals, so Hewett could persuade himself that defrauding them was a moral act. No one was going to go into Cuban waters to search for the *Beau Belle* and no one was going to get hurt.

'Foolproof, except that the charges went off by accident,' Trent said.

Skelly emptied the canvas bag onto the table and counted twenty-five small pebbles: 'A dozen men have been killed for these. That's obscene, Mr Trent. Obscene.'

Only an acting genius could have portrayed such strength of disgust and anger. Trent said, 'Hewett got conned. He was used as a mule. There's thirteen million dollars of gold on the *Beau Belle.*'

He was watching Skelly and saw the shock in the Superintendent's eyes. He could almost hear his brain whirring into a new gear. 'Drug money from Angola so it must be Cuban,' Skelly said and Trent nodded. But there were also those who had paid the Cubans in bullion. The American mafia. Now that they had no further use for the Cubans, the mafia might well try to retrieve the gold.

Skelly crossed to the window and looked out across the channel towards Cuba: 'Castro had three generals shot for involvement in the drug trade, probably their gold. Whoever inherited intended parking it for a while. Is that how you see it, Mr Trent? The *Beau Belle* sank by accident and they didn't know where? So they found themselves a bird dog?' Still facing the window, he added: 'O'Brien told you where the yacht sank.'

And Captain Pedro Gomez y Roig, alias Pepito, had put Trent in touch with O'Brien. Thirteen million would buy a lot of protection. Trent said: 'They must have had transducers on my Zodiac and on the *Golden Girl*.' He wondered who had placed them. He was certain that Richard was innocent. Which left Auria Rocco or Marco. Auria had put up the $200,000 bond – and there was her fear. She must be under a lot of pressure. 'I'll need to do an electronic sweep of the cat,' he said.

Roddy de Sanchez flew Mexicana to Cancún in Mexico. He queued at the left hand of three passport inspection kiosks. The immigration officer flicked through the Cuban diplomatic passport, glanced up to compare face and photograph, slid a folded tourist visa between the pages, and waved him on. Roddy rode a cab out to the beach strip and booked into the Carib Mar Hotel. Up in his room he read the instructions for the meet written on the back of the visa by his contact in Mexican Intelligence, Captain Pedro Gomez y Roig. Roddy and the Captain had co-operated a couple of times in the past and the big Mexican was Roddy's key into the Americans . . .

He changed into briefs under a pair of red swim shorts, and a white T shirt. He strolled out to the beach at ten minutes to two in the afternoon and turned left. The tide was running and he kept to the wet sand. He reached the second ice cream stall from the hotel at two minutes to two. He stood facing the sea and, at exactly two o'clock, charged into the water. He swam straight out for a hundred metres.

Captain Pedro Gomez y Roig idled an open dive boat between Roddy and the beach. As he passed Roddy, he dropped a face mask overboard. Roddy dived for the mask and stripped off his shorts and T shirt before surfacing. The dive boat curved back towards him and a hand the size of a butcher's block plucked him on board.

Sprawled on the floorboards, Roddy glowered and said: 'Whoever planned this meet has a perverted imagination.'

Pepito grinned lazily and motored gently a further hundred metres out from the beach before opening the throttle wide.

They raced south at thirty knots parallel to the shore. After half an hour, Pepito eased the helm over to bring them closer in. There were no houses in sight, nothing but palm trees and silver sand unmarked by footprints. Pepito pointed to a solitary figure seated in the shade and slowed briefly while Roddy dropped over the side.

The American, Smith, had found a chunk of driftwood to sit on. He wore a seersucker suit and wire-rimmed glasses through which he had been reading the sports section of the previous day's *Miami Herald*. He folded the spectacles carefully and replaced them in a metal case which he slipped into his inside pocket. 'Nice to have you call on me again,' he said, with a friendly smile, and offered Roddy the newspaper to sit on.

Declining the paper, Roddy squatted down and said: 'I hope you found the names I gave you useful.'

'They certainly checked out,' Smith said. 'Is that what we have here, more drug names?'

'Real beauties.' Roddy could barely make out the wake of Pepito Gomez's dive boat away to the south. 'How far are we from the road?' he asked.

'Two miles or thereabouts,' Smith said. 'The big Mex has a couple of his men at the intersection. He sets a good meet. A little complicated sometimes, but safe, and that's what matters. Washington finds out I've even walked down the same road as you, they'll have my badge. And here we are holding hands on the sidewalk like a couple of lovers.'

Roddy said: 'The *paseo*, Señor Smith. The rules say twice round the square and the engagement is official.'

Smith raised an eyebrow: 'So it's not official?'

'No,' Roddy said. He wanted to be back in Cuba but it was already too late. The CIA would have his photograph on file so Smith probably already knew his name. If he didn't now, he would by sunset. But still he hesitated.

Smith said: 'Nothing's easy except getting a bullet in the head. I can say you should trust me but that's what I'd say whatever.'

Roddy distrusted all Gringos and distrusted this Gringo

more than most, quiet as a spider and courteous. And Smith's Spanish was unusually fluent and idiomatic where most Gringos were ignorant. Most Gringos were also loud, brash, ill-mannered, arrogant, racist, and as easy to read as a road sign. Smith was very different. Roddy said: 'You know who I am?'

'Rodrigo de Sanchez, Lieutenant in Naval Intelligence, son of Admiral Antonio Maria de Sanchez. You want promotion, you're going to have to play less tennis. That's official. It's in your personal file. And you need to be a little more careful over whose wife you screw.' Smith shrugged and grinned. 'What did you expect? Only fools believe in secrets, Lieutenant. The way the world's progressing, the credit card corporations probably have more on you than your own department. Mind, they're more trustworthy, seeing they want your cash rather than your job.'

Roddy laughed despite himself and Smith said: 'Like I said, watch the wives and the tennis. You and me could be on the road to a useful relationship and I'd prefer to have you climb the ladder than mess up.'

'I need to cool off,' Roddy said. He walked back out into the sea. With the water up to his chest, he turned and beckoned the American. The American hesitated, but finally stripped reluctantly to a pair of patched boxer trunks before joining Roddy. 'You're very careful, Lieutenant.'

'It's an allergy I have to microphones,' Roddy said. He moved round so that his back was to the shore and spooned water up in both hands, dribbling it through his fingers as he spoke. 'A half-dozen senior Naval officers plan to defect to the US with a naval vessel, Señor Smith. They wish a four-point guarantee in writing from your State Department.'

Smith's expression didn't change. 'Give me the points.' Roddy remained silent and Smith shrugged. 'OK, so I'll set up a meet. There's a time scale on this thing?'

'Short,' Roddy said.

The police helicopter buzzed the *Golden Girl* before landing Trent on South Andros. With the Zodiac and outboard lost, Marco had brought the catamaran in bow onto the short jetty.

He had laid only one anchor where Trent would have laid two and he hadn't buoyed the anchor, which was Trent's habit in the Caribbean. Then, if the anchor got jammed under coral, it could be hauled out by the buoy rope.

Marco charged down the jetty and danced Trent round in a bear hug: 'Hey man, you're one tough *hombre*.' He held Trent back so as to be able to look into his eyes: 'Saved my kid sister from the Commies. I owe you, and that's personal, Trent. Plus Dad says to tell you, you eat free at the top Italian restaurant in Newport, and that's for life.'

Having had his own say, Marco grabbed Auria and thrust her into Trent's arms like a Christmas package: 'Welcome the hero home from the wars.'

Auria jerked free from her brother and pushed Trent away. Rik Hewett stood a little apart, waiting to be noticed, and Trent said: 'Hi, how did the voyage back go?'

Rik said: 'I wasn't much help. I think I ate something.'

'Sick as a pig,' Marco said, clapping Rik on the back. And to Trent: 'Listen, I'm sorry we weren't there to pick you up. We had a Cuban patrol boat sitting on our tail. Nothing we could do.'

'That's what I guessed,' Trent said. Needing to talk to Rik, he asked Marco to load the BMW: 'I'd like to sail over to Nassau to replace the equipment we've lost.'

He walked Rik down the jetty and along the beach to a patch of shade beneath a palm. He sat down on the sand. Rik waited, watchful, but at ease with Auria absent. 'Your stomach's all right now?' Trent asked.

Rik said it was fine and Trent asked when he'd got sick.

Rik said that he had felt a little queasy while Trent and Auria loaded the anchor warps. Wanting to stay on deck, he had taken the helm after they left. Marco had brought him a mug of soup but that hadn't helped. On the contrary, he had vomited and had had to take to his bunk. 'I was unconscious for a couple of hours,' he said.

'You're not the first person to be sick,' Trent said. 'You might as well sit because we have to talk. I'm afraid your father's dead.'

Rik sat, his back against the tree-trunk, bony elbows resting on drawn-up knees.

'It was quick. He wouldn't have suffered,' Trent said. 'There was an explosion in the engine room, something that happens on yachts every once in a while. Probably a build-up of gas in the bilges from the galley. The stove and the icebox ran on butane.'

Rik nodded. The skin across the bridge of his nose and along his cheekbones had gone very white, as had his knuckles.

'My father shot himself,' Trent said. 'Money troubles.'

'I'm sorry,' Rik said. He looked across and Trent said: 'I don't know why I told you that. Sharing, I suppose.'

'It's all right.' Rik watched the sea as if it were a screen on which to play his thoughts and memories. After perhaps quarter of an hour, he said quietly: 'He was nice, really. Not a very good man, I suppose. A bit thoughtless. Somehow stuck in his early twenties. But he was nice. I mean, I loved him. You know, despite everything.' He looked at Trent. 'What about the other men?'

'The New Zealanders died too. I didn't find the fourth man.'

Rik picked up a handful of sand and watched the grains run out through his fingers. The last grain dropped and he asked: 'Was he doing something wrong? Illegal?'

'Not very,' Trent said.

'I was always frightened he would. He wasn't good with money, which was all right as long as he got jobs. And he wasn't very clever so he would probably have got caught. He would have hated prison. Getting caught must put a stop to fantasy for a while. I think that's what he lived in a lot of the time.'

'Fantasy?' Trent asked.

Rik nodded: 'The grass was always greener, jobs and women.'

Trent stood up and walked to the public telephone. He called O'Brien first only to be told that the DEA man was away till the following day. Next Trent called Cancún in Mexico. He didn't mind if the line was tapped. The pot needed

stirring. When Pedro Gomez y Roig answered, Trent said:
'No questions, Pepito. You are a dumb fisherman who knows
how to dive. Take a week's leave and get yourself on a flight
to Nassau.'

He walked back towards the jetty. Auria came to meet him.
The anger in her was as strong as it had been the previous
morning when he had been dropped by helicopter into the
water alongside the dory. He was reluctant to lie to her. He
thought that there had been enough lies between them. He
thought of asking who had put up the bond money. But she
would have told him to mind his own business, or that it was
hers. He thought of telling her that Rik was worth a lot more
than she seemed to think, but all he said was: 'Rik's father
died on the *Beau Belle*.'

She said, 'Oh,' and, after a pause, 'What else haven't you
told me that you found?'

'Not a lot. I thought I should be the one to tell Rik,' Trent
said.

21

Roddy's instructions came sandwiched between two white tennis shirts in a gift-wrapped package from the hotel shop. The meet was for twenty past midnight. Roddy tried to look indecisive as he threaded his way through the night crowd on the sidewalk. His first choice was the Café Presidente, where he drank a cuba libre at the bar. He ducked into a couple of discos without staying and finally settled on the Disco Boom. Already half deaf from the thud beating from the multiple speakers, he shouted for a second cuba libre at the bar and made it last while he watched the dancers.

A blonde in a tight T-shirt and dayglo eye make-up shimmied up to him. The T-shirt bore the logo of a Florida tennis club. The girl felt Roddy's biceps and shouted in his ear that he looked like a tennis player. He felt like punching her in the belly, or punching Smith.

They danced for a while before she led him out onto the sidewalk. She put her hands to his cheeks, kissed him, and whispered in his ear loud enough for the doorman and a couple of cab drivers to hear that she had a suite at the Hyatt Cancún Caribe so there'd be no trouble with the front desk.

At the hotel she strode over to the concierge as if she owned the place. The concierge called her Señorita Baugarden and warned that her father had arrived soon after midnight. She cursed, hesitated, then said, 'To hell with it,' took her key, and led Roddy to the elevators.

She held a finger to her lips as she slid the key into the lock. Dragging Roddy into her room, she shut the door so that they were in the dark and kissed him again. Roddy hoped that she was the right girl. Fumbling for the light switch, she opened the connecting door to a big drawing-room. Smith was there in standard striped seersucker over by sliding glass doors that opened to a terrace. He looked frustrated and angry enough to hit someone.

A slim younger man in a made-to-measure grey suit, blue button-down shirt, and well-polished English Oxfords lounged in an easy chair with his feet up on a coffee table. Smith introduced the young man as Mr Jones and Roddy as Señor Mendez. Jones said: '*Buenas noches y bienvenido, Señor.*' Like his clothes, his upper-class Madrileño lisp was a little too perfect. Smith grunted his disgust and crossed to search Roddy while Jones went to the door leading to the second bedroom and knocked quietly.

A heavily built man in his sixties came out. His thick grey hair was untidy and he wore a cashmere bathrobe over his shirt and monogrammed velvet slippers. He inspected Roddy with some interest, then looked over to Smith who shrugged and said: 'That's him, Baugarden. He's clean.'

'Baugarden,' the older man repeated, either reminding himself of who he was meant to be or introducing himself to Roddy.

From behind Roddy, the girl said: 'I'll wait up, sir, so he can leave through my room.'

Baugarden dismissed her with a nod and asked Roddy if he'd been offered a drink.

'He's just arrived,' Jones said.

Baugarden pointed to the laden drinks tray on a sideboard: 'Help yourself. And I'll have a small whisky.' Turning to Smith, he said: 'You'd better listen to this seeing you set it up.'

Smith grunted a bad-tempered monosyllable and parted the curtains with one finger so that he could look down at the beach.

First switching on the TV and a portable radio, Baugarden seated himself at the small round dining table. Jones scurried over with a leather desk set which he opened and laid in front of his chief.

Roddy handed him a whisky and Baugarden nodded his thanks. 'This suite's been swept, Lieutenant, and the radio's designed to transmit interference, but we can sit under the shower if that makes you more comfortable.'

Roddy said they were fine where they were.

Baugarden pointed him to the chair opposite his own: 'You know who I am, Lieutenant?'

Roddy nodded. Baugarden, under a different name, was the man to whom the Assistant Secretary of State with responsibility for Latin America turned for whispered advice at conferences. Baugarden leant back in his chair with his hands clasped behind his head and studied Roddy from under lowered lids: 'Smith tells me your father wants to cross over. Possibly some others?'

'The Admiral, two flag captains, one commander, thirty-two enlisted men,' Roddy said.

Baugarden smiled. 'You've left yourself out, Lieutenant.'

Roddy shrugged. He wasn't there to play games. He said: 'Before defecting, Admiral de Sanchez wishes for a four-point guarantee in writing.'

Baugarden took a gold-capped pen from the desk set: 'Give.'

Roddy spoke slowly so that the American had ample time to write the points down: 'First, the US government will consider the Admiral and all members of his party as political refugees. Second, the US government will legitimise all funds and valuables brought out from Cuba by the Admiral and members of his party. Third, the US government will facilitate the banking of all such funds and valuables. Fourth, the US government guarantees that no investigation or criminal proceedings will be instituted against the Admiral or any of his party with regard to any of their actions prior to their defection.'

Baugarden frowned at the grunt of indignation forced from

177

Smith over by the terrace doors. Finished writing, he replaced his pen in the desk set and read the points through, not because he couldn't remember them but because he needed time to think. He tapped the bottom of the sheet of paper with a blunt finger and chuckled softly as he looked at Roddy. 'Someone who didn't know better might suspect that your father had robbed a bank. Who do you expect to sign this mythical piece of paper? God?'

Jones tittered and Baugarden glared at him.

'The Assistant Secretary will do,' Roddy said. His father wanted copies of the document lodged with a Cuban banker in Miami who also owned an Hispanic TV station, with a Cuban monsignor at the Bishopric, and with an Hispanic Florida state senator.

'Intelligent and comprehensive.' Baugarden rolled his whisky glass between his palms as he studied Roddy. 'An admiral, two captains, a commander, a navy vessel, and possibly a lieutenant. That's one hell of a propaganda disaster. The way the Cuban economy is right now, maybe even big enough to bring Castro down. What do you think, Lieutenant? You think he'll survive?'

'My concerns are with my father,' Roddy said.

'Jesus! What are you? The last of the true believers?'

Jones tittered again and Smith turned back from the window. Roddy looked up and their eyes met. He sensed that Smith hoped that he would lose his temper and blow it. He could feel the rage in the DEA agent, his frustration at not being in control, at being reduced to a minion.

Roddy said: 'Señor Smith will tell you that I am only an amateur tennis player, Señor.'

'With a sideline in adultery,' Smith said.

Roddy smiled and said: '*Si, Señor*, that is correct.' He got up from the table and carried his glass over to the drinks tray. Turning back to Baugarden, he said: 'With your permission, Señor.'

'Help yourself.' Baugarden looked over at Smith: 'I want this thing to happen, Pat. Start running interference and you'll end up on the beach down in Patagonia without a pension.

That's a promise, so call your dogs off.' To Roddy, he said:
'The documents will be in Miami by noon tomorrow,
Lieutenant.'

Roddy bowed perhaps a couple of inches: 'I will inform the
Admiral, Señor. Now, with your permission . . .'

'Sure, run along.'

Roddy said 'Thank you for your help,' to Smith. His
stomach began to cramp halfway to the door leading through
to the girl's bedroom but he kept to a slow stroll.

The girl had showered and washed her hair and sat wrapped
in a towel in an easy chair watching cable TV. She looked up
and said, 'Hi,' and smiled as Roddy turned the lock.

He said, 'I need to use the bathroom. I don't feel too good.'

Pepito was due into Nassau Airport at noon and Trent brought
the *Golden Girl* into the marina on New Providence Island
with an hour and a half to spare. Trent asked Marco and Rik
to swing the BMW ashore and trotted up the wooden dock to
the marina office. He was halfway through filling in forms
when a neat young American in a neat blue suit and rimless
spectacles entered the office. Trent completed the paperwork
and the American followed him outside. The suit was too well-
cut for him to be a Mormon on missionary work but he
radiated the same earnestness.

'Trent?'

'Trent,' Trent agreed.

The young American said that he was from the Embassy.

Trent asked which Embassy and the American looked
confused.

'The US Embassy, of course.' He had the remnants of a
west coast accent overlaid with east coast prep which he had
picked up escaping from his schoolteacher parents, and he had
left his sense of humour behind, or perhaps there was nothing
humorous in having to wear a suit in the midday heat. 'Mr
O'Brien is away for two days, Mr Trent. You are to stay here
till he gets back. Mr O'Brien said to tell you that is an order.'
He had said enough, but he pushed on, determined to
impress: 'Is that understood?'

179

Trent said, 'Yes.'

Back on the *Golden Girl* he listed the supplies and equipment they needed if they were to dive again and gave it to Marco. Auria asked when he planned to sail and he said that he'd been ordered to wait in port by an official from the US Embassy. 'They probably want to get a statement from me about the Lobos Cay killings.'

22

Captain Pedro Gomez y Roig slouched through customs and immigration with a blue nylon dive bag slung over one massive shoulder. He gave the impression of being a little drunk or a little simple, smile sloppy and a permanent fixture. He had converted to designer stubble or needed a shave, and his hair hadn't been brushed. Bleach had drained most of the colour from his tan chinos and the soles of his sandals were carved from an old car tyre. 'Earth Mover Incorporated' was the slogan in big white letters printed across the front of a scarlet T-shirt from which the arms had been chopped. He hugged Trent and boomed: '*Hola Señor Jefe*, you a good man to give me a job.' He presented Trent with the remains of a bottle of tequila and looked pleased with himself.

Trent hustled him out to the car park.

They were halfway down the main street when Trent spotted Auria striding towards him on the sidewalk. He would have waved but a van pulled out from the kerb and he had to brake and swerve. Auria walked straight past without recognising the BMW or even noticing it. Instead of shouting after her, Trent said to Pepito: 'This is where you get off,' and gave him the name of the marina. He let Auria get well ahead before making a U-turn and following. From across the road he had a broad angle of vision so that he could afford to keep well back, idling the engine in first gear as if searching the shop windows.

Tourists crowded the sidewalks. Untrained in leisure and on foreign soil, there was an aimlessness to the way they walked in little groups of temporary friends. The North Americans were better dressed than the British, their suntans less puce through a more meticulous reading of the holiday magazines in which skin specialists warned of cancer and advised on creams and lotions. In comparison with the tourists, the Bahamians had purpose, if only in patrolling their own territory. They had friends to greet, business to attend to, proper shopping lists.

Auria turned up a side street under a 'no entry' sign. Trent accelerated and reached the turn in time to see her check her wrist watch before entering a restaurant under a pink neon lobster with a red eye that winked for attention. He circled the block and found the kitchen entrance. He parked, took off his helmet, and knocked before poking his head round the door with a twenty-dollar bill ready.

A thin Bahamian cook in a white hat and white apron looked up from frying fish over an open grill. Two old men for whom tourist affluence had come too late washed dishes at a pair of double sinks while a fat woman bossed them.

'I think my girlfriend's in there,' Trent said to the woman. He put everything into his smile, acknowledging her as the source of power, and more than that: she was a proper woman of the world who would understand. 'I'm on a bike, can I look?'

The twenty-dollar bill disappeared into the front pocket of her starched apron and she said, 'Help yo' self,' and to the cook: 'Bob boy, yo burn that fish and I have yo arse.'

A waiter came through the double doors with slow dignity that turned into a speed trial as the door swung shut. But Trent had already seen Auria and her companion. It was enough. 'Damn,' he said, and grinned at the woman as he backed out. 'She's with her husband.'

'Yo be careful you don' get your white tail in a mess,' the woman warned.

Trent rode two blocks back from the main street before turning down and parking on the corner, from where he could see the entrance to the restaurant. Auria reappeared almost at once; she hadn't wanted to stay for lunch or hadn't been invited. An hour later an empty cab drew up at the door. Auria's companion came out with a waiter scurrying after him to open the cab door. So the man tipped well. Late thirties, Trent guessed, clean shaven, and probably, like Auria, Italian American. Trent followed the cab, constantly varying his distance. The driver headed out of town and Trent eased in behind a truck.

The driver braked at the white sentry box at the entrance to the private development where Rogerton-Smithe had his house and Trent rode on past, keeping watch in the rearview mirror. He made a U-turn as a security guard raised the striped barrier to let the cab through. The cab was still in sight as he reached the barrier. Wearing a helmet, there was no chance of his being recognised, and it wasn't the same guard as had been on duty on his last visit. Trent showed him a ten-dollar bill: 'I've got a yacht that I need to berth for a few months. I want to see the secretary of the marina.'

Boats were big tips and the guard grinned as he took the bill: 'Yes, sah, nice bike. Ride right on through. The marina's first on the left past the golf club.'

Trent passed the turn and braked on a slight rise from where he could see across the fairway. The cab had pulled up alongside a fast-looking motor yacht. Trent couldn't make out the ensign. He counted four men under the awning that shaded the after deck, knee-length shorts, sports shirts, and sneakers. They were too far off for Trent to fill in the details. None of them looked to be in a hurry but two of them stood up as the man Auria had met came up the shore companionway. The taller of the two followed him through sliding doors into the saloon.

Trent thought about Auria. He was sure that she was acting under duress but he wasn't sure what to do. Finally he turned the key and rode the BMW on past the golf course. Swinging into Rogerton-Smithe's drive, he tucked the bike away in the shade to the right of the house by the garage, left his helmet on the saddle, and rang the bell.

Robert opened the door to him. The young Bahamian wore a swimsuit and a short white bathrobe. His feet were bare. The bracelet had been joined by a thin gold chain with a plain crucifix. Nothing gaudy – Rogerton-Smithe had good taste.

'Hullo,' Trent said. 'I've been at sea for two weeks. I wanted to take a walk along the golf course. Green grass.'

Robert was close to panic. He said, 'I'm afraid Mr Rogerton-Smithe's resting. He's not very well.'

'Then we mustn't disturb him. I parked by the garage.'

Robert came down two steps and his face lit as he saw the big scarlet BMW. Trent asked if he had a licence and watched his brief struggle with temptation. Robert led the way to a spare bedroom and brought Trent shorts and a T-shirt left behind by a previous guest and a wide-brimmed planter's hat to protect the shaved front of his skull.

'Keep the speed down,' Trent warned. 'And don't go off the estate.'

Stripped to the waist, Trent slid his knife from its sheath to clean the blade of any sweat and heard the BMW purr down the drive. A moment later the door opened. Rogerton-Smithe saw the knife first, then the scars and the fresh bandages. There wasn't any fear that Trent could see but the dark violet eyes were difficult to read and the underwiter was already sweating despite the air conditioning.

Trent slipped the knife back into its sheath and explained that he had wanted a walk where he wouldn't be bothered by touts. 'Robert was kind enough to find me some clothes. He's ridden my BMW down the road.'

Now the fear came: 'A motorcycle? Damn you, Mr Trent. That wasn't fair.' Rogerton-Smithe looked over at the planter's Panama lying on the bed. 'And Robert's lent you his favourite hat.'

Though the connection was ambiguous, Trent said: 'I'm sure he'll be all right.' He dragged the T-shirt over his head, smoothed what remained of his hair, and adjusted the wide brim of the Panama so that it would shade his face. He checked his image in the looking-glass and glanced at Rogerton-Smithe's reflection. Their eyes met. 'I found the

Beau Belle,' Trent said. He picked up his sunglasses. 'I'll be gone about an hour.'

Trent bought the latest *Yachting Monthly* at the marina and found a table in the shade of an awning at the dockside café. The yacht was sixty foot long and flew the Honduran ensign to protect the owners from having to pay US taxes. The wheelhouse lay forward of the deck saloon with a fly bridge above. There were two searchlights on the fly bridge and the mast tower behind the bridge carried a radar dome and three aerials. A sixteen-foot ski boat sat in chocks behind the fly bridge with a second boat hanging in davits at the counter. The engine room, amidships with big ventilators, split the lower accommodation fore and aft, presumably with the owner's stateroom under the after deck and probably a second cabin. A fixed aluminium awning shaded the after deck.

Four men lounged in cane chairs under the awning. One of them was fair-haired and wore white overalls – probably the engineer. The man from the restaurant and the tall man who had followed him into the saloon were absent, so the yacht carried a minimum complement of six. There wasn't anything special about the men except that they were all clean shaven. A fair number of Americans gave up shaving while on holiday, particularly men on yachts, feeling real men, if only on a temporary basis, rather than the office variety. And no women.

Trent asked the bartender for a ballpoint and drew on the inside cover of his yachting magazine a sketch of the Cuban reef and adjoining islets he had found after his last dive.

He strolled back across the golf course. The BMW stood on its stand in the shade. Trent rang the bell and Robert came to the door full of thanks for the ride. He looked pleased with himself so, if there had been an argument with Rogerton-Smithe, he'd been the victor. But Trent thought Rogerton-Smithe too pragmatic to have chided the young man.

Robert showed him out to the pool terrace and went back into the house for drinks. Rogerton-Smithe lay on a sunbed, his head resting on a pillow. It wasn't that hot but he was still sweating. Without looking at Trent he said, 'Do sit down. Perhaps I was a little short. My older brother was killed in a motorcycle accident. I was very fond of him.'

'I'm sorry.'

'It was a long time ago. As one grows older there is a temptation to burden the young with one's experience.' He rolled his head on the pillow and his deep violet eyes rested on Trent: 'I said nothing to Robert. He enjoyed himself.'

'Good. Or bad?' Trent saw the beginnings of a smile.

'Precisely. Though, in the end, all one can achieve is to accept responsibility for one's own mistakes. I try to do that, Mr Trent. You said that you had found the *Beau Belle*? Would you kindly tell me how she sank?'

Trent detailed the explosives, Hewett's death, and the murder of the New Zealanders.

'Dreadful. Quite dreadful.'

Watching Rogerton-Smithe, Trent was sure that he was deliberately picturing what had happened in all its horror, the struggle of the two young men as they drowned.

Rogerton-Smithe said: 'Life is a slide, Mr Trent. You choose to climb the steps; how far you slip is mostly chance so there are no degrees. Call someone a fat Jew boy and you join the Commandant of Auschwitz.

'With Lloyd's, the top of the slide comes when you set up a small syndicate for your friends and immediate family and funnel the best of the firm's business into it. Common practice in the Thatcher years, Mr Trent. Next you move the syndicate offshore to protect the profits from tax. Set up a brass plate company. Now murder.'

Robert came with Trent's daiquiri and Rogerton-Smithe's mint tea. Rogerton-Smithe smiled his thanks and touched the young man lightly on the wrist. 'You haven't visited your mother for some time, Robert. I think now might be a good moment. Why don't you take the car? Perhaps you'd come back on Saturday? And do remember to collect the dry cleaning.'

The young man hesitated. His concern was obvious and Rogerton-Smithe said: 'Don't be silly. I'll be quite all right. If

I don't feel like cooking for myself, I can always telephone the marina to send something up. Run along now, and call in at the flower shop on your way through town. Roses,' he added, in sudden decision and enjoying himself, 'yellow roses – at least a dozen – and make sure your mother crushes the stems before putting them in water.' He turned to Trent as the young man closed the terrace door. 'There is fun in having money, Mr Trent, even when, strictly speaking, it's not one's own.'

'No "Drive carefully" or "Remember to leave the car somewhere safe"?'

'Good heavens, no. And anyway I'm hardly in a position to advise people as to their conduct.'

'Only to tell them to keep away when you think they're in danger. You brought a lot of Italian Americans into your syndicates,' Trent said. 'They must be what you'd call rather cross and I'd call furious and bloody dangerous.'

'Actually I would have said extremely cross, Mr Trent. And, yes, some of them are dangerous. I must say that at the time I wasn't aware of who they were. Perhaps deliberately unaware, but it can be quite difficult to be certain of where the division lies between one's conscious and subconscious and I was under quite intense pressure. The ones I dealt with had quite good manners and dressed well, though I suppose their shoes do give them away.'

'Do, as in the present?'

'Yes, Mr Trent. It is both impolite and tiresome to play games. If there is something you wish to know, ask, and I will answer if I consider the question suitable.'

'I'm sorry.'

'Oh dear, how very British, and somewhat inappropriate, Mr Trent. Surely I should be the one to be sorry? I'm a fraudster. I stole a great deal of money. Now I am associated with two ghastly murders. Ask your questions.'

Rocco had been the first of the Italian American investors. Trent asked if Rocco had introduced the others to Rogerton-Smithe, and how much Rocco had known of Rogerton-Smithe's business then and now.

'So that you can make a judgement, Mr Trent? How very brave.' Rogerton-Smithe thought a moment, remembering. 'Mr Rocco is a very nice man and an excellent restaurateur but perhaps a little naïve in financial matters.'

Rogerton-Smithe had eaten at Rocco's restaurant regularly over three summers before suggesting that he become a member of Lloyd's. He put him into one of his syndicates that was in good shape. 'I used him to gull the others, Mr Trent. I'm never quite sure whether that makes them gulls? I rather hope so, because the description suits – refuse collectors with beady eyes. The Oxford Dictionary of Slang is imprecise on the point.

'Mr Rocco was quite unaware of my intentions towards his customers. When informed of their problems, he was most upset. It was they who insisted he charter the *Beau Belle*, obviously to keep their own names out of some nefarious activity. Smuggling I presumed, but murder I didn't expect.'

'I haven't told the others but there's thirteen million in gold on board. I'm going to dive for it tomorrow night,' Trent said. He folded back the cover of the yachting magazine he'd bought down at the marina and dropped the magazine beside Rogerton-Smithe's sunbed.

The underwriter saw the sketch of the Cuban reef. He pushed himself up, crossed slowly to the drinks tray, and poured himself a small brandy in a balloon glass. He swilled the alcohol round and, facing Trent, elevated the glass. The sheen left by the liqueur on the sides of the balloon glowed in the sun. 'You wish me to tell them? Rather than have the girl do so?' Rogerton-Smithe suggested with a wry smile: 'Surely you should be wearing a white wig and black cap Mr Trent?'

23

Trent rode back from Rogerton-Smithe's house. A quarter of a mile short of the marina, he spotted Skelly at the roadside pretending to change a rear wheel on a white Ford pick-up truck. Trent braked and offered to help.

The Bahamian's smile was a little bitter as he replied that Trent was the one in need of help: 'There's a forceful request from the Americans to keep you in harbour.' Trent had expected as much. Skelly said: 'I made a promise to you, Trent, and it stands, no politics. But I'd like to cover myself.'

'Eleven o'clock tonight,' Trent said.

'We'd better make sure you aren't followed.' Skelly took a small electronic de-bugger from the pick-up and Trent thanked him.

Trent found Rik, Marco, and Auria in the *Golden Girl*'s cockpit while Pepito lay half asleep on the netting forward between the hulls. Trent checked the stores and equipment against the list he had given Marco earlier in the day then suggested to Marco that they take a walk ashore. They stopped at the marina's bar for a cold beer. Taking the bottles outside, they sat on the edge of the dock and, as dusk approached, watched a dozen or so yachts enter the marina.

Though Marco was a professional 'yachty', he was never spiteful regarding the manner in which the holidaymakers handled their craft and twice he ran down the dock to take a line. Trent found him good company. He said: 'The internal iron ballast on the *Beau Belle*'s been replaced with gold bars.'

Marco said: 'You're kidding,' and took his eyes off a brunette armed with a boat hook in the bows of a Nicholson 36. 'I mean, gold, for real? Come on, you have to be kidding.'

'Around a ton, say thirteen million dollars.'

Marco whistled. Hands flat on the dock, he eased his weight off his backside. 'Thirteen million. Now I know you're kidding.'

'Drug money put on board in Angola after the Cubans pulled out. Think about it,' Trent said. 'Blow a couple of holes in the *Beau Belle* when she's inside the Cuban reef and the gold's safer than it would be in a bank.'

'Not so easy to collect.' Marco shifted weight again, spat down between his feet, and watched the rings spread across the surface. He shook his head and looked up at Trent: 'This is for real, right? Thirteen million.'

'A million either way,' Trent said. 'That's the good news. The bad news is that a kid from your Embassy ordered me not to take the *Golden Girl* out of the marina so maybe somebody else knows about the gold and they don't want us getting our hands on it. That's a guess, but there has to be a reason why I'm not allowed to sail.'

'Screw the reason,' Marco said, 'this is the Bahamas. No kid from the Embassy has any right telling you what you can or can't do.'

Trent shrugged fatalistically and stayed silent.

For Marco, any infringement of his liberty was like a red rag to a bull. 'Hey, come on, for Chrissakes. You're a Brit, Trent. So is the *Golden Girl*, and the *Beau Belle*'s in Cuban waters.'

'So what do you want me to do? Write to my Member of Parliament?' Trent returned their empties to the bar and bought replacements.

Marco thanked him and said: 'You meant to pick the gold up, right?'

'No one seems in a hurry to claim it,' Trent said.

Marco chuckled. 'A ton, that's some salvage operation.'

'We would have needed two full nights,' Trent said.

They watched a professional skipper ease a sixty-foot flush deck motor cruiser into a berth close to the *Golden Girl*. A party of three men in their late forties with younger wives or girlfriends were drinking on the after deck.

'Pity.' Trent kicked his heel a couple of times against the dock. 'Once in a lifetime.'

'So what's stopping us?' Marco asked.

'In all probability the Bahamian police.' And Rik wasn't one for breaking the law. Nor was Auria.

'Screw them. Come on, Trent. Stop being so goddamned negative,' Marco said. 'How about the big Mex?'

'He's a great diver but a little simple. He does what he's told.'

Two of the men on the motor yacht had jumped ashore to make the stern lines fast. The third walked up the dock past Trent and Marco to the marina office with the ship's papers.

'Think, for Christ's sake,' Marco urged.

'That's what I've been doing all day.' Trent handed Marco his empty bottle: 'Your turn to buy.'

Marco fetched fresh beers and sat down again.

Trent toasted him and said good evening to the man from the big motor yacht returning from the marina office. 'Nice boat,' Marco said, and the man thanked him for the compliment and carried on down the dock.

'You're good at making friends,' Trent said to Marco. 'Try starting a party on the motor yacht that gets noisy enough so I can complain.'

At a quarter to eleven at night the party on the motor yacht had overflowed onto the dock. The laughter was louder than the music because one of the men on the yacht had turned the record player down a few decibels in response to a word from the duty guard at the marina office. A lot of flesh was on show and AIDS might have been lost in history judging by the dancing on the after deck. A couple of women came out from the galley with dishes of cocktail niceties that no one was going to remember eating.

Trent had cooked pasta on the *Golden Girl* to absorb the beer he'd drunk with Marco earlier. Once Auria had eaten, she joined Marco at the party. She danced now with a Bahamian while Rik crouched in a corner of the catamaran's cockpit, watching. Looking round at Trent, he said quietly: 'Loving my father, loving Auria, it's a pattern. I must seem like a fool. Although I'm good at my job. Very good,' he added, and pushed the hair back out of his eyes as he faced Trent: 'Understanding balance sheets helps. Reliable, caring, promising future, but not a lot of fun. My father being who he was made my mother frightened of fun. Perhaps I should take lessons? The talent must be there, genes and all that.' He smiled suddenly, amused by his own pretensions.

Trent said: 'Yes.'

Rik returned his attention to the party on the motor yacht, Auria dancing. Trent was about to leave him, but the young accountant said: 'Being good with balance sheets is mostly sensing when something's been omitted, Trent.' The lift of his shoulders was less nervous than usual as he turned to face Trent again, and there was determination in the set of his jaw and narrowing of his lips. 'He was my father, Trent. I don't need protection from the truth.'

'I don't know the truth, not all of it,' Trent said. He told the young man about the gold and the murder of the New Zealanders and why he believed that Hewett had been innocent of involvement in the larger crime.

Listening to Trent's account, Rik sat with his elbows on his knees, chin cupped in his hands, eyes hooded as he sifted the facts. Finally he said: 'We thought we came to you for help. You were waiting for us. You're a policeman of some kind.' He nodded to himself and looked up, angry and bitter: 'Using us as bait. A girl . . .'

Trent thought of replying that he was the bait but the explanation would have taken too long and there remained too many gaps in the evidence. And Rik said: 'No, if it was like that, you wouldn't have told me.' He looked across the marina to where Auria danced on the after deck of the motor yacht and the pain came with realisation: 'Auria's involved.'

'I think she's being blackmailed. It's something I have to sort out,' Trent said, and made his way forward to join Pepito, who had spread a sleeping bag on the webbing and appeared fast asleep. The Mexican had played the simple fisherman right down to eating by himself out on the foredeck. Trent, to support the image, had hardly talked to him but he had to now. He squatted down beside the Mexican but, without opening his eyes, Pepito said: 'Go away, compañero. I don't want to know.'

'Thanks,' Trent said. Alone but for Pepito, he searched the catamaran with the de-bugger Skelly had given him and found a small Russian-made transducer stuck to the back of the radio. Leaving it in position, he called to Pepito that he was going ashore.

Marco caught his eye as he strolled up the dock and Trent saw the American take his stepsister by the arm. Skelly and a police constable were sipping beers in a corner of the marina office. Trent said to the duty guard: 'I don't want to make a fuss but I can't stand the noise. I want to move berth.' He spoke quietly and with deliberate politeness. The guard looked round at Skelly and Skelly said: 'My constable will give you a hand.'

'Thanks,' Trent said: 'I'll find a berth over on the outer dock.'

The constable removed his boots before following Trent. On the way to the *Golden Girl*, he said: 'Superintendent said I was to tell you I had a cousin on Lobos Cay, Mr Trent.'

Marco and Auria had returned and Trent said to Auria, 'Hi, I'm sorry to pull you out of the party but I really need the sleep.' To Pepito, he said, 'Go below so you are not in the way.' He said the same to Rik and to Auria: 'I'm not being rude, but three of us on deck is enough.'

Auria was about to argue but Marco whispered something which silenced her, and she followed Pepito and Rik into the saloon.

A gentle breeze blew off the shore and Trent raised the mainsail while Marco shackled the lightest of the big running sails to the forestay. The constable let go the stern lines and jumped on board. Trent hardened the sheet and the mainsail filled, drawing the big cat silently from her berth.

With Marco standing by the jib halyard at the mast foot, Trent eased the helm over and steered for the far corner of the marina beyond the entrance. He slackened the sheet a little, turned, and with his own body covering the constable, hit him in the belly. As the constable doubled up, Trent hit him on the jaw, then grabbed him as he fell and levered him over his thigh to the side. He felt the constable's hand squeeze his thigh for a moment as he slipped him overboard. Trent raised a hand to Marco and the huge white foresail broke free of its lashings. They had the remains of the night and the following day to reach Cuban waters.

'Well?' Admiral de Sanchez asked Roddy.

'It's done,' Roddy said: 'Four copies of the document lodged as you requested and Smith was told to pull his dogs off the case. Trent . . .'

'Trent is halfway to Cuba,' the Admiral interrupted. 'Rocco telephoned before they left Nassau that they will dive tonight and tomorrow night.' He chuckled softly. 'What could be more perfect, my son? They do the work. We wait for them outside Cuban waters.'

The *Golden Girl* lay at anchor in six feet of water between the two islets on the Cuban reef. The dozen or so palm trees on each patch of sand and coral camouflaged her mast and Trent, though knowing her position, soon had difficulty distinguishing the catamaran in the darkness as he motored away from her in the new Zodiac.

Marco had bought the twenty-two foot model in Nassau, and an 80 horse Mercury, so there was ample power and room for their party of five, the eight dive bottles, and the lines and heavy anchor warp. Trent had relied on Marco to explain to Auria why they had skipped port and Marco in turn had left Auria to silence Rik's protests. They had slipped across the reef an hour after dark and, once safely anchored, Trent had sketched for them the position of the *Beau Belle* in the cavern and how he intended gaining access to the holes in the engine room.

Marco had understood at once that Trent must have been in the yacht when the roof fell. And that he had therefore made a third dive. 'You went back? Alone?'

Trent explained that he had thought first that the roof of the cavern would affect the readings on the magnetometer. When he realised that it wouldn't, he had borrowed a Zodiac from the lighthouse keeper on Lobos Cay: 'It had to be the ballast.'

Trent and Marco dived first, taking with them the new anchor warp. They inspected the old anchor warp where it dipped over the cavern lip. Trent tried not to think of his last dive but the memory was too strong, and he shivered as he followed the warp down the cliff face, sensing that Marco was aware of how he must feel.

The pale circles of light cast by their flashlights led them down into the darkness, 143 feet, and he felt the weight of the water pressing on him as he repeatedly cleared the pressure in his ears on the long descent. He could feel the pressure above and the waiting depth of the cavern below, open and empty as a toothless mouth, and he shivered again as he saw for the first time the shattered remnants of the *Beau Belle*'s superstructure.

Of the wheel-house and saloon nothing remained but a few scraps of timber and panelling that protruded mere inches above the deck line. The engine room companionway and the companionways down to the fore and after accommodation were blocked solid, but the already crushed prow of the yacht had been torn away so that the forecastle gaped open and empty, the bodies of the two New Zealanders lost to the greater depths. The rigging and shattered masts had gone with the prow and bowsprit, as had the stanchions and teak rails, but the heavy brass fair-leads on the after deck remained bolted through the main deck beams.

The *Beau Belle* lay with her starboard side against the cliff and Trent pointed to the stern fair-lead on her port-side. Marco made the new anchor warp fast and they turned together, ghosting up the cliff face with no need yet to decompress. They led the anchor warp at an angle forward across the sunken yacht's bows, hauled it taut, and made it fast to a big coral head thirty or so feet back from the lip of the cavern. Trent let go the old anchor warp and they followed their air bubbles up to the surface and sat waiting for an hour in the Zodiac while the *Beau Belle* settled.

Pepito accompanied Trent on the next dive. The Mexican carried a saw and crowbar while Trent carried four dive lamps. As the *Beau Belle* had fallen onto the new anchor warp she had ground chalk from the side of the cavern and the fine powder reflected the beams of their flashlights so that they sank into a softly glowing cloud in which small fish hunted for crustaceans. The *Beau Belle* had swung round on the new warp and hung now bow down with her deck against the cliff. Trent raised a thumb to Pepito and led him along the starboard side to the hole in the engine room which he had already enlarged.

Trent rigged the lamps while Pepito sawed. And they kept an eye on each other, wary of the depth and the risk of narcosis. Six minutes was enough at that depth, and Trent signalled Pepito up. Again they waited an hour in the Zodiac before Pepito dived with Marco.

The cavern below and the proximity of the Cuban coast forced the three remaining in the Zodiac to restrict their conversation to brief whispers. The sea lapped the rubber hull and they could smell the coast and hear the occasional car or truck on the shore road and the soft thud of a single-cylinder diesel engine pushing a fishing boat along the edge of the reef. Trent could see sometimes, as the beam from one of the lighthouses swept over them, the air bubbles burst. The bubbles shone silver as they broke the surface and Trent thought of the gold. He would like to have said something to Auria that would have taken the fear from her and the anger that she had focused on him. Perhaps to tell her that he understood. But now that they were lifting the gold, he was less sure of the outcome than he had been at Rogerton-Smithe's house, and he remembered that Rogerton-Smithe had mocked him for usurping from God the right of judgement.

Marco surfaced and Trent hauled his equipment on board. Seated astride the hull, Marco took a dive tank from Pepito and held it up in front of Trent for a moment before dropping it back into the sea. The tank was the one that Trent had abandoned in the engine room.

The four of them dived now, leaving Rik alone in the Zodiac. Trent and Marco swam down with two weighted duffel bags to the *Beau Belle* while Pepito and Auria waited on the lip of the cavern with two more bags on lines leading up to the surface. Trent loaded the ingots into the duffel bags and Marco manhandled them out of the hole and signalled Pepito or Auria to haul them up to the rim, where they transferred the gold to the other bags which Rik then hauled to the surface. It was slow work. After ten minutes, Pepito replaced Marco. Both Trent and Pepito rose to the cavern lip after a further fifteen minutes and decompressed before surfacing.

24

Trent loosened his harness. Pepito took his tanks and belt and heaved him into the Zodiac. They squatted facing each other. The gold lay neatly stacked down the centre of the varnished floorboards, dive tanks on each side so they wouldn't roll. It should have been a time of celebration. Marco sat beside his stepsister on the port hull while Richard was in the bows, distancing himself from Auria.

'There may be difficulties. We have enough fuel to make the run back to Lobos Cay with the Zodiac,' Trent said quietly in Spanish to Pepito.

'With you there are always difficulties. We play it your way, compañero.' Pepito watched as Trent adjusted the string of beads round his neck so that his knife lay hidden in the nape of his neck beneath his hair. The Mexican's teeth flashed white as he grinned: 'And may God be with us.'

Trent started the big Mercury. For a moment he thought that Auria would say something. The moment passed and he opened the throttle, feeding in the power till the laden Zodiac finally lifted onto the plane. Pushing the helm over, he headed for the islets between which the *Golden Girl* lay at anchor. In fifteen minutes he rounded the tip of the sandbank and headed in towards the catamaran.

A searchlight hit them and he was immediately blind. An American voice called through a loud hailer: 'Put your hands above your heads, all of you except the man at the helm. Come straight up the beam of the light. Make a mistake and we'll shoot the girl first.'

Trent couldn't touch her so he had to do it with his voice. 'I know they are threatening your dad but it's going to be all right. You have to trust me,' he urged: 'There may be a time when you can make a scene. Remember.'

As he nosed the Zodiac alongside the motor yacht, a second searchlight came on from the saloon doors, focused the length of the after deck. The voice called down: 'You there, the young guy in the bows, throw up a line.'

'That's you, Rik,' Trent said.

A rope ladder dropped down the side of the yacht and the voice called: 'Come on board at a time when you're told. The guy with the long hair at the helm first.'

Trent clambered up the ladder and stood on the after deck with his eyes closed against the light.

'Take your wetsuit off slowly with your left hand,' the voice commanded. Trent undid the poppers between his legs and unzipped the jacket. He pulled the jacket open from the collar so as not to disturb his beads. His scars must have looked impressive in the brilliant light. A second voice said: 'Holy shit.'

There were chuckles as a third said, 'The guy's been hiring himself out for target practice.'

'A real loser.'

'Better than being a dead loser.'

Fresh chuckles.

'Throw the suit straight in front of you,' the first voice ordered: 'You're the Brit, Trent?'

'Correct.'

'Take your pants off. Kick them over here.'

They were careful, very careful, Trent thought as he stood naked under the light. Someone threw his pants back and he bent, blind, fumbling for them, and pulled them on.

'Now walk straight ahead into the saloon.'

The light went off his eyelids as he passed the deck searchlight and he opened his eyes. The saloon was decorated in yacht designer safe ; nothing in bad taste, nothing good, but pleasant enough. Two six-foot couches and two easy chairs upholstered in oatmeal tweed formed a square round an oblong coffee table at the after end. Forward, a companionway led down to port. The L-shaped bench built against the companionway and the after bulkhead half surrounded a polished teak dining table ; add the four directors' chairs scattered round and the table would sit eight in comfort, ten at a squeeze. An open door to starboard led through to the galley and wheel-house and to a further companionway down to the forward cabins.

There were two men in the saloon, one sat on the dining table, the other in one of the easy chairs. The one on the easy chair held a shotgun ; the other was armed with a Colt. The man with the Colt said, 'You want to sit, use a towel. We don't want salt on the cushions. And no games, because we don't want blood either.'

Taking a towel from a pile on the coffee table, Trent spread it on the easy chair opposite the man with the shotgun. Sprawled out as if he were exhausted by the dive, he watched from under half-closed lids.

There were only the six men whom he had seen at the marina. Auria's companion at the restaurant in Nassau was the leader. Alfredo, one of the others called him. He was well-dressed, unsuitably so for halfway through the night and anchored offshore. Fawn cotton trousers, red sports shirt, expensive deck shoes.

Like a package out of an advertisement in the *New Yorker*, Trent thought as he took in the details : cashmere sweater draped over his shoulders, wafer-thin Patak Philip watch on a slim gold bracelet. It was all too new and too well-ironed. The six were identical, members of the new executive generation, slimline readers of health fad magazines who jogged mornings before catching the inter-suburban to the office. Gone were the traditional thugs with their scarred knuckles, bent noses, muscle-heavy. Perhaps muscle was no longer tax deductible. But the viciousness was there. The evil.

Rik came next up the ladder. Stripped, he crossed his hands

to protect himself and the men laughed cruelly. 'Richard Hewett,' Alfredo said. 'We'd rather have your Old Man.' He ordered Rik through to the saloon where the accountant stood in a corner by the deck doors as if that was as far as he could walk. Trent didn't think that he was afraid for himself. But he was afraid for Auria, and his need to understand what was happening had emotionally exhausted him. He might crumple at any moment.

Alfredo called Marco next. 'You're the "yachty" stepson, right?'

Marco nodded. He didn't seem afraid. He sat in one of the directors' chairs in the corner opposite Rik.

'Now the big guy,' Alfredo ordered.

Pepito staggered onto the deck. All his muscles had gone slack, shoulders stooped, so that he looked like a badly-stuffed sack. He stammered in almost indecipherable English that he was a diver. He used his hands a lot to make up for deficiencies of vocabulary. He was a Mexican. He had been hired by the Gringo – he immediately apologised for using the word. '*No es un isulto, Señors,*' he implored, vast hands flapping like plantain leaves in a storm. 'I have much respect, Señors. *Mucho respecto por los Norté Americanos.*'

He had a wife, four children. He showed their heights. He knew nothing. There was more gold. '*Mucho más, Señors.*' They had brought less than half to the surface. If the Señors would dive with him, he would show them. '*Muy profondo . . . si,* deep, Señors.'

It was not his fault that they had failed to complete the salvage in one night. Each ingot had to be lifted and passed from one man to the next. '*Al minimo, cuatro personas, Señors. Muy lento, el trabajo.*' At the least, four men. Very slow, the work . . .

'Shut him up, for Chrissakes,' Alfredo said, and the tall man slammed Pepito in the stomach with the butt end of his twelve gauge. Pepito whimpered and clutched himself, crumpling onto the deck where he tried to peel off his T-shirt: 'Please, Señors. See . . .'

But Alfredo had lost interest. 'Mexicans!' He spat his

disgust. 'Get your arse into the saloon and keep your mouth shut.'

Crawling past the men on the deck, Pepito knelt at the threshold of the saloon, shaking his big head, bewildered at what had happened to him, shamed by his cowardice. Not wishing to be associated with the others, he staggered aft and bowed clumsily, hands joined in prayer, to the man with the Colt who sat on the dining table. '*Con su permiso, Señor . . .*' he begged and parked himself on the very edge of the L-shaped bench like a kid at school waiting to be bawled out by the teacher.

'OK, you can come up now,' Alfredo called down to Auria. 'Take your wetsuit off.'

She stood in her swimsuit with her forearm covering her eyes. The light made the thin cloth transparent.

'She's sure as hell not carrying a gun,' the blond engineer said, and Alfredo laughed with the others.

'She's one of us. That right, Auria?' Alfredo put his hand on her backside, feeling her as if she were a cushion in a second-hand shop he considered buying for his dog. 'So what stopped you calling us at the marina like you were meant to do?' he asked for the pleasure of letting Trent and Richard and Marco know that she had betrayed them: 'Get yourself a seat and you can watch the gold come up.'

'Nice,' Alfredo said as he inspected the ingots piled on the saloon carpet. The three men who had helped him transfer the gold from the Zodiac had gone to their bunks in the forward accommodation leaving the two in the saloon on watch.

'If we're going to dive tomorrow, I need sleep,' Trent told him: 'There's a couple of things I'll need from my boat.'

'Give one of the boys a list. If you're thinking of the two twelve-gauges under the saloon seat, we have them on board. We've been in this game longer than you have.'

The man with the shotgun opposite Trent laughed as if Alfredo had said something funny. Alfredo beckoned Auria: 'Let's go below.' He probably didn't even want her. It was the power that excited him, showing them that he had it.

'Auria!' Richard cried. He moved forward two steps before Alfredo back-handed him across the face. The blow was perfectly timed and Richard dropped to his knees. Alfredo kicked him in the stomach. Marco hadn't moved.

Alfredo took Auria by the back of the neck, pinching hard as he propelled her towards the stateroom companionway. She went like a beaten dog. 'Bitch,' Trent said to her back: 'Have fun, but you'd better remember . . .'

Two, Trent thought as he looked from the man with the shotgun to the one with the Colt. 'Bitch,' he repeated, and Pepito glanced over as he stretched and lolled right back in the easy chair with his hands folded behind his head.

From beneath half-closed lids, Trent gauged the man with the shotgun. Pepito seemed to have gone to sleep but he'd moved round a little on the corner of the settee, not much, but perhaps enough – his reach was easy to underestimate. And he didn't look quick. As far as the mafiosi were concerned he was only a diver, a little dumb, but probably competent at his job for a Mex. The timing had to be right and Auria had to remember.

Feel the boat, Trent warned himself. Feel the way she moves, the way she lifts to the slight swell. He looked down at Richard: 'Fine little whore you picked.'

He sneered as Richard forced himself up onto all fours and crawled towards him. 'Snivelling little clerk,' Trent said as the yacht rose to the next swell. He had her now, the way she moved, the slight pause at the top of the rise, then the fall away to port.

Auria screamed and they heard a slap.

Richard cried, 'Auria!' and raised his head. The man with the shotgun looked down and kicked him in the face as the yacht rose to the next swell and the man with the Colt laughed as Rik beat into the carpet with his clenched fists. The man with the shotgun kicked him again. It was the moment of hesitation at the top of the yacht's rise and Trent's right arm whipped over to point straight at the man with the shotgun. The man dropped the gun and tried to get his hands to the handle of Trent's knife, which protruded two inches from his throat. Trent heard a snap as he turned and saw Pepito lower the man with the Colt to the carpet. His head was at the wrong angle.

Auria screamed again.

Trent retrieved his knife. He went down the companionway on bare feet. A third scream from Auria told him which of the two doors and he turned the handle. Alfredo faced him across the cabin. The mafioso had looped his belt round Auria's neck. She knelt at his feet, her back to the door, and she choked as Alfredo yanked her up to shield his body. Alfredo snatched under the pillow on the bunk for an automatic and fired over Auria's shoulder as Trent dived. Trent's shoulder smashed Auria aside. His left hand slammed the pistol against the bulkhead as Alfredo fired again and the heel of his right hand slammed up into Alfredo's nose. The force of the blow drove the bone up into Alfredo's brain.

Trent rolled off the bunk and lifted Auria to her feet. There was gunfire above and he grabbed Alfredo's automatic. He went up the companionway in a crouch and a shotgun fired twice in the wheel-house. Trent crossed the saloon without a glance at Rik and Marco. Pepito blocked his view of the forward companionway. The wheel-house was low for the Mexican and he stood leaning against the bulkhead, bent-legged, as he thumbed shells into the magazine of the 12-gauge he'd taken from the mafioso in the saloon. He looked round at Trent and said: 'The shots your end flushed them out.'

'All of them?'

'*Si, compañero.*'

'*Gracias.*' Trent turned back into the saloon as Auria came up the companionway. She wore a sheet knotted above her breasts. Alfredo's belt had left a red weal round her throat and there were further marks where he had slapped her cheek. She stood balanced like a boxer at the head of the companion-way, her feet at an angle to each other and eighteen inches apart. 'All right?' Trent asked.

She nodded and he turned to Richard, who sat crunched up in one of the easy chairs. Bruises darkened his face and blood caked his right eyebrow. Trent said: 'Well done, both of you. We'd better shift the gold to the *Golden Girl.*'

They loaded the ingots into the catamaran's cockpit lockers, port and starboard, leaving two ingots on the motor yacht, and Trent replaced his two shotguns under the saloon seat. Leaving Marco to transfer the dive gear from the Zodiac, he clambered back onto the motor yacht. Pepito followed. In the tropical heat, the yacht already smelt like an abattoir.

Trent needed evidence for the Mafia, evidence that the gold had been in their hands and that therefore its loss was their responsibility; Auria and her father had done what they could and were free of blame. The gold ingots were the key to the scenario. The men had fought amongst themselves. Who started the fight was unimportant. What mattered was that they were dead and that one of them had had sufficient strength to set the automatic pilot.

'We'll drag one of the men you shot up into the wheel-house,' he said.

Pepito, the policeman, said: 'No blood.'

'Mop some up with a towel,' Trent said: 'We prop him over the wheel with the towel wrapped round his waist. It'll look as if he crawled there from his cabin. We give the shotgun back to your man with the broken neck in the saloon and tip him backwards down the companionway to the forward cabins. He shot the remaining two men from the forward cabins. Bad luck that he fell.'

Pepito nodded at the man Trent had hit in the throat with his knife. The knife was Trent's hallmark, and too many people knew of it.

'Put a bullet through the knife wound. The blood's there already,' Trent said: 'Alfredo we can leave where he is.'

'You think it will play?'

'Who's going to care? Six mafiosi? You're the cop.'

'I'd be interested,' Pepito said. 'A chess problem, I'd try to work out. But you're right. Six mafiosi – I wouldn't much care that they were dead. What I'd do would depend on the kind of pressure that came down from the top. The Mafia have influence so that the pressure could be tough. Where do we send the boat?'

'Cuba.'

Pepito looked towards the coast as he gauged the politics that were so much a part of all Latin American and Caribbean police work. The Mafia had exploited Cuba in close friendship with the Batista dictatorship and remained the sworn enemy of the Revolution.

'In Cuba, it will play,' Pepito said: 'We'd better take the yacht a few miles down the reef before sending her in.'

25

Estoban called Roddy soon after dawn with news of a motor yacht that had run aground on the north coast and Roddy drove out to meet him at the wreck. The yacht had ripped her bottom out on the coral close to shore and, with the tide out, lay in a few inches of water. Having attached cables to her bow, the coastguard waited on the beach for the rising tide to help them haul the yacht clear of the waves. For the moment, Roddy and Estoban were alone on board with the corpses and the flies.

As always, Estoban wore a brown suit and he kept his hands in his pockets, not to preserve fingerprints for the forensic squad, but because he didn't give a damn. He emphasised his contempt for what they found by pointing with a foot at the evidence. 'Big yacht, expensive clothes, guns, what do you think, Roddy? Did they kill each other over a few kilos of gold?'

'No way we can know,' Roddy said.

'We know they were scum.' Estoban clambered down the yacht's side and climbed the sand towards his Lada. Roddy followed. The dead were more of the Brit's work and he felt uneasy rather than grateful that the Brit had ended the Mafia's attempt to steal back the gold they had paid Roddy's father. Roddy recalled that he had thought himself very clever in using Trent to find the *Beau Belle*. The Russians and

Americans had thought themselves clever in inventing nuclear weapons, he thought, and smiled for a moment, but then he remembered that it had been Estoban who had presented him with the Trent file.

There had been no departmental rationale for Estoban to have called him out to inspect the yacht and less reason for Estoban's presence. The wreck and murders came under the jurisdiction of the police and coastguard. Uncomfortable in his thoughts, he watched Estoban ease himself in behind the wheel of his car.

The morning sun had turned the Lada into an oven and Estoban cursed as the heat burnt through his trousers. He grinned up at Roddy: 'Rich kids learn about car seats in first grade but I'm a peasant, Roddy, that's my trouble. But I like you. Do yourself a favour and take a long drive along the coast. See if you can find another yacht.'

A warning, Roddy thought. He watched the square ugly Russian car bump away up the track to the highway. Looking out to sea, he thought of the Brit again, and Rocco, and Rocco's sister. And of his own father who had made him a criminal.

Pepito had fallen asleep under the awning in the *Golden Girl*'s cockpit, leaving the forward trampoline free. Trent lay face down on the webbing in the morning sun. He had known that he would be unable to sleep.

He heard bare feet come down the side deck and Auria's scent drifted to him on the breeze. She sat a little away from him. She didn't speak and finally he turned his head and said: 'I didn't thank you. Remembering to scream saved us, that and Rik's theatricals in the saloon.'

'What will you do with the gold?'

For the present, he needed it as bait. He said: 'We set the scene to make Alfredo's associates believe that the Cuban authorities have it. If the Mafia believe it's available, they'll come after it.'

'Why don't we give it to them?'

'Why should we?' Rik asked.

They looked up to see him watching them from the cabin-top. Bruising discoloured his cheeks and jaw and had almost closed his right eye. He sat cross-legged, seemingly at ease with himself.

Auria glared at him, shoulders squared and with an upward tilt of her chin. 'Leave us alone.'

Rik said: 'No. I want the truth.'

'What truth?' She gave an angry shake of her head, eyes stubborn. 'That I deceived you right from the start? You don't mean a damn thing to me, Rik. Alfredo said that I had to find out where the *Beau Belle* sank or they'd kill Dad. That's what they do in the States. It's not some kids' game.'

Rik said: 'I'm not a kid, Auria.'

'So I should have told you? What could you have done?' She turned away from them, shoulders hunched and tight with anger so that the muscles stood up in twin ridges each side of her spine.

Rik said quietly: 'There had to be some way.'

'Yeah, tell me!' She turned on Trent. 'Maybe I should have guessed that you were a goddamned killing machine. Where do people like you advertise, Mr Trent?'

Rik said: 'Trent's a policeman, Auria.'

'What?' She spun round, lips parted, eyes round with shock. 'Is that true?'

'Unpaid and at a couple of removes,' Trent said.

Auria dug her thumbnails into the sides of her index fingers as she remembered Alfredo beckoning her over to his Merc parked across the road from the tennis club. He had directed her to persuade her father to charter the *Beau Belle* from Rogerton-Smithe and, later, to contact Rik, and had told her how to begin the search for the sunken yacht. 'You want your father alive, do it right,' he'd said. 'Nothing personal. I'm talking business.'

She had never bothered to plead or cry. She would have done both had there been any point – or even offered herself. But she knew them too well. They were users of women. Even their wives, kept at home and out of the business, were tools, there to breed, cook, and pick up the wash. She hated them.

She always had, even as a child, when they had come to visit her father, bearers of candy and sweet words for a little girl. 'Hey, Tony, look at her, will you. An angel, for Chrissakes.' She had been frightened of them always. Frightened of them because she could smell, even as a small child, the fear in her father as he scurried to do their bidding, all fake friendship and familiarity, making little jokes, hands washing each other while hurrying his waiters to spread fresh table linen, the table already immaculate.

At first she had been unable to understand why her father, a big, laughing man, strong and warm in his love, could shrink, and his proud belly suddenly sag, the muscle gone from it, while his face aged as she watched. Once she had understood, she had determined never to permit her own life to be touched by the vileness of it. Yet here she was, trapped. She said: 'Dad never did anything wrong. All he did was have a restaurant and introduce people to Rogerton-Smithe. He'd made money with Lloyd's. He thought he was doing them a favour. This charter business was my doing.'

'Who did you tell?' Trent asked.

'You think I'm crazy?' She shrugged, rage against her entrapment holding her body tense. 'I wrote Marco at the beginning that things might work out for him long-term if he wanted to settle down, but that was all. He'd written me from the Med, some race he crews in, sounding a little depressed.'

'I think we can probably work something out,' Trent said. 'Try to get some sleep. We're going to be up all night.'

'They won't dive much before ten o'clock,' Admiral de Sanchez told Roddy as they studied the wall chart of the north coast of Cuba and the Old Bahama Channel in the Admiral's office. He tapped the patch of shallow water separating the two islets where the *Golden Girl* lay at anchor: 'Pity we don't have a transducer on their tender, but at least we'll know the moment the catamaran moves.'

Auria insisted that she was competent to dive to the *Beau Belle* and Trent believed that it was important that she be given the chance to redeem herself in her own eyes. They worked as two teams, Pepito and Marco diving first to the yacht while Trent and Auria hauled the gold to the cavern lip. They waited an hour and a half in the Zodiac before making the second dive, and now it was Trent and Auria's turn in the wreck. The last dozen ingots were jammed at what was now the bottom of the engine room under a steel chest of spare engine parts that had broken loose from lashings already weakened by the explosions. Trent tried unsuccessfully to lever the chest free with a crowbar.

He considered abandoning the ingots but to do so seemed feckless and lazy and a failure, so he signalled Auria and they ghosted up to join Marco and Pepito on the edge of the cavern, decompressed, and continued to the surface. They waited an hour in the Zodiac, then all four of them swam down together with four duffel bags. They made the lines from the duffel bags fast above the cavern lip and continued on down with the bags to the *Beau Belle*. The three men entered the engine room. Trent and Pepito manhandled the chest up a couple of feet and held it while Marco retrieved the twelve ingots. They loaded the gold into the duffel bags outside the hull and began the slow ascent out of the cavern. The nitrogen had accumulated over the three dives and their dive computers held them at seventy feet for three minutes and again at thirty-five feet.

The moon had risen and, resting against the cliff face, they watched their air bubbles dribble up towards the slight paling of the surface. Pepito saw it first, touched Trent's arm, and pointed at the shadow that glided along the cliff edge. Even as he felt in his belt, Trent remembered thinking, as he dropped backwards out of the Zodiac, that the dangers were over and that this last dive would be short with no need to carry a bang stick. Two minutes remained before they could rise to the next depth level and they waited for the shadow to return.

The divers watched the dark shape of the shark circle against the moonlit surface. They had drawn close together for protection and hung fifteen feet below the lip of the cavern. They were comparatively safe, grouped, and with their backs to the cliff, but they would be helplessly vulnerable once they rose into open water.

Trent calculated that they had sufficient air for a further fifteen minutes but they must decompress for at least five minutes at twenty feet. Twenty feet was the depth at which the shark swam now, and for those five minutes they would hang like slabs of meat. Above and to their left the Zodiac showed as a black blob, close but out of reach as long as the shark patrolled its territory.

The breeze grew in strength and a bank of dark cloud had built over the past hour along the northern horizon but the moon continued to glass the surface so that Richard could see into the water directly below the Zodiac. Twice he had thought that he had seen something within the compass of his peripheral vision and now, as the shadow slid beneath the Zodiac, he recognised one of the monsters that had peopled his childhood nightmares of the sea.

He had studied marine biology as a boy in the hope of pleasing his mostly absent father and could remember still the different sharks and their characteristics. This was a Tiger, at least twice the length of a man, twelve to fifteen feet. Tigers were territorial and savage. He thought of Auria below and the three men. He understood the need for decompression but was ignorant of the tables ; however, the second dive had been shorter than the first and Trent had said that this third dive would be shorter still. They had dived with the same bottles that they had worn on the second dive and he was uncertain of how much air remained in the bottles.

He supposed that there must be some air left from their first dive and, looking back at the bottles wedged against the hull by the ingots, he saw the two bang sticks protruding from Trent's dive bag.

The shark circled again, so efficient in design that its muscles barely moved. Richard imagined the crescent mouth closing on one of the Zodiac's hulls. The air would hiss out, the bottles and gold ingots spill against the collapsed tube. All the weight on one side, the boat would tip, spilling him into the water. In his nightmares he had been in a small wooden boat that rocked as his father jumped down onto the rear seat and laughed at Richard's terror. He felt the same terror now as once more the shadow slipped beneath the Zodiac and he recalled the frenzied screams that had summoned his mother to his bedside.

He thought of Trent on the Mafia's motor yacht and how calm he had looked in the moments before he had become, like the shark, a killing machine. The antithesis of panic, as Richard was when faced with business accounts. This was no different, simply a problem to solve.

The 12-gauge cartridges for the bang sticks were packed in a waterproof box in Trent's dive bag. Richard loaded both sticks and propped them against the transom. He tied the small white anchor buoy to the anchor line, and opened the large blade on the pocket knife he had carried for twenty years, one of the few gifts from his father, and he took a rough bearing at the closest of the coastal beacons with the compass in the knife's handle.

The Mercury outboard fired at the first press of the starter button. Richard set the throttle to idle and heaved in on the anchor line until the Zodiac lay directly above the anchor. He dropped the spare dive bottles overboard, let go the anchor line, held his left arm out over the water, and drew the blade of his pocket knife across the inside of his forearm. The blood trickled and he pushed the Mercury into gear and motored slowly away from the blue hole in the direction of the closest coastal beacon.

He thought that two hundred metres was far enough from the cavern, but judging the distance was difficult. He put the outboard in neutral and knelt looking over the side with his arm dripping.

He had to stay very calm and he tried not to think of Auria, but ten minutes had passed since he had first seen the shark and perhaps they were already desperate for air. The blood dripped from his arm but seemed too little and he cut again. This time the blood spurted and he held the bang sticks over the side in his right hand. He thought for a moment that he saw a dorsal fin break clear of the sea, then the now familiar shadow turned beneath him. He waited and it came again, closer now to the surface, and, as it turned away, he saw briefly the pale crescent of its jaws.

Seconds or minutes passed. Already he felt dizzy from loss of blood. The backs of his calves and thighs tingled, there was an emptiness in his stomach and a sour burning, and his bowels threatened to void. The shark hit the bottom of the Zodiac, not hard in attack, but as if feeling the consistency of the boat. A sudden whirlpool in the water twenty yards away signalled its turn and it came at him. Rik sensed its decision and it came fast and rolled at the last moment, rising out of the water to take his arm and he slammed both bang sticks into the side of the head. As the explosions tipped him back, he saw a huge bloody hole gape where the shark's head had been.

His belt pulled tight above the cuts in his arm, he scooped water over the hull and scrubbed away with the other hand all traces of blood with his T-shirt so that no further predators would catch the scent. On a back bearing, he motored slowly back towards the blue hole.

Noise travels great distances through water and Trent heard the Mercury start above them and the slap of the air bottles as Richard dropped them overboard. Convinced of Richard's commitment, he wondered what bait the accountant would use to tempt the shark away. But the shark had gone and he led the dive party up over the cavern lip and across the sand to the coral head under which he had jammed the Zodiac's anchor, where he saw the scattered dive bottles. He signalled Auria with his flashlight and gave her his mouthpiece as he changed her tank. Pepito and Marco changed their own tanks and Trent did the same.

Back on the cavern lip, Marco hauled up the first of the duffel bags. The thud of an explosion echoed through the water as they drifted up to fifteen feet and they heard the outboard beat to their right. Ten minutes more and Trent surfaced and signalled their position with his flashlight.

The Zodiac turned towards them.

The first cut Richard had made in his arm had been too shallow, the second too deep. Back on the *Golden Girl* Trent stabbed a local anaesthetic into the arm and sewed the deeper wound, but he knew that Richard would require surgery to reconnect the muscle, nerves, and a small artery. While Auria bandaged the arm and held the tourniquet, Trent helped Pepito and Marco transfer the last of the gold from the Zodiac to the cockpit lockers.

Auria passed mugs of soup out to them and Trent ducked into the saloon and swept his right hand behind the radio, feeling for the transducer. The cloud bank had rolled in across the Old Bahama Channel and the first drops of rain spattered their faces as they swung the new Mercury onto the *Golden Girl*'s transom. Trent dropped back into the Zodiac and coiled the anchor line down while Marco went forward to shackle the smaller genoa to the forestay. With his dive knife, Trent slit the Zodiac's anchor buoy, slipped the transducer in, cut the buoy loose, and dropped it over the side.

Back in the cockpit, he signalled Pepito to raise the mainsail and Marco to haul in the anchor. With the mainsail backed, the catamaran swung slowly round to face the open sea. 'Raise the genny,' Trent called to Marco as Pepito dropped down into the cockpit and winched in the sheets.

Marco joined them as the catamaran cleared the spit of sand at the end of the inner of the two islets. Trent said: 'The closest hospital's Cuba.' Pepito played the dumb Mexican peasant while Marco hesitated for barely a moment before supporting Trent by slackening the sheets as Trent eased the helm and set course for the Cuban coast.

Cloud hid the stars and moon. The rain thickened as they approached the coast and squalls concealed the beacons at the entrance to the small fishing port. 'You'd better call on the radio,' Trent told Marco: 'Tell them we need an ambulance.' With a mile to the harbour, he ducked into the saloon. Auria leant forward, elbows on the table, coffee mug cupped in both hands as if to stop herself striking Rik, who lay on the settee beside her. Striking him or shaking him. It was the waiting that she couldn't stand. 'How much further?'

'Ten minutes . . .'

The eighty-foot Cuban patrol boat rolled in the swells of the Old Bahama Channel. The Admiral had ordered his daughter to the skipper's cabin to care for her mother, who lay on the bunk, her head over a bucket. For the past two hours Roddy had watched the direction finder but the *Golden Girl* hadn't moved from her hiding place between the islets. 'They must have had problems underwater,' he told his father as the Admiral ducked into the radio room.

The radio operator shushed him, scrawled a message on his pad, and handed it to the Admiral: 'On the emergency frequency, sir. The *Golden Girl* is less than a mile offshore. They've asked for an ambulance.'

The Admiral cursed and jabbed a finger at the chart as he rounded on the skipper: 'Full speed. We have to get ashore and cut off the road.'

26

The little town nestled in the crook of a stumpy peninsula on gently sloping land between the shore and the mountainside. A river divided the town in two. In the early years of the town's life, boats had moored in the river, but in the eighteenth century the Spaniards had built a mole parallel with the shore to protect the river mouth from the storms that blasted across the Old Bahama Channel. These same storms had swept the sand and silt from the river mouth. No official would admit that the mole was a mistake so the harbour silted up, the town became a backwater, and now the only berths lay on the outer side of a wooden jetty that stuck out from the shore at right angles to the mole.

Trent and his companions from the *Golden Girl* stood in the rain on the jetty and watched the tail lights of the ambulance carrying Richard climb out of the town and vanish over the ridge. They were surrounded by men and women in uniform, a few of them armed, customs, immigration, police, coastguard. Auria had wanted to accompany Richard but the officials had forbidden her. These Cubans had no experience of foreign tourists and were suspicious and watchful; one of them said that the *Golden Girl* was the first yacht in forty years to have visited the harbour.

The lights of a car bounced down the quay through the rain, an old Lada, or perhaps a new Lada – with Ladas it was difficult to tell. The officials shuffled back as if pried apart. There was just the one man. He would have appeared nondescript to the superficial observer: medium height, medium build, face undecided whether to be a little plump or not; brown suit, striped nylon shirt with the top button missing, plain red tie that had been tied and retied so often that the edges were frayed. His eyes were tired, dark, careful, and with enough stored behind them to overload most data banks. Castro's Director of Bureau Three. Estoban Tur.

Unsure of protocol, Trent and the Cuban stood looking at each other, their faces faded yellow in the pale lamplight. Rain pattered on the flagstones and there was the soft sucking lap of the sea between the pilings.

'Mahoney,' Estoban said. 'Patrick Mahoney.'

'I prefer Trent.' Trent could feel Pepito behind him, watchful; Marco almost disinterested; Auria tense as a gundog held back on a leash.

'You sailed in here.' It was a statement, no surprise. Nothing had surprised Estoban in years; not even the drug dealing and corruption of General Alvarez, head of Fidel's personal security.

'I had a wounded man on board.'

Estoban nodded back at the aerial on the Lada's roof: 'They told me.'

Trent said: 'We were diving out on the reef. He used his blood to lead a shark away.'

'A brave young man.'

Trent said: 'It would be a kindness if you would allow the young woman to follow him to the hospital. She is not part of anything.'

Estoban beckoned a police officer.

Trent turned to Auria. The rain glistened on her cheeks in the dim yellow lamplight. 'They'll take you to the hospital,' he said: 'Everything will be all right.'

The police officer took her by the arm and led her down the jetty to a car. Then they were alone again, Trent and the Cuban, alone in their own space, isolated from the others by years of undercover warfare.

'Mahoney,' Estoban said as he remembered, and looked at Trent: 'You could have sailed for Andros. Once you were into Bahamian waters, a helicopter would have picked up the young man. What difference would it have made? Four hours? Three?' He looked down at the slender racing lines of the *Golden Girl*: 'Less.'

Trent shrugged: 'I brought a gift for Fidel. Port and starboard cockpit lockers.'

Estoban toed his shoes off before stepping on board. His right big toe stuck out through a hole in his sock. Trent watched him open the port-side locker. The Cuban didn't bother to look in the starboard locker and he didn't ask how much, nor was there any surprise that Trent could see.

'A gift for Fidel?'

'I understand that he can use it,' Trent said. 'It's not mine and I don't want it.'

Estoban called to the Cubans to unload all but two of the ingots onto the jetty. When they had finished, he said: 'Go away, all of you. Take the Mexican and the American with you. Do something useful. Drink. There must be a bar open somewhere.' And to Marco: 'You have American dollars?'

Marco smiled, the only man there apparently at ease.

'Good,' Estoban said: 'For dollars they will serve you whatever the hour. The new Cuba . . . or the old Cuba.' He shrugged his disgust at the circle of history that had fetched Cuba back into whoredom and watched the men and the women walk away down the dock, Marco and Pepito at once the centre of the group, the Mexican's deep voice rumbling and sudden laughter shattering the tension.

Estoban picked up his shoes. He didn't seem to know what to do with them. One of the soles had split. Finally he sat down on the dock, his feet dangling over the edge. Trent sat beside him, not too close. They sat in silence. The rain marked the lamplit sea with overlapping circles as it had marked the lake in Ireland where Trent had first fished as a small boy with his grandfather, also christened Patrick Mahoney.

Trent threw a pebble. They watched the rings spread and Trent nodded at the ingots. 'There were four crew on the yacht carrying the gold. Two of them were murdered. The Mafia were waiting for us the first night we dived.'

'The white motor yacht ? You did well.'

Trent thought of saying that Pepito had done more than his share but there wasn't any point. 'Would you like a drink ?'

'Rum ?'

Trent fetched a bottle of dark Dominicano from the saloon. It wasn't a night for glasses. His wet trousers dragged on his thighs as he sat down again on the puddled quay beside the Cuban. Estoban drank and passed the bottle back, waiting. Trent said: 'It's the generals' drug money from Angola, but you know that.'

'Gold is a great temptation.' The Cuban tilted the bottle, then examined the label. 'We also make good rum,' he said sadly, and without faith in Trent's belief that anything of quality was made in Cuba.

They heard the soft throb of turbo diesels at quarter-throttle and a patrol boat nosed round the end of the mole. A squall cloaked her in rain, but they heard her chains clatter as her skipper anchored fore and aft to block the harbour mouth. The squall passed and now two sailors manned the twin-barrelled cannon mounted on her foredeck. Three hours at forty knots and the patrol boat would be safe in Florida with thirteen million in gold on board.

Trent said: 'There had to be an admiral involved as well as the Air Force and Army generals.'

'de Sanchez. If he escapes, the Americans will make him a hero.' Estoban nodded towards the cannon on the patrol boat. 'They won't shoot till the Admiral comes. Like a cockerel, he will want to crow a little.'

Three sets of headlights dipped over the crest of the hill above the harbour and the two men watched the vehicles wind their way down through the trees towards the town. Twice they were hidden by rain as squalls chased off the sea.

The Cuban looked up through the rain at the scudding clouds: 'I have men standing by with helicopters but only the President can permit such troop movements. To find him at night is never easy.'

Trent knew from the files that Castro slept in a different house each night to avoid assassination. With the wind shrilling through the *Golden Girl*'s rigging, he said: 'Helicopters won't get through. How is the telephone?'

'Cut ten minutes after you called on the radio. We die together.'

'I'm not ready to die,' Trent said, and Estoban chuckled.

The vehicles were in the town now, their lights slipped over the cottages and illuminated a small, tree-shaded square with a statue in the centre. As Trent had expected, the vehicles halted briefly then reappeared in the main street that led to the harbour. A Russian jeep came first, followed by two military trucks. The jeep and trucks halted at the end of the jetty and marines dropped down over the trucks' tailgates. A non-commissioned officer shouted orders and one group fanned out across the road while the others followed three officers up the jetty, a Marine Commander, Admiral de Sanchez, and a young Lieutenant who was probably the Admiral's son. Marco was with them, and Trent said: 'When the time comes, the American is mine.'

Trent presumed that the Admiral had ordered the patrol boat to stay outside the harbour for fear that the crew might grab the gold and run, but the delay was dangerous because he had to be clear of Cuban waters by daybreak or have the Cuban Air Force blast him.

The marines carried machine pistols at the ready but no grenades, and the three officers kept their pistols holstered. Estoban called to the Admiral's son: 'You are in the company of scum, Roddy. I had hoped better of you.' They were close now, the three officers, and Trent and Estoban were between them and the machine-gun on the patrol boat.

The Admiral said: 'You talk of scum, Tur. You! With a father who was a field labourer.' He needed space for his scorn and had stepped a little to one side of his companions. For a moment Trent and Estoban were screened from the marines and Trent slammed Estoban forward. As they hit the water, he yanked Estoban by his coat collar back between the pilings and to the right so that the *Golden Girl* protected them.

The Admiral shouted at his men to kill them and wood chips flew as a marine lay on his stomach and hosed under the jetty with his machine pistol from the opposite side to the catamaran. Trent whispered to Estoban to dive under the *Golden Girl* and they surfaced between the two hulls. Trent pushed Estoban over to the far hull and made him lie underneath it with only his face out of the water. Ducking under the hull himself, he cut the Zodiac loose.

Again and again the marines hosed the pilings and cursed as they crawled on their bellies along the jetty, searching its underside. Only two of them had flashlights and the night was dark with the rain and cloud and the tide high so that there was only a couple of feet between the planks and the sea.

With the marines concentrating on the jetty, the Zodiac had drifted to the outer boundary of the dim lamplight before one of them spotted it. Machine pistols shredded the hulls. Through the barrage of small arms fire, Trent heard the grind of the patrol boat's anchor chains. The Admiral must have ordered the skipper in to load the gold.

He heard the Admiral shout at a marine to sink the *Golden Girl* and Marco say that the catamaran had positive buoyancy and wouldn't sink.

'Then cut her loose,' the Admiral commanded. 'Check her first,' he snapped as an afterthought, and rubber-soled combat boots landed heavily in the cockpit. Trent counted two men.

The patrol boat's diesels roared as the skipper brought her round in her own length. One of the marines on the *Golden Girl* leant over the transom and sprayed bullets between the two hulls while his companion entered the saloon. Roddy called, 'Forget it, they must have been with the Zodiac.'

'Just get the cursed thing out of the way,' the Admiral yelled as the patrol boat edged towards the jetty. 'Stay on board,' he charged one of the marines, or perhaps both. The lines hit the deck and the catamaran rocked as one of the men shoved her clear. A squall blasted under her bridge deck and swung her round towards the town waterfront.

One marine dropped down from the saloon into the port hull, probably searching for valuables. Trent thought that the other marine must have jumped onto the jetty. He ducked under the hull, signalled to Estoban to stay where he was, and floated aft along the port hull. A carelessly opened locker lid struck the side of the cockpit as he grabbed the boarding ladder and he froze as the marine he had thought safely ashore gasped: 'Mother of God!' Then, softly: 'Toni, come look.'

The second marine's boots crossed the saloon as Trent slipped back under the bridge deck. Estoban watched as he grabbed the handle on the hatch opening up into the saloon. He eased the hatch open and drew himself through. In the cockpit the marines whispered over Trent's share of the gold, which Estoban had left on board.

Trent lifted the seat and took a 12-gauge from its mountings. He poked the saloon doors open with the barrel and the marines looked up. 'Don't move, don't speak, don't even think,' he warned them. 'Estoban,' he called softly.

The Director of Bureau Three clambered heavily up the fixed boarding ladder on the port hull transom and took the shotgun while Trent tied and gagged the two marines and dragged them into the saloon. The *Golden Girl* had drifted a hundred yards from the jetty and, hidden by the darkness, Trent ran forward to drop the anchor.

He kept a ninety-foot coil of stainless steel rigging cable in the bridge deck locker at the foot of the mast, sufficient to replace a stay. Stripped, he pulled on his wetsuit, fins, mask and tube. A hollow fender made fast to the coil provided sufficient flotation and he jumped overboard.

The patrol boat lay alongside the jetty. The gunners had swung the cannon round to cover the main street. Half a dozen marines handed the gold ingots up to the after deck where sailors passed them down through a hatch. Others continued their search of the pilings. The marines were expecting flight rather than attack, but Trent had to be careful not to splash with his fins. He knew that he had a few minutes at most.

As he reached the patrol boat, he heard the Admiral shout

up at the bridge and a siren immediately summoned the marines from town and those guarding the end of the jetty. The cable over his shoulder, Trent pawed his way aft along the hull, dived, and hung the cable over one of the patrol boat's twin propellers. He cut the lashings with his knife before surfacing, sucked in air, and dived again. The cable would have been difficult to handle on land – underwater it was a battle, but he managed to weave a loop round the blades of the port propeller.

An officer yelled at the marines to hurry or they would be left behind and Trent, as he gasped for air, heard their boots pound up the jetty. Back underwater, he wrapped the second propeller, gulped air again and threaded slack over one propeller shaft and back round the other shaft. He hadn't time now to worry whether he was seen or not. He surfaced at the stern for air, filled his lungs, and dived to twist the cable ends into a loose reef knot.

The turbo diesels thundered and the wash from the propellers rammed Trent back and down and tore the mask from his face. He fought for the shelter of the jetty but he was blind without his mask and the deadly maelstrom sucked and beat at him, and rolled him over, so that he lost all sense of direction. One end of the cable slashed across his back. His right foot hit timber. He piked round, grabbed with both arms at the piling, and forced his way under the planking. He surfaced into the ripping currents of the propellers as the skipper forced the patrol boat clear and charged for the open sea. Pulling himself up onto the jetty, Trent yelled at Estoban to cut the *Golden Girl*'s anchor line.

The patrol boat's propellers spun ninety feet of plaited wire cable with a breaking strength of four tons into an ever-tightening cat's cradle. First the mounting for the starboard propeller shaft buckled, then the shaft snapped. The broken shaft slammed into the other propeller and the blades sheared. The roar of the twin turbo diesels rose to a shriek as Trent raced down the jetty and along the shore to meet Estoban as the wind drove the *Golden Girl* ashore.

He passed a sixteen-foot hard chine sailing dinghy pulled up on the beach and thought it would do. Pepito and the Cuban officials had smashed their way out of the bar where they had been locked in by the marines and ran to meet him. Trent yelled at Pepito to get the mast out of the dinghy and get the dinghy into the water. Reaching the *Golden Girl*, he told Estoban what he'd done and that the patrol boat must have broken down not far beyond the mole. 'We have to stop the Admiral getting away in one of the tenders,' he gasped.

While Trent fetched his two 12-gauges, Pepito mounted the Mercury to the dinghy's transom and connected the gas tank. For speed and safety the dinghy had to be kept light but Trent needed one man up in the bows to keep the boat from rearing up on its stern. One man only, and this was Cuba. For Estoban, the Admiral was a personal vendetta.

27

The patrol boat carried liferafts for thirty men and two twenty-foot tenders. She lay a mile offshore and already a marine had grabbed a single ingot and leapt overboard in a lifejacket to swim for the shore. Almost immediately a second marine followed, then a sailor, a steady stream of enlisted men abandoning ship, every man for himself.

The skipper and first officer stood guard while the marine officers and Marco swung out the two launches. The officers grabbed their own gold, enough for a fresh start in the US, and divided into two groups, the de Sanchez family with Marco in one tender, the remaining officers in the other.

A Russian gasoline engine powered the launch and Roddy was surprised when it started at the first press of the button. He turned the bows out to sea and opened the throttle wide. Marco Rocco had armed himself with a Kalashnikov and was in the bows while Roddy's sister sat amidships with their parents. The rain had eased as had the breeze and the heavily built launch made twenty knots as it ripped through the small waves.

The beam from a lighthouse lit the other tender for a moment and Roddy saw that they were already on divergent courses, his father transformed by failure into a pariah. Roddy imagined his parents incarcerated in a Miami apartment, his father exiled from his mistresses and his uniforms; his mother

in her permanent black banished from the funerals she loved
and the family tombs. His sister would survive, she had been
taught by their father to sell herself – though neither she nor
their father would recognise her relationship with Marco as
prostitution but as a merging of common interests.

Marco, the murderer. Roddy hated him.

Kalashnikov at the ready, the American swayed as supple
as a dancer to the pitch of the launch. Occasionally he glanced
at Roddy's sister, his smile lazy, not with desire or fondness so
much as with conceit of ownership. His hands tightened
suddenly on the gun and Roddy looked back at the next sweep
of the lighthouse and saw the spray of a speedboat fountain in
their wake. The Brit, he thought, the Brit and Estoban Tur –
the final chase in a Western, except this was real. And he had
never imagined himself on the wrong side. To the contrary,
the romantic in him had always identified with the Lone
Ranger. He slipped his pistol from its holster and tucked it
under his thigh as a small break in the cloud opened.

Estoban knelt right forward in the spray that curtained the
dinghy's bows and Trent shifted forward a foot to help weigh
the bows down. He opened the throttle on the 8o-horse
Mercury an extra notch as the two launches ahead split away
from each other. The launches made stable gun platforms
when compared with the leaping dinghy, but the dinghy, at
full speed, was a difficult target. But which launch?

As if in answer to his question the left-hand tender turned a
further five degrees off the direct course to the reef and, in the
next sweep of the lighthouse, its wake had vanished. The
helmsman must have cut power, choosing to hide in preference
to flight.

Certain that the Admiral would run, Trent eased the helm
over a fraction and gave chase to the other launch. Racing at
twice the tender's speed, he passed it at a distance of a
hundred metres, then changed course to intercept.

Roddy slammed shut the throttle in automatic response to
his father's shouted command and Marco steadied himself,

Kalashnikov to his shoulder, and waited for the beam to sweep the dinghy.

The dinghy drove at the launch like a missile.

The beam came and Trent saw the women. He cursed and shut power as he rammed the steering arm over. The sudden change of speed and direction tumbled Trent and Estoban to the floorboards as the dinghy skittered broadside towards the launch. One burst from Marco's Kalashnikov and it would be over.

The beam from the lighthouse swept across the water and Roddy saw Marco smile, his lips damp and parted by the pink tip of his tongue. The tongue that had pried open Roddy's sister. And Estoban Tur was Cuban. Arrogant Gringo son of a pig, Roddy thought, and shot Marco through the side of the head.

The Admiral leapt to grab the Kalashnikov as it fell and pivoted to face Estoban Tur, still helpless on his back. Roddy held his pistol in both hands. He shouted at his father not to shoot and the Admiral hesitated. Estoban grabbed one of Trent's shotguns. He didn't seem to aim but suddenly a dark shadow covered the Admiral's chest. The Admiral folded at the knees and knelt for a moment at the feet of his wife and daughter before slowly tipping over onto his side.

Roddy squatted beside his father. He would have said that he was sorry but it was too late. And he wasn't sorry. Rather, he was relieved that it was over and that the good guys had won – even though he had been on the other side and had earned a ten year jail sentence. He looked up as Trent brought the dinghy alongside. Estoban clambered, unarmed, into the launch. To Roddy's mother, he said: 'A boating accident, my condolences, Senora,' and to Roddy, quietly: 'Your orders were to search the north coast, Lieutenant. Don't let disobedience become habitual.'

For a moment Roddy didn't understand.

The helicopters landed on the town's waterfront as the cloud lifted from the mountains and the Special Forces fanned out along the coast in search of the enlisted men from the patrol boat while coastguards sought the second launch.

Pepito had towed the *Golden Girl* back to the wooden quay and he brewed coffee while Trent and Estoban showered and changed into dry clothes. The Mexican was too big for the catamaran's saloon, but he set the mugs and percolator on the table and slouched opposite Estoban, shoulders hunched, mop of black hair out of control so that his eyes were hidden from Trent in deep shadow.

Trent said: 'If you were smaller, I'd beat your brains in for getting me into this. That goes for you too, and your chum, O'Brien,' he added to Estoban: 'A great little Troika.'

A radio operator trotted up the quay with news that Rik had been transferred to hospital in Havana. Estoban said that it would give him pleasure to introduce Trent to his wife: 'We can have breakfast at my apartment.'

'I'll bring a care package,' Trent said.

Leaving Pepito on the *Golden Girl*, Trent flew by helicopter with Estoban to the capital. A second and more ancient Lada awaited Estoban at the military airport. Children's safety seats were strapped in the back. Sweet papers and broken crayons littered the floor and the chewed beak of a yellow plastic duck poked out from beneath the driver's seat.

Estoban drove into Havana slowly and with concentration while Trent cradled a second bottle of rum between his thighs. Turning uphill from the Malecon, Estoban parked in front of a concrete apartment block. He took the rum bottle from Trent and tucked it under the seat. They rode the elevator up to the sixth floor, Trent carrying the food parcel he'd brought from the *Golden Girl*.

Finger to his lips, Estoban opened the door carefully. A bedroom opened off the narrow entrance hall. Estoban beckoned Trent to look at the two small boys in the twin beds. The room was cramped and airless and a slight sheen of sweat darkened the children's eyelashes.

School exercise books were piled on the table in the living-room, one of them open with a red pencil lying along the spine. Estoban's wife came out of the second bedroom. She wore a cotton nightdress down to her feet. Thirty years old, short, slim, eyes with the sleep still in them, sockets bruised with fatigue, probably a little African blood. She pushed a mass of long, black, tightly curled hair away from her cheeks.

Estoban put an arm round Trent's shoulders: 'Maria, meet my best enemy.' His smile lacked confidence and his wife didn't answer it.

Trent dipped his head in a half-bow. '*Muy cantado, Señora. We brought food . . .*' He held the plastic bag up as proof.

'For breakfast,' Estoban said, still without confidence: 'Eggs, bacon, real coffee.'

Maria Tur nodded at the exercise books on the table: 'You know I must work.'

For a moment Trent thought that Estoban would take her in his arms but they had played the same scene together too often and Estoban said only: 'I am sorry. I had forgotten.' He turned to Trent, his emotions buried: 'We will eat at one of the hotels.'

'You said that you would look after the children.' Again it wasn't a complaint. Merely a statement of fact.

Parking the Lada outside the Museum of the Revolution, the two men walked up the hill, hand-in-hand with the children, to the Hotel Inglaterra. 'Foreign currency only. You'll have to pay,' Estoban told Trent.

They discussed details while they ate, then walked to the hospital where a duty doctor reported the success of the operation on Rik's arm. Rik had been given a private room. Still groggy from the anaesthetic, he lay propped in a 'V' of pillows with his arm in plaster resting on a hard bolster. Auria was with him – or at least she was in the same room, but slumped in an easy chair over by the single window that opened onto a bare courtyard. She looked up at Trent and was about to speak, but the younger of Estoban's boys retched at the cloying hospital smell of cheap soap and disinfectant.

Estoban gentled the boy and called a nurse, asking her to play with the children out in the corridor. Then he crossed to the window and stood looking down at Auria with the sunlight behind him so that she wouldn't be able to read his face. 'There has been a misadventure, Señorita Rocco,' he said with the same gentleness that he had shown his son.

She turned to Trent: 'Marco?'

He had expected her to ask questions, take shelter in rage, but she remained calm, her fingers interlocked on her lap, one thumb prying absently at a flake of dry skin on the other.

Estoban said: 'Our relations with the United States are difficult, Miss Rocco. Given your permission, I will arrange for the burial to take place here in Havana.'

Auria thanked him and he crossed to the door with a murmur of apology to Trent that he must occupy himself with his children. The door closed on the Cuban and Auria said quietly and without looking up: 'Marco was the American on the *Beau Belle*.'

For hours now she had been trying to recall at what moment she had been sure. She thought it was when she had told Trent that she had written to Marco in the Mediterranean about the proposed charter. Even then she hadn't accepted it immediately, but all the threads had slipped into place, most of all Marco's concern for her father's predicament when he had never cared before for anyone but himself. Marco, the big brother whom she had idolised, the lover, capable of turning on the charm as if he were plugged into a power-point; that was what she remembered from her childhood, the bewildering changes of mood.

'No one will ever know. It's over, all tidied up,' Trent said. 'The Cuban Ministry of Marine will issue a report for the insurers so that Rik's mother gets her pension.'

'And my father?' Trent's silence goaded her and she twisted round, trying to burst free of a trap. 'He's done nothing wrong.' But she was repeating herself. She thrust herself out of the chair.

'Rogerton-Smithe won't make a claim for loss,' Trent said.

'Thanks, but that's not what I'm talking about.' Her shoulders slumped and she sighed and was about to turn away but the injustice was too much and the rage flooded back. 'The Mafia will kill him, Trent. Do something, for Christ's sake !' She looked away. 'I'm sorry.' She would have left it at that but for Trent's silence. She spun back to face him. 'I mean I'm not sorry, Trent. You can, you goddamn know you can.'

He held her by the elbows. Rik moaned and coughed and she shook herself loose, crossing quickly to the bed. She wiped Rik's lips with a Kleenex and tried to get him to drink but he had slipped back into sleep and she looked round to find Trent watching her.

'So I enjoy sports but that doesn't mean I'm stupid enough to think a cut arm makes us a relationship,' she said. Trent smiled, and she said, 'You know what I want. I want life to be like it was before this thing happened. My life. It was so goddamned good. Give it back to me, Trent.'

Trent said, 'All right,' because that was what she wanted him to say.

She said, 'Thanks, you're a good man.' She walked to the window and looked down at an elderly couple warming their bones against the south wall in the courtyard. The strain had left her and, as Trent joined her at the window, she gave him the same open uncomplicated smile that she had brought on board the day she first swam out to the *Golden Girl*.

Trent felt as if he had reversed an evil spell. He said: 'Who's the top man of the group, Alfredo's boss?'

'Mr Syracusa.'

O'Brien laid down his newspaper and folded his spectacles as Trent walked up the beach below the Chickcharnie Hotel on Andros. 'Glad to see you, Mr Trent. Cold beer?' He nodded to the bartender and waited for the drinks to come.

'Your very good health, Mr Trent, a real pleasure.' He chuckled softly and tapped the *Miami Herald*: 'There was a report in the paper a few days back that Admiral de Sanchez met with a boating accident. A senior man at State is accusing me of having saved Castro's hide. Fortunately we have a kid here with the Embassy swears I had him order you to stay in the marina and there's a Superintendent in the local police who backs that up.'

'Nice for you,' Trent said.

O'Brien nodded, sipped his beer, and smiled lazily. 'Like I told Estoban Tur back when we were putting this operation together and Pedro Gomez came up with your file, you're dependable, Mr Trent. Tell you what to do, and you do the opposite. You'll need to keep away from Washington, at least till there's a change in Administration. That's no loss to your social life, and you've made yourself friends here in the islands so, all in all, you shouldn't complain too much.'

'I haven't complained,' Trent said.

O'Brien took another neat little sip at his beer and wiped his lips. 'Think how bad you would have felt with that son of a bitch Admiral living the good life in Miami. And the Rocco boy . . .'

'What do you want me to do?' Trent asked: 'Congratulate the three of you for having set me up?'

'It was a good operation,' O'Brien said.

Trent said, 'So leave it at that. Did you order lunch?'

O'Brien said he had: 'Pond crab with rice.' He raised a hand to the waiter to fetch fresh beers and took a letter from his pocket. He handed it to Trent. 'Seems your friend, Rogerton-Smithe, killed himself.'

Dear Mr Trent,

I have lived over the past months with the fear that a small number of American Names in my syndicates may choose to punish me for their losses by harming Robert. My own death seems the only viable insurance against this possibility and, given my health, it is an option which I take without regret.

Your actions in regard to the *Beau Belle* have aggravated my position and it is therefore fair that you should accept some responsibility. I have therefore named you as executor of my will and trustee of my estate of which Robert is the sole beneficiary. Wealth can be difficult to deal with and Robert is already blessed with youth and beauty. I will lie more tranquil in my grave in the knowledge that he will benefit from your counsel and protection. It also appeals to my sense of humour. I must advise you not to invest in the Lloyd's Insurance Market until such time as the Committee institute independent regulation.

Though ceasing to be, I remain yours gratefully,
David Rogerton-Smithe

Trent folded the letter. He would like to have copied it to Auria's father with a reminder that entertaining the devil was never a social occasion, but he had made a promise to Auria. He said to O'Brien: 'Time to start paying your dues. I need the address of a Mr Syracusa.'

EPILOGUE

The wind chased a fresh flurry of snow across the driveway as the guard opened the gates. Ten acres of open lawn and flowerbeds separated the public road from the house which lay beyond a slight rise. There were no shrubs and the few ornamental trees and ancient oaks were too well spaced to offer cover to an intruder.

The drive had been salted but the uniformed chauffeur eased the stretch Mercedes with great care up between the white cloaked borders. The house had been designed by Frank Lloyd Wright, a 1920s fortress of smooth concrete and armoured glass. A Spanish American manservant in a black suit hurried down the steps with a golf umbrella as Trent's chauffeur held the car door open.

Once in the house, Trent let the manservant take his overcoat, scarf, and gloves. He wore a double-breasted Savile Row suit, plain cream cotton shirt with Regimental tie, and Edward Greene brogues burnished mirror bright. His hair was grey and military short as was his moustache. Blue contact lenses coloured his eyes. British Establishment, rich, in his mid fifties.

A dark young man in grey flannels and a yellow jumper apologised for patting him down. Search completed, the manservant led him across the hall and opened double doors to the library: 'Mr Patrick Mahoney, Sir.'

The American had been standing in front of an open fire. He strode across the big room to meet Trent midway and held out his hand: 'Syracusa. What will you have? Scotch? Martini?'

Trent said: 'Perhaps coffee, if it's not too much trouble. Black.'

'Espresso?'

'Please.'

Health club slim and in his late forties, the American wore dark green corduroys and a red turtle neck, embroidered house shoes. His face was remarkable for its lack of lines and a manicurist had attended to his hands. The lid was up on a Bechstein grand by the east windows and a folder of sheet music lay open on the stand. The columns of books were sufficiently untidy to have been dipped into frequently and the three tortured figures above the stone mantelpiece had been painted by Francis Bacon. Two comfortable armchairs upholstered in worn leather faced each other from opposite sides of the log fire.

Syracusa waved Trent to a seat: 'You have an interesting way of introducing yourself, Mr Mahoney. Letter from the senior partner in the most prestigious Philadelphia law firm saying you've been associated in the past with the British and American Governments and enclosing a copy of an order of sequestration issued by the Havana High Court on a ton of gold bullion. What can I do for you?'

Trent said: 'You know who I am?'

The American raised one eyebrow perhaps a quarter of an inch: 'We checked with our sources.'

A knock on the door heralded the manservant's return with a single cup of espresso on a silver tray. Trent thanked him and waited for the door to shut: 'The Rocco family are friends of mine.'

'The restaurateur?' Hands clasped, Syracusa watched the flames dance against the iron fire guard. His eyes shifted back to Trent; no other part of him moved. 'You've gone to a great deal of trouble to tell me this, Mr Mahoney.'

'It's that sort of friendship,' Trent said. 'The gold's lost and

Rogerton-Smithe is dead. Close the book and I'll owe you a favour.'

'What kind of favour?'

'Just so as it's inside the law.'

Syracusa stood up and walked over to the piano. He caressed the keys, then hooked the piano stool back with his heel. Before sitting down, he adjusted his trouser legs to protect the creases. He played the opening bars of a Greig sonata and looked round at Trent. 'What did you expect, Mr Mahoney, something lushly baroque and Italian? You could threaten me. Or is being Patrick Mahoney the threat?' Through the bulletproof window to the left of the piano, he inspected the smooth slope of the snow covered lawns, the big oaks and the ornamental trees with their lower limbs pruned to insure that an intruder would be seen by a guard or register on the surveillance electronics. His fingertips stroked the ivory keys as he again looked at Trent. 'One of our sources said you retired. Maybe retirement doesn't go with the territory.'

'Not easily,' Trent said.

Syracusa smiled for the first time. 'That's what I've always thought. Tell Rocco he can relax.'